"There's an office the line."

Katherine was worried by the operator's monotone. Did she understand the urgency? Katherine watched in disbelief as the shadow figure moved toward the shed attached to the waterwheel. Too late, she thought to get a picture after the person disappeared inside the shed.

"Oh no," Katherine muttered. She spoke into the phone, "Hurry. I think it's the killer, maybe looking for something left behind? Hello?" Had the operator hung up?

"Yes, the officer is on the way. Please stay on the line." The operator's voice now sounded bored.

A sharp ray of light from inside the shed cut through the darkness. The light jumped around. Sweat collected on Katherine's upper lip as she imagined the killer looking through her things for something, maybe critical evidence. Fear gave way to irritation at the invasion. Irritation gave way to anger. Someone had to stop that killer from removing whatever incriminating thing was so critical it had driven a return to the scene of the crime. Katherine wanted to scream. Where were the police? Maybe MJ was right about them. She pressed against the French doors. The light in the shed went out. Her breath caught in her throat. The silhouette walked out of the shed toward the alley leading to the maze that burrowed throughout Bayside and beyond.

Katherine spoke gruffly and fast, "Hello. Where's your officer? The suspect is getting away."

"Ma'am, please stay calm and hang on the line. They're on the way."

Katherine unlocked the door to the yard and whispered to the 911 operator, "I'm in pursuit."

Praise for *KAT OUT OF THE BAG*

"Inside every handbag are artifacts—pieces of personality, glimpses of the past and often the deepest secrets. Vintage purses have a story to tell and for Kendall's mystery, these stories unveil more than just purse-sonal history; they're the clues to catch a killer."

~Esse Purse Museum, Little Rock, Arkansas

~*~

"Captivating characters, and a tight, tricky plot, *KAT OUT OF THE BAG* is a curl up under a blanket, grab a cup of tea cozy mystery that you'll be reading—and enjoying—into the wee hours of the morning."

~Laura Childs, Author of Tea Shop Mysteries, Scrapbooking Mysteries, Crackleberry Club Mysteries

~*~

"Spellbinding, stylish, and completely engaging. Wendy Kendall fashions a charming setting and delightful cast of characters. The perfect weekend escape reading. I'm feeling a need to buy a new purse. Something sparkly. A clutch perhaps."

~Keenan Powell, Agatha-Nominated Author of the Maeve Malloy Mysteries

~*~

"A sophisticated page-turner in the tradition of Laura Child's novels and the small-town charm of Louise Penney's novels. A gutsy protagonist with a handbag for every occasion, a murder, and a love interest. When Katherine lays aside her voluminous handbag collection to find the murderer, she puts her life in danger. Will she regret coming back to her old home of Bayside?"

~Valerie J. Brooks, Author of Revenge in 3 Parts and Tainted Times 2

Kat
Out of the Bag

by

Wendy Kendall

An In Purse-Suit Mystery

Kat Out of the Bag

Cover Art by *Kim Mendoza*

The Wild Rose Press, Inc.
PO Box 708
Adams Basin, NY 14410-0708
Visit us at www.thewildrosepress.com

Publishing History
First Mystery Rose Edition, 2020
Print ISBN 978-1-5092-3071-6
Digital ISBN 978-1-5092-3072-3

An In Purse-Suit Mystery
Published in the United States of America

Dedication

To my beloved parents, John and Pam Kendall

Chapter One

All That Glitters Is Not a Judith Leiber

Katherine Watson slumped in a heap, littering the side of the road, all branding for her prestigious purse and fashion company, K. Watson Designs International abandoned. She struggled to sit up in her muddied Kevan Hall designer gown. The strategically seductive slit up the left leg of her gown was now in tatters, and a hole was growing under her left arm. Her once upswept, auburn hair hung flat like the dense suede fringe on a poorly made Coach knock off.

A teenager walked by her, talking on his cell phone. "I'm not kidding. The mayor's dead. She was hanged."

Katherine's tears blended with the misting rain, and she gently rubbed her scraped knee, although it wasn't the knee she was crying over. She watched the ambulance drive up the hill carrying her best friend Brenda. Her dead friend, Brenda. Russ, Brenda's devoted husband of twenty years, followed in his silent Tesla. Katherine had never before seen Russ angry. Tonight, he'd gone from zero to furious in a sudden burst, with eyes blazing red and fists clenched, shouting his rage at the two paramedics who had physically stopped him from riding with them. They'd come between him and his murdered wife.

Brenda and Russ Dirling fit together like a kiss clasp on a coin purse, Katherine had always said. Love at first sight, they'd treasured each other through raising a family, starting a business, and pursuing Brenda's political advocacy to Bayside Mayor. They'd always had a glint in the eye for each other, until the very end.

Sometimes Katherine missed that glint in her own life. It had been replaced with a steely, cold stare when her ex signed their divorce papers, slammed the pen on the desk, and told her he'd make sure she'd end up penniless and alone. Despite all his efforts, he was wrong, well, about the money anyway.

Trust was like a delightful, Judith Leiber jeweled clutch masterpiece. If handled carelessly and some of the precious, crystals fall off, then there are unsightly and critical gaps. You can try to reattach the glittering jewels somehow, if you can even find them all. But no matter how hard you work to put it back together, you still feel the damage. It's never the same again.

The end of her marriage was tough, but not brutal like this. The paramedics had forced Russ out of the ambulance and away from his beloved wife. A police officer had made an appearance to stop the enraged husband. Russ had raced off to his car and Katherine had, of course, run after him. As he got to the Tesla, his crazed look had pierced her sorrowful daze.

She'd told Russ he was too upset to drive. She'd reached for the door handle, and he'd roughly pushed her away. She'd landed hard on the curb, in mud puddles and rain. Without a glance, he'd jumped behind the wheel and raced off.

Another wind gust, and she gulped in air. Shivering, she shifted her weight forward over her knees and rubbed her sore wrist, watching as goosebumps covered her arms. She twisted to observe the scene behind her. Shock had masked all the noise, but now it roared at her.

The giddy Bayside residents partying at the gala opening of Katherine's Purse-onality Museum had transformed into a mob. An evening of hors d'oeuvres and exclamations praising indoor exhibits on Women's History and Fashion degenerated into sobbing groups gathering outside and piercing shouts across the yard. Bright, glittery fashions swirled with the fall leaves in the storm under the spotlights. The grounds of the renovated, historic farmhouse, so meticulously decorated earlier for the event, were trudged through and torn apart by the upset crowd. Police searched for anything or anyone of interest to the murder, indifferent to flowers, shrubs, and ornaments.

Herding a dozen or so guests from the garden onto the front porch and through the front doors of the museum, the police were spreading out now. One large team stood on the lawn where Brenda's body had laid when it was dragged from the pond. More police stood at the museum door. Just tonight, she'd stood right there and greeted and laughed with Brenda. She'd have to go home through that door. She missed her quiet Los Angeles condo.

Katherine reached for her muddied K. Watson Designs limited edition Shimmering Cherie clutch. The gathered fabric had soaked in splotches of mud, and the delicate pearls sewn into the front were gone. The clasp had broken, and the contents spilled out, including her cell phone which lit up with her new background picture. Katherine recoiled. There she was arm-in-arm with Brenda, both of them all smiles after cutting tonight's ceremonial ribbon. Mayor Brenda had made time to do the honors. Friend Brenda had been Katherine's biggest supporter. It had been a perfectly glittering evening gala, until the murder.

Katherine's nylons were torn. The Louboutin had fallen off her left foot and vanished. She flexed her toes as her thoughts tormented her. She groped inside the purse. Where was that death threat note? She was sure she'd stuffed it into her clutch. As the chaos swirled, more unwelcome thoughts taunted. Should she have called the cops when she first found the note? She indulged in a long sigh of relief when she found the note in the zippered pocket. She held it up to the bright, police lights and squinted at the terrifying cut out newsprint letters. Her shoulders froze, paralyzed as her guilt screamed from within. She had the note, and she did nothing. It was as if she'd killed Brenda herself.

Bright flashing lights on top of yet another police car broke through her accusation. This car was speeding right toward Katherine on the curb. She barely had time to roll out of the way. After a stunned self-affirmation she was still alive, her head hung heavy as she moved to a sitting position again. The siren stopped as a loud, vicious barking from inside the car started. Katherine stared at a huge German shepherd jumping against the car's back window. A car door slammed.

A man kneeled next to her in the mud, leaning close. "Are you all right, miss? Are you okay? Do you think you can move?"

Katherine's first thought was *that's a big gun*, as she stared ahead at the sidearm in the holster hanging from his belt. Katherine nodded at bright blue eyes that reflected the pulsing light from the police car. Grief, shock, and confusion yielded to the strong enchantment that hit deep within her scarred heart. The feeling left her speechless.

He steadied her as she stood lopsided with only one shoe. "You're sure you're not hurt? Lucky I was able to swerve out. It's not safe to be sitting on the curb, in the dark like that."

Katherine couldn't look away from his gaze. She just nodded again.

"Let me help you into the house. I need to report in to do some tracking." He raised his hand in a gesture at the car, and the dog was silenced.

Katherine found her voice. "You've got to find the killer. Brenda was my friend."

"Yes ma'am, Bayside PD is on it, and we'll get to the bottom of it."

Katherine glanced at his badge gleaming in the light and his name underneath it, Jason Holmes. Wait, why was that name familiar? He turned her arm toward the house. She needed to make him understand what this case meant, to her. She stopped abruptly and fumbled with her shattered purse. Pulling out the folded note, she held it out to him. "My name is Katherine Watson. I'm K. Watson Designs, fashion from Los Angeles and New York." She hesitated, waiting for a glimmer of recognition from him. He showed no reaction. She held the paper up higher. "This is my home and I opened this Purse-onality Museum here. Brenda and I found this note just as the gala started. It's . . . it's a threat. It must be from the killer."

Jason kept his eyes on her and grabbed a small flashlight from the shoulder pocket in his vest. She searched her addled memory. Where did she know that name? He took the note and read it. His eyes had been inviting, but now they clouded over into what she interpreted as concern. Then they stormed into something dire. He read it out loud, "*Shut this down or bag a corpse. You won't ruin Bayside.*" He looked at her again. "You received this death threat in advance, and you did nothing?"

Katherine stepped back, facing him squarely. "I didn't do 'nothing.' I planned to contact the police after the gala."

Katherine noticed she was speaking faster and louder. She wanted to calm down, but the violence, and the cold of the storm, and the misunderstanding of this man wore her down. "The gala was for local guests and a small group of media. There wasn't any indication a killer would sneak in unnoticed. As I said, I'm a fashion designer. I'm well known." She paused again, waiting for his recognition of her celebrity.

When it became uncomfortable that no indication was coming, she continued, "Threats and crazy people are not unknown to me and my extensive network. I was sure I could handle the situation for one evening. There was so much planning and work in the gala. I thought the threat was directed at me. I never intended to put my friend in danger." Katherine squinted at his unblinking expression. "You think I don't regret what's happened?" Katherine fought back tears. She wasn't going to cry in front of this regimented stranger.

Jason shook his head. "We're here to serve and protect, ma'am. Citizens like you can quickly get in over your head. Don't wait to bring in trained professionals. We'll take it from here."

His tone intensified her guilt and anger. It didn't help that he was a couple of inches taller and looked down on her as he spoke. His eyes glinted like sharp-edged, broken glass. That's when she remembered why she knew his name.

Brenda had commented months ago about the Afghan war veteran who they were proud to have just hired onto Bayside's finest. She'd said that he'd worked with a dog on his two tours of duty in Afghanistan and would be on the K-9 patrol here. Brenda also said that he impressed her, although she had an uneasy gut feel about him.

Holding her palm out to him, Katherine lowered her eyes. Her voice was quiet now and formally polite when she asked, "Can I have my note back, please?"

"No ma'am, this is evidence." He slid the note inside a clear, plastic bag.

One tear rolled down her cheek, but she ignored it as she softly said, "Not ma'am. My name is Katherine. So, you're just going to take that then?"

Katherine thought he hesitated. She thought he started to reach out to her. He gazed at her then, with both hands, sealed the bag and turned away toward his car. "Yes."

Katherine held her head up, stuffed her clutch tightly under her arm, kicked off the remaining shoe, and walked stiffly across the lawn toward her front porch. The car door slammed behind her as she looked at the vinyl banner across the porch. Its welcome hung at a slant now,

Time to let the Kat out of the bag
Women's History and Purse-onality Museum
At the house Katherine recognized the police chief.

7

He was talking into the radio attached to his shoulder while directing the small band of excited, local paparazzi behind the front path. She introduced herself to him.

The chief wasted no words. "We need a list of all your guests tonight, Ms. Watson. And we want to ask your guests and you questions. You live here alone?"

Katherine nodded. "The first floor is museum exhibits and also a little café. The upper floors are my private home. My grandparents live across the property in a cottage at the end of the backyard."

The chief made a quick note. He swiveled away from her and said, "Jason, we've been waiting for you and Hobbs."

"Yes sir."

He'd followed her. His German shepherd was leashed and sitting attentively at his side.

The chief continued speaking to Jason, "We've got evidence you might be able to use to track." He waved at an officer inside the entryway who walked past Katherine with a clear plastic bag containing Brenda's chain strapped purse.

Katherine became dizzy seeing that purse and couldn't catch her breath as death scene images flashed. First, she remembered the large waterwheel attached to the shed on her property, as it turned and churned the small pond, although it had been turned off for the night. She'd been confused. The wheel had been turned off for the night, why was it moving? It was the murder weapon. She re-lived the shocking, dull, repeating thump of Brenda's body against the wooden boards.

She closed her eyes, trying to avoid it, but her mind showed Brenda's body hanging by a long, thick Chanel style chain wrapped around her throat and caught at the top of this giant water wheel. The body bounced relentlessly against the spokes of the waterwheel that was turning in its devastating circle. The contorted face strained at the end of the chain, staring but not seeing the terrified crowd. Clashing with the grisly sight, a Swarovski jeweled panel, visible on the front of the purse, glittered in the yard lights below. That left no doubt in Katherine's mind. It was her embossed designer crossbody she'd gifted to her friend Brenda. Katherine put her hands to her ears now, vainly trying to block the memory of the panicked voice that had echoed from the middle of the shouting crowd, "Turn that wheel off. Where's the switch? Where's the switch?" Then the leather purse broke from the weight, and there was a collective gasp as Brenda fell thirty feet straight down into the pond.

As the officer now handed the bagged purse to the chief, Katherine stumbled as she struggled to breathe. Her stomach heaved. Another officer helped her sit on the porch step. She saw Jason remove something from his vest. Staring at Katherine, he handed the bag to his chief. "I have this for you, sir. It's a note that was found by the museum owner earlier tonight. It looks like it may be from the killer. It was handled extensively before I got it."

The chief nodded. "Who's seen it?"

Katherine waved her hand to get the chief's attention. Jason scowled, but she refused to be intimidated. She said, "Brenda and I were inside the house, in my office. I showed her the prize purse she was going to present to the raffle winner at the end of the gala fashion show." Katherine took a breath.

"Brenda opened the prize purse and found that note inside. We were both surprised. I have no idea who could have put it there. Brenda read it first, and then she handed it to me with a strange look. When I read it, I could see why."

Katherine's voice cracked, but she was determined to finish. "I was the one who said it would all be fine for tonight. I promised Brenda I'd report the threat to the police as soon as the gala was over." Katherine paused and wiped a tear from her cheek. "I never thought I was endangering my own friend. I told your officer, if I could take that moment back I would in an instant. I'll never forgive myself for waiting to call the police."

"Who else did you tell about it?"

"No one, and I asked Brenda to keep it quiet. She agreed she wouldn't say anything during the gala as long as I promised to call the police right away, as soon as the party was over."

"So as far as you know, only Brenda and you were aware of a death threat."

Katherine nodded. "Just Brenda, me, and the murderer."

Chapter Two

The chief kept his eye on Katherine as he fingered the clear plastic bag holding the death threat. One of the officers handed the evidence to Jason. The dog was watching his partner attentively. Jason got down on one knee. Opening the bag with the purse, he held it out to his K-9. Katherine vaguely remembered the dog's name, Hobbs. The dog's hair rose stiffly on the back of his neck as he sniffed at what was offered. He stood up facing the shed and strained at the leash with a whine.

Jason handed the bag back. Katherine noted the excitement in his voice when he said, "He's got it. I'm in pursuit."

Katherine watched Jason and the dog run, dart sideways, then disappear out of sight behind the shed. The chief was talking into his radio again. Katherine sighed and moved into the house. The police had set up a command center in the front room of the museum, where the 1920's decade of purses and women's history exhibits were displayed.

Katherine went straight to her office and wrapped herself in a warm comforter. She stopped in the kitchen and encouraged the caterers to keep the coffee and beverages available to guests. She silently walked to the back of the room to watch the police question. The detectives wrote down names, and contact information, as witnesses approached and sat on the 1920's mahogany salon seat with the barely padded bench, nonexistent back and stubby legs. It was built for sturdiness and exotic shape, not for comfort. Her guests squirmed as they answered their interrogators. There was tense handholding between couples and hugs between parents and children. An officer took pictures on his cell phone and recorded what was said. Katherine's own phone screen flashed too as she typed some notes.

The interviews continued through the night and Katherine's tired stare sometimes wandered from the scene. At times she focused on the intricate beading on the small flapper dance purses displayed in the room. They were made from brilliant metals available at the end of World War I. They were made to reflect happier times after the devastating fight abroad.

There was a clash of present and past when a detective knocked over a couple of the beaded flapper bags in the case. From the shadows of the room Katherine jumped, but forced herself to ignore the blatant insensitivity of the officers to her priceless collection. Then more clumsy gestures knocked one of the Whiting and Davis purses onto the floor. Katherine gasped. A sudden heat flame ignited inside her. Callous treatment of this historic piece, made by the leading manufacturer of art deco, was indefensible. Katherine leaped to her feet and picked up all three treasured, antique purses. She noted the officer's badge name, Grace Adams. Oh hardly, thought Katherine. She stamped her foot, as the officers ignored her. She pulled the display further out of their way.

Katherine sat down again at the back of the room and laid the vintage pieces with care on the table in front of her. She thought about the detailed renovation of not only this room, but the house. It had been a big effort to bring this dream of hers to life.

It's so appropriate Purse-onality Museum is housed in this hundred and fifty-year-old, four storied farmhouse. When she'd come to Bayside to visit her grandparents, she'd had no idea she'd be managing her extensive business from here for this long. Her gran and grandpa were very persuasive about needing her here for now. With an absent father and a mother who disappeared on periodic adventures, they'd been her home. The day would come for her return to Los Angeles' Rodeo Drive, her real world, but until then creating a sweet legacy in Bayside was exciting. She had the staff in place to run Purse-onality when she returned to her celebrity life.

Katherine sighed heavily as the police stomped around the chic museum exhibits. This had been her great-grandparents' family haven. She'd lovingly restored its glory, as a tribute to her great-grandmother, Ellen Stedman. That grand lady had inspired and fed Katherine's inner fire for celebrating women's stories. From its back mudroom to the foyer entrance, from the below ground basement to the gabled attic, dear Ellen Stedman's spirit embraced her home. Katherine could almost hear her great-granny's voice calling her with that childhood pet name, "Kat, join me for cookie time." No more the sound of faint scraping as the top lifted off the cat shaped china jar. Fond memories lingered, like snuggle-up times together on the kitchen's bay window seat telling stories, giggling, and dreaming. Sometimes the walls did talk.

At the gathering after her great-grandmother's

funeral, Katherine had sat in this same spot watching her parents talk with other grownups. Kids were outside playing. It was unusual weather in an otherwise dreary February. Her mother had held her close and said, "The world is remembering your dear granny with sunny warmth as she joins Grampa in Heaven." Grateful for open arms, Kat had hugged her close.

Late in the day Kat had climbed the long, steep stairs to the top floor attic, and gripped her crocodile skin purse. The croc's face draped over the top of the little shoulder bag and its snout extended onto the front. Granny had given this first purse to her. Isolated inside the attic, Katherine had sat on the old cloth couch. Its fabric faded, the material still showed the engrained, daffodils planted across soft cushions covering bulging, metal springs. The shiny crocodile's eyes seemed to pool with giant tears just like hers. She gave her croc a kiss and leaned him against the back of the couch. She opened the giant trunk, as she'd done so many times with Granny, revealing the store of amazing treasures.

Filled shelves hung from inside the lid, and assorted delights piled in the great depth below. The big, top shelves held the dear purses. She'd gently touched some of the bags and she'd thought of the many stories they represented.

One favorite purse had been a durable, tan, lizard skin satchel with a sturdy shoulder strap. That had been high fashion in London post World War II. Kat had remembered reaching inside to feel the luxurious, chocolate brown silk lining as her great-granny had remarked, "Your dear Grampa treated me to this when we left England for America after The War. He'd said 'Ellen Stedman we're putting The War and its horrible memories behind us forever. Throw out that olive-drab satchel of yours. Dear, I'm told this purse is all the rage. It's called a Fassbender and it's made for style, not durability. That's our future in America."

Adult Katherine was well aware that Fassbender was indeed the company that made the Post War modern, luxury purse. Grampa had certainly splurged with this gift. Vintage Fassbender alligator skin handbags were exhibited at the Victoria & Albert Museum, London's permanent fashion collection. And this one was now displayed here at Katherine's museum. Finished with gilt hardware, this one was even complete with its original compact mirror intact in a small, interior pocket. The original clasp on the front of the bag opens revealing one zipped compartment, and two internal pockets on either side.

Remembering her great-granny's funny, oversized straw tote bags with the beaded and bejeweled designs gave Katherine a chuckle, even on this dreadful night. One of the straw totes had been decorated with a peacock, one a beach scene, and one with a watchful poodle. Made in China, Great-Granny had bought them on vacations in Florida. Her great-granny had laughed with her but sniffed, "In the 1950's at least these had more style than those horrible see-through Lucite boxes so many of the American companies made. Can you imagine? They sold plastic purse boxes." Katherine still remembered the horrified expression on her face, and then they'd laughed together again.

Young Kat had realized that day that every purse packed a fascinating story. These stories needed to be remembered and told and celebrated. And as Kat's own purse collection had grown, and she'd made a name for herself selling her own line, it was time for her dream of a venue telling women's stories. Now Katherine leaned her chin on her fist and gazed at the remains of this tragic opening party.

Detective Grace Adams walked toward her and said, "We're done here. We need that guest list now, and we'll let you know when we're done with your signed guest book."

Katherine handed her the guest list she'd printed while in her office.

"Thank you. We've cleared the house but prefer that you stay out of the shed and the roped off area in your yard until we finish there."

The front door slammed. Katherine looked to see a soaked Jason, with his drenched four pawed partner Hobbs standing in the entry. Katherine followed Detective Adams and the chief who walked straight up to Jason and asked, "What did you find?"

Jason shook his head. Hobbs shook the rain off his coat.

The chief moved to the front door. "Get your report filed by oh-four hundred, then head back out for another try." He disappeared into the night. The officers followed him, except for Jason who had just noticed Katherine.

As a celebrity who was often interviewed, it was unusual for her to be caught speechless twice in a night. She noticed he hadn't taken his eyes off her. He shifted his weight to his other foot. "I have to ask. You've handed over all the evidence that you have to an officer. Correct?"

Surprised at her own disappointment at the question, she instinctively squinted at him. "Yes.

Listen, I'm trying to help, not hurt the investigation. You can tell me not to be involved, but just look around you. I am involved." She stared at the assortment of paw prints and boot prints amidst the rainwater on her exhibit room floor.

Jason reached in his shirt pocket and handed her a small business card. "We could be dealing with a very sick and dangerous person. For your personal safety, don't be involved. If you do think of something that could be helpful, or run across something suspicious, please contact me first. Don't try to do anything foolish on your own." He gave a commanding pull on the leash and walked toward the door.

Katherine wanted to shout at him, "I'm not foolish." They were interrupted when the department radio attached to Jason's shoulder spluttered a brief conversation. She missed the first few words but caught "suspect in custody". Jason touched the button with his left hand. "Copy that. On my way in."

The voice boomed through the speaker then, "Negative. Report to Coroners. Backup needed for Russ Dirling arrest. He is charged." Jason turned back and looked at Katherine as she shook her head at him, mouth gaping open. He responded into the radio again, "Copy."

Katherine's mouth moved and her voice had to catch up. "That's wrong. Russ Dirling was never violent in his life. He loved Brenda. He would never hurt her."

"You may not know him as well as you think you do. Either way, I have my orders." She tried to give a quick response but ended up watching him tug the leash and walk out.

She slammed the door shut and stomped her foot. Then she leaned against the door frame thinking of poor Russ, arrested. His wife murdered. His heart broken. His family ruptured. What could possibly have made them think Russ did this? She knew Russ and Brenda better than anyone. Russ was innocent. She would prove it.

Katherine took a step forward to her office and stopped. Had everyone really left? There was no sound, but had the police searched the whole house? The police have the wrong person, so the killer is still at large. Was she alone here or was someone hiding?

Chapter Three

Glad to seclude herself in her office, Katherine was nervous, tired and as weighted down as a shoulder bag saturated with hardware. She pulled the blanket off and her hand brushed part of what was left of her gown. Brenda had been the one to find this gown online and had emailed her the link with the note—*Fabulous Dress, Fabulous Bag, Fabulous Friend.* Katherine had been surprised when it turned out to be one of her Southern California colleagues' designer dresses.

When she'd arrived tonight, Brenda had hugged Katherine and said, "You bedazzle us all." The shimmery, black dress had slinked tightly down her body, accentuating her curves. The low scoop neck had been framed beautifully with a matching shrug jacket. No dazzle now.

She'd been trudging around in her gown all night, through the heart break, the push by Russ, the speeding police car, those deep blue eyes. Jason. Then she remembered his lecture and that look in those eyes as he'd told her he'd keep the note as evidence. She slammed her broken clutch down hard on her desk disrupting the sleeping Purrada, who meowed in a loud complaint. The shiny black haired, sleek pet reclined on a fluffy cushion on the window seat next to the desk. Now that Purrada was startled and on the alert, Katherine could see the white fur patches scattered on her nose, chin, and along the front of her neck. The cat then feigned nonchalance and casually began licking the top of her front paw.

"Oh Purr." Katherine gave the cat a gentle pet under the chin and a meandering caress under the ear, and her pet treated her to vibrato, loud purring. She sat in her armchair as she surveyed the purses lining her office shelves. She thought of the funny remark Russ had made at the beginning of the evening. She even relaxed a little, sinking deeper in the chair and snuggling with Purrada as she thought back on how well the evening had begun.

Russ had smiled as her grandmother had approached the museum with her vintage friends for the gala. He'd said, "Please excuse me Katherine, but I see a parade of purses headed this way. I'm going to say hello to my favorite 'ladies of the round table' and help them through the crowd." Russ had deftly made his escape out of the foyer of gathering guests leaving Brenda and Katherine together.

Katherine said to Brenda, "Your husband is a sweetheart. The dear old ladies went to their weekly, round table early dinner at Al's Cafe tonight."

"It's so cute how Al reserves their round table for them at his restaurant so they can all see and hear each other," Brenda remarked.

"You mean so they can see all, and gossip unapologetically to each other." Katherine had watched the Bayside seniors make their way up the path, each vying for Russ' attention.

Her gran entered first. "Brilliant. It's all lovely." Her English accent fluttered gently. It matched her English look with pearl necklace, brooch, and charming yellow, long sleeved dress tied with a decorative pussy bow collar over one shoulder. Despite the cane, she proudly managed a tan Osprey London handbag in the crook of her other arm—Katherine's Christmas gift last year. It was a classic British luxury leather brand for a classic British lady.

Katherine hugged her. "You look beautiful. Glad you're here."

"Where else would I be?"

Brenda stepped forward with a hug. "Hello, Pam, it's so good to see you."

"Hello, Brenda. That young man of yours is very nice to help us."

Russ had returned to the front yard to help the rest of the purse parade up the ramp next to the stairs, onto the porch and through the front door. Katherine had paused to notice. Of course, Peggy was next and overtly flirting with Russ, who was giving her an arm to balance on. Behind her Judy and Elizabeth were gaily chatting to each other, the two youngest in the group at 72 and 73. Incurable world travelers, they had returned from their recent trip to Russia. Margaret was a few paces behind them using her walker; she moved with a smile as she enjoyed a word with Russ who had walked back out to be at her side. Instead of a purse hanging from her walker, Margaret had a souvenir book bag from the New York Public Library. Bringing up the rear were sweet Winifred and her caregiver, Amanda. Winifred had been an artist of beautiful landscape and floral paintings. Her sight loss had been gradual. She was almost blind now at ninety-two. Not one to let anything defeat her, Winifred remained the most cheerful of optimists. They entered the foyer to hugs and greetings.

"One of those Paparazzi took our picture as we came up the ramp and onto the porch," Peggy said with a blush.

MJ, the Purse-onality historian hugged Pam and gestured toward the doorway to the first exhibit room. "Can I invite you ladies into the next room to browse some exhibits? And some hors d'oeuvres?" The ladies' enthusiasm spiked.

To Katherine, MJ is her museum historian, her friend, and her mother who had often been absent during Katherine's childhood. MJ is the living embodiment of the 1960's free spirit, flower child. Many people were taught about this time in history from books or movies. Some experienced it through Katherine's mother Moonjava. Sometime during her sojourn to San Francisco decades ago she'd christened herself as Moonjava, which Katherine had shortened to MJ. Tonight, her long, braided hair was interspersed with daisies, and she wore a peasant style blouse draped with brightly colored bead necklaces and dark black jeans. Her only concession to this evening's gala event had been some decorative studding on the jeans. MJ wanted to teach women's history to give fashion a deeper meaning beyond its artistry, at least until the wind blew her off in another direction again, thought Katherine.

More guests arrived and Katherine remembered busying herself greeting them. She remembered Brenda's official mayor-style voice in her ear. "Looks like the city council are arriving as a group."

Several of them had stiffly walked past Brenda, merely nodding in her direction. Unfazed, Brenda smiled at each and then gestured to Katherine. "Where's the brand-new design I get to hand over to the lucky raffle winner at the end of the purse fashion show? Do I finally get to preview it?"

Katherine thought back on how carefree she'd felt as they'd started down the hallway toward the back of the house, pausing at the gift shop entrance for a small group crossing in front of them. Katherine remembered how they'd passed Ida Hansen, Bayside's Historical Society President. Ida had cornered three of the Seattle reporters. Ida's hand had been resting on one reporter's arm as she batted her lashes at the mesmerized man. Katherine had blinked hard as she'd overheard Ida say, "Bayside is a town with a lot of history. I'd love to tell you some stories about my hometown sometime. I'm from a proud, founding family. As a community leader I'm one of the models in the purse show. Do you like my 1920's outfit for it? Should I spell my name for your article?"

She was dressed all in white, a close-fitting dress with tiered fringe all the way to her knees. The fringe shimmied with every move. Her heels were pumps, and she featured loops and loops of white stringed pearls hanging from her neck. Her crowning detail was a white headband around her forehead that sported a very tall, white feather. Katherine remembered recognizing with envy the antique purse. It was a chainmail Chatelaine Flapper Antique Sterling Bridal purse with a large blue sapphire stone shining at the clasp. No doubt, that beauty was Ida's family heirloom.

****

She and Brenda had ducked into the office. She'd joked to Brenda, at Ida's expense, "Oh Brenda, I get such a kick out of Ida's haughty air of self-importance and her search for immortality. Did you hear her bragging about being a runway model in tonight's little runway raffle show?"

"Well, it is a big deal in her life. We don't want to spoil her moment."

"Right, all this is for her and her hysterical family."

"Historical. Historical family," Brenda had corrected with a laugh.

Katherine nodded with a grin. "I'm telling you, she's not carrying a full coin purse these days, if you know what I mean."

"You mean not enough bills in the billfold," Brenda taunted her.

"Well, more like no credit cards in the holder," Katherine giggled.

"Ah yes, a knock off with a counterfeit label." Brenda winked.

"That's a little close to home," Katherine had playfully protested, and they'd both laughed.

The office's bright, white walls, with the warm, brick red accent wall, and the oak desk, and the large bay window had provided the background for a dramatic centerpiece on the large mahogany conference table. There had stood the K. Watson 'Bayside Chic Tote' in all its ivory and gold colored glory. It was the first of a limited-edition design celebrating Purse-onality's opening. The square shaped, pebble leather had held the ladies' attention in an aura of sophisticated fun, until hearing a loud and indignant yowl bounce off the walls.

The velvety, black Purrada had stepped around from behind the ivory and gold with a complaint about an interrupted nap. Her extra-long tail had twitched sporadically. She'd rubbed the side of her face against the "Bayside" and maintained a sidelong glance at the intruders.

Brenda had made a soothing little sound toward the cat. "This can't be that dirty, soaked cat from the alley out back? Is she the one that hissed and scratched at anyone within a block? Is she the legendary evader of Bayside's finest Animal Patrol?"

"She's sort of adopted me. Brenda, let me properly introduce you to Purrada."

Brenda clasped her hands together. "You clean up real well, Purrada. Now step aside and I'll admire your owner's handiwork. Katherine, look at this purse. It's pure artwork. Can I see inside your masterpiece before I give it away?"

"Of course." Katherine said. Pride bubbled in her throat.

Brenda had picked up the tote and stroked the richness of the exterior leather with her thumb as her fingers sank inside into the satin of the gathered fabric lining. The sturdy, leather handles appeared delicate and light. The magnetic clasp was accented with a shiny, clear Swarovski Crystal, sparkling like a lighthouse beacon. When Brenda had popped it open, she noticed the logo. With her finger Brenda had traced the sketch of the sitting cat with a front paw reaching out high, and its long tail stretched out from behind to the right in a small w. "A new logo? I like it. The cat is your K and the tail curled into a W down front is for Watson."

"Yes, inspired by Purrada and her crazy tail that seems to twist and snag incessantly. I'll continue the original logo out of Los Angeles and New York. This is for a new museum line."

"It almost sounds like you're putting down roots here."

"Sounds can be deceiving then."

Brenda had crossed her eyes at Katherine, mocking her, and then diverted her attention back inside the tote with a mumbled compliment on its capacity and organization. Katherine had crossed her arms. "You know my plan is to return to California. I can sponsor the museum from out of state. You know I'm an L.A. woman."

"It's meant so much to your family, and friends, for you to be here. Hasn't it meant anything to you?" Katherine remembered how Brenda confronted her then. "I think you're looking for a place to belong. You haven't figured out that you don't belong in that cold condo where you sleep and store your things while you go to work."

Katherine had said, "It's an elegant condo." Right then she'd noticed Brenda's face pale to a stark white with such a puzzled expression. She'd stared at a paper she'd pulled out of the purse. Katherine didn't want to remember anymore. She got up, left Purrada on the chair and walked over to her closet.

She reached up with one hand to pull on the cord for the overhead light. Her eyes focused on jeans and on a turtleneck on the shelf above. She struggled to reach the zipper on her dress and pull it down. It started, with jagged stops and awkward catches. If only dresses used the smooth zippers on those Dooney satchels that never seem to fail, Katherine thought. Desperate, she grabbed both sides of the back of her tattered dress and pulled hard. The silky material ripped loudly, and sequins fell. She tried pulling it apart again, and with a groan what was left of the material gave way. She tore the dress off, and it fell to the ground in a puddle. She stomped out of it, pulled the jeans on, slipped on the turtleneck and shook out her hair.

She indulged her anger by grabbing the gown of muddy sparkles and throwing it against the wall. It didn't change what had happened. It didn't ease Katherine's heart. It didn't stop the agonizing guilt. It didn't get the police here in time. It was like popping the button off very tight jeans - an ugly situation revealed but not fixed.

She pulled the cord to turn off the closet light and walked back into the office. Her feet began to warm up as soon as they contacted the fleece lining in her suede loafers. The rest of her felt numb. She sat down in her chair and pulled a brush out of her desk drawer. She brushed her tangled hair and stared at her cat.

Katherine could see that in blissful ignorance of the tragedy around her, Purrada was now getting active and playful after hiding in the office during the gala. The tail was twitching as she investigated the designer dress toy that had suddenly flown into her arena. First, she investigated by pawing and swiping at the remnant of fashion with caution.

Purrada tested the toy again with her paw and then pounced onto this unprecedented cat opportunity. Some interesting light reflections appeared to entice her. With a couple of meows, Purrada jumped forward onto the soft fabric. She nosed her head under a part of the fabric, and the rest of her body soon followed. Her extraordinary, long tail didn't quite make it all the way under the fabric, as Purrada turned to curl up amidst the folds. As she lay down and her head peeked out, the end of her tail gave one last twitch and she grabbed an edge of the fabric in her teeth for a happy tug and chew.

Katherine gave Purrada a half-hearted grin, as she took a brief respite in the cat's antics. The rain hit against the windows, drawing her attention back outside. Her thoughts turned back to Brenda. Katherine grabbed Kleenex out of the desk drawer and wiped more tears. Brenda's work as mayor of Bayside had brought on growing tensions between her and the council members. Could there have been a conspiracy to permanently remove her from office?

Chapter Four

Katherine picked up her cell that had fallen out onto her desk when she'd slammed down her clutch. She started looking at pictures she'd taken at the party. She studied a picture of Jim, one of the city council members. He was talking with Brenda. Ida was in the foreground. As usual Ida was submerged in attention seeking, pointing at one of the exhibit's historical artifacts.

Jim was a short, stocky man who was clearly beyond middle age but dressed much younger and wore his black hair in a very small man bun. In the picture his complexion was blotchy, and his finger was sharply pointed in conversation at Brenda. Katherine recognized the stance Brenda had been caught in. Hands firmly on her hips and feet apart almost shoulder width. Brenda seldom took that stance, except when she was gravely serious. Were they arguing about the city council's building heights proposal? Was it something else? Had the issue escalated beyond discussion? Jim's own businesses had been questioned as a conflict of interest in local news editorials. It had been raised that he may have to exclude himself from voting. Had his self-interest raised the stakes to murder?

She viewed more pictures on her cell phone, realizing how little she knew about the stresses in her friend's life. Katherine stopped at the picture where

Rob, the local reporter at the Bayside Herald, was interviewing her own museum historian, MJ. It reminded her of a conversation she'd overheard between Rob and Brenda.

She'd seen Rob abruptly step in and block Brenda's way, cornering her into the isolated alcove near the kitchen entry. Katherine had made her way near them, as Rob's voice heated.

Rob's back had been to Katherine, yet his threatening gestures toward Brenda were obvious as he lowered his voice to say, "Mayor, you're going to pay for the favors you've given, and the families you've hurt."

Brenda hadn't even hesitated to reply, in her professional, calm tone, "Is that from the press, or is it personal, Rob?"

"It's personal, Brenda." Rob had shoved her aside and walked in long strides toward the bar.

Brenda had later attributed it all to an overly zealous reporter, ambitious to be the Woodward or Bernstein of Bayside. She'd added with a shake of her head to Katherine, "Big dreams of a little man." She'd said it would all be forgotten tomorrow. She suggested that he needed to sober up. Could Rob have taken his personal grudge into the realm of murder? She'd known him almost her whole life, a tattered history between them.

Skimming through more pictures, Katherine wanted to find others that included Rob. Her brain churned and she had an idea for organizing some of her thoughts. Katherine put down her phone and pulled out from against the wall her large, wheeled whiteboard usually reserved for designing, and turned it around so she could use the blank side. She shoved all the day's data on purses, inventory, sales and scheduling, along with the new leather and suede samples out of the way to the end of the conference table.

She stood with her back to the office door that led to the kitchen, leaned back on the conference table, and periodically scribbled names and ideas on the whiteboard. Occasionally she'd pause to look at the pictures on her cell, and then scribble again. She took a moment to notice that Purrada had moved from her sequined dress toy back to the tabletop, staring wide-eyed from the samples at Kat's feet to the moving marker in her hand. That's when both cat and Katherine suddenly froze in place. A loud bang sounded from the kitchen. Katherine was barely breathing as panic seized her. Now there were footsteps in the hallway, and right outside her office door. She looked in every direction for a weapon.

Katherine abruptly jumped and screamed when the office door groaned open. MJ walked in and jumped with an involuntary scream of her own. "Katherine, it's me. What's wrong?"

"Oh my God, you scared me to death. I thought I was alone in the house."

"Sorry. I was doing some meditating and yoga to center myself, and then I saged the entire museum and house. I guess my meditation for today was right." Katherine picked up Purrada and petted her.

Katherine always tried to ignore MJ's daily mantras that she said came to her from the Universe, just as she absorbs life itself. Katherine disagreed, thinking that MJ chose her focus for each day just as she'd chosen her Moonjava name, randomly.

"Today's mantra was—'Develop your intuition.' I'm still meditating on that."

Katherine quietly repeated it. Would a better developed intuition have improved her judgment with the death threat? She thought of the day MJ decided to work at Purse-onality. She'd said her mantra that day had been—'to learn, read; to know, write; to master, teach' so joining with a designer on this project was her unlikely way to teach women's history. In retrospect, Katherine was sure her own mantra that day must have been 'destiny works in strange and mysterious ways.'

MJ was saying, "Do you think you'll be able to sleep tonight?"

Katherine shook her head. "Maybe."

"Let me know if I can get you anything. Some herbal tea might help. What's all this, by the way." MJ waved her hand toward the whiteboard.

Katherine tapped her marker lightly against her chin. "That's my list of suspects to help the police find Brenda's murderer. I won't let them get away with killing my friend. I can solve this. The police seem distanced from it, not completely engaged. If they don't make headway they'll just move on to other things and the trail will grow cold. I'm determined."

MJ walked to the board. In silence she took the marker from Katherine and popped the cap over the tip. "Here you go again. You're Katherine the crusader wanting to make things right. It's Katherine the fixer. You just brutally lost your friend. You need to grieve. It's okay to feel the hurt, the sadness, the anger."

Katherine paused, and brushed away a stray tear. She saw MJ's hand tighten around the marker. Katherine sat heavily in the nearest conference table chair to try to contain her frustration. Gravity and solitude were her new companions. The whiteboard captured her full attention through shining eyes, and an intensity of an eagle on the hunt.

Katherine lowered her voice. "You think I should take time to recover. Feel every emotion of grief, miss the beautiful person Brenda was, meditate, or pamper myself. Sit in quiet contemplation. Cry. Rebuild myself." Katherine was gripping the arms of the chair with white knuckles. "I should sit and gain strength, and in that time a killer gets away with this, and maybe kills some other beautiful person. All this so I can sit and cry? Well, I won't sit, and I won't stand either. I'm going to move and get into action and solve this mystery. I won't stop now. I can help."

"That's heavy, girl. Because it happened here doesn't make you responsible. The murderer is responsible. Help the cops? Avoiding and protesting them works better for me. These cops, it's just the man stamping heavy footprints all over, and in the end, they just go in circles. Don't let the man keep you down."

"Brenda, Russ, her family, her town for God's sake. She was our mayor and she cared about this town and the people in it. Brenda deserves someone who cares for her as a person, not like the police who just worked for her. I wasn't the friend she needed tonight. I owe her."

"What makes you think you can solve a murder?"

"Because I desperately care."

"Love is friendship reverberated in an electric guitar riff. Repeated over and over again, or played just once, it's still deep. You're hunting for a dangerous murderer and I can't stop you?"

Katherine nodded, and Purrada took the opportunity to jump down into her lap for a soothing pet. "You can't stop me. No one can. I'll stop when that murderer is caught."

"Well then, you need more than your background in reading mysteries." MJ uncapped the marker. "You should create this as a visual timeline that is hour by hour, right across the middle of the board, like this." MJ picked up another pen. "And color code each of the suspects along that timeline to see where they were at all times. Then you'll know who had opportunity." Katherine was now sitting up in rapt attention with her back straight, hands clasped, a focused stare following every turn of the marker, with a growing grin as she welcomed each word.

"Oh, don't look so surprised. I know a thing or two about planning events. This is like planning an event after the fact. I have a visual that may help you determine motives too." MJ handed her a marker.

"I was checking the pictures of the Gala on my phone so I could try to place people in the crowd and see what they were doing, who they were talking with, and maybe figure out anyone missing because they were outside the building. I wish we had a video camera outside." Katherine shuddered along her spine as she feared she'd invited a killer to her party. When she noticed MJ watching her, Katherine said, "I'll try matching my photos onto your timeline Thanks MJ." Katherine gave her a smile, surprised she felt grateful to have MJ's sympathetic ear and helpful advice.

"You're welcome. Oh, I also emailed you video Amber took on my phone of your Paparazzi Q&A. Now don't get mad, but she left her friend Michael in the gift shop watching the register so she could film some of the gala."

Katherine petted Purrada. She really didn't care about gift shop sales right now. MJ gave her a hug. "Maybe you'll see something helpful on Amber's video of the press people and some of the guests arriving. One thing I want you to keep in mind. We don't know what happened out there in that dark shed. Was Brenda the only target? Did that thought even occur to you? This happened at your home and your party. You need to watch out if you're a target."

Katherine waved MJ off. She started writing on the board, deep in thought about potential suspects. Purrada tried to get her attention by rubbing her leg. Failing to get what she wanted, the cat jumped back up onto the abandoned chair and squeaked out an indignant meow.

Katherine started pacing, and in her periphery saw MJ walk to the door. The timeline began to grow with markings methodically added. MJ said good night and Katherine nodded as she went back to adding suspect information beside the timeline.

She printed 'Rob' in broad, heavy capital letters. Ambitious. Self-righteous. Those were the first words that came to mind when Katherine thought about the local reporter, based on their long history growing up together. She pressed her lips together tightly and glared at the board as she printed the words under his name. He was just a couple of years younger than her and there had been a time they could have been friends. No chance of that following his middle school stunt designed to embarrass her. She shook her head and whispered to convince herself, "I'm not naming him because he's a jerk. I'm suspecting him based on evidence." She became absorbed with the notes she was writing about motive under Rob's name—'personal threat' and 'ambition' and 'accused Brenda took favors' and note in news headlines. She had nothing to add under the categories of means or opportunity, yet.

Katherine thought this might be a good time to watch the video that MJ had mentioned. She sat at her desk and turned on her pc, and the images appeared on the big screen that hung on the wall. She sighed as she noticed the many emails waiting to be read. She clicked on MJ's and started the video.

Amber had started her filming as guests arrived. She showed a group joining others in the 1920's and 1930's room, the former living room. Her camera zoomed in on the far wall and the musicians who were set up there. As if in a single sweeping motion, the string quartet from the Bayside Youth Symphony began playing *The March of the Penguins*. The city council members with their spouses and friends nodded and commented to each other as they surged forward from the foyer toward the music. Tom Corey, a local Developer who was always sniffing for new ventures, entered the main room and peered around the archway. Katherine had assumed he was there more for business rather than pleasure. He and his wife Janet stepped forward and joined the natural, gently swaying flow of some other guests, dressed in their best finery for the night, gliding clockwise around the room, pausing at each exhibit that was set up on the perimeter.

Some young children ran from the hallway at the back of the house and burst into the people circling the main room's perimeter, including Brenda and Russ who were standing beside the quartet chatting and holding champagne glasses. The kids were laughing and jumping, carrying the small, children's history books that MJ had suggested to give away. Katherine was happy to see their excitement as they ran up to their parents showing the gifts they'd been given. Guests watched the children and applauded the young musicians who had finished their song. As council members Erica Tandy and Tracy Elliot joined in the applause, Katherine noticed they nudged each other in Brenda's direction and then shook their heads.

Katherine's own voice came through loud and clear on the video now. "James thanks for coming." The screen filled with Katherine and James in a hug, surrounded by some others belonging to the Fans of the Bayside Library group who were smiling and waving at her. Some were saying congratulations.

James stepped back and put his arm around his wife. "Of course. I love history and my Lori loves fashion so what a perfect match for us."

Lori added, "I'm so excited to be in the runway show. Thanks for including me Katherine." She reached out to hug Katherine. "And look here's someone else with us." Stepping around the tall blonde now hanging on James' arm came the deliciously familiar Sandy who was grinning and carrying a large covered tray with the Sandy's Bakery label on top. Katherine noticed that James motioned his arm in Brenda's direction. He shook his head and frowned at Lori.

She saw herself in the video hugging Sandy. "Hi Sandy welcome. What have you done here? Oh wait; I can smell bacon and cheese, and something, what else?"

"Well, it's my mini quiches. I know you have this

catered, but I just wanted to contribute for you. Peter is bringing in more trays from the truck to the kitchen from the driveway."

"You're a wonder. Thank you so much. I'm looking forward to featuring many of your creations in our café. It's going to be an amazing partnership. Oh, let me have a taste." Even now in her office Katherine still savored the tangy fingertip quiche on her tongue, with the perfectly light and flaky crust. The fluffy egg with onion and bacon bits just popped. Katherine paused to make a note on her phone to order these from Sandy for the café for opening week.

Back on the video, James and Lori were also sampling as Katherine thanked Sandy and moved to help take the goodies back to the kitchen.

"Oh no worries Katherine, I know my way and will get them circulating for everyone. You stay here and enjoy your night." The camera caught Sandy walking down the hall and the Library Fans group moved into the main exhibit.

Katherine skipped over to the next video. It turned out to be her greeting the press. Frequently invited on entertainment news shows and on televised red carpets, Katherine was used to seeing her own image on the screen, but she winced now as the screen showed her wink at MJ and step out on the porch. Amber had followed her outside with her phone recording. It wasn't visible in her screen image, but Katherine remembered how she'd struggled to hide her disappointment at seeing half a dozen reporters, compared to her Beverly Hills days when couture press events overflowed with Paparazzi. Her forced smile was caught on film.

Amber panned the group on the front yard lawn standing under the bright spotlights along the path to Purse-onality. They stepped forward facing Katherine. Cameras clicked, and cell phones pointed for pictures and video. A couple of reporters spoke into their phones. She paused the video as it focused immediately on the person right in the middle of the screen. There he was, the bane of her existence since middle school, in rugged jeans, hiking shoes, and a black raincoat. He wore a baseball cap with the Bayside News insignia. It rested low over his dark, curly hair. She wasn't fooled. He may be working for the Bayside Herald, but he was also a syndicated freelancer. He could sell an event-gone-bad story faster than cheap knock- offs sell from the trunk of a car. He was right in the front of the group and watched her on the porch attentively. She didn't trust him for a minute.

Behind Rob was that young, twenty-something Purse blogger Samantha Wagner. A notorious fashion fan and reporter in training, Samantha was in tan, plaid Burberry from head to toe including scarf, tailored coat, wristlet, tote bag, skirt peeking out from the coat, and even shoes. She was holding up her cell phone and practically jumping up and down in anticipation.

Dave Sheldon from the competing local paper was smoking a cigarette under the big magnolia tree, a little apart from the others. He was pacing and looking at his watch.

The other couple of reporters near Samantha were people Katherine didn't know. She stopped the video again and zoomed in. The one gal stood out because she wore a baseball cap that had glittering sparkles completely covering the front panel and they gleamed in the outdoor lights. The insignia for the Seattle Times danced on the panel amidst the sparkles.

Amber became artistic with the shots, focusing off to the side and down the street. Her side yard and backyard were dark. The camera shot zoomed in down Main Street. In the ambient light she could see the clouds moving in fast from the Peninsula and off the Bay directly toward them. The phone shot back to the porch, and showed Katherine pick up a microphone lying on its side on the porch banister. In retrospect the microphone was overkill.

On video the light shimmered through her black dress slinking tightly down to her ankles. It made her think about the tedious appointment to hem the dress appropriately for her 5'9" height. She noted she was showing just enough leg through the side slit. The time and money were worth it, she thought. Having her auburn hair swept up in a loose style had been a good idea, especially outside with the building wind gusts. Of course, all of this was no comfort for how it had all turned out. At this point in the night no one had any idea what was ahead. The sound of the banner hanging over the porch as it flapped and snapped in the breeze annoyed Katherine now on the video as much as it had then.

Katherine picked up the microphone. "Welcome to Purse-onality on National Handbag Day."

"Who are you wearing?" Samantha called out.

She slid her right hand down along the side of the dress, giving it an extra shimmer in the lights. "This is my friend Kevan Hall. I find his designs to be a modern twist on the old-time tinsel town glamour." Then she shifted feet to feature the clutch in her other hand. "And of course, my evening bag is my own Katherine Watson 'Shimmering Cherie.'"

Pausing for everyone to get a good look at the bag she continued, "I just want to say, this has been an unexpected journey, but I'm so proud of Purse-onality where fashion and history converge."

Then he shouted, "Rob Tomlinson with the Bayside online news. What about this location, this old house?"

"I'm especially proud to be back in my hometown…"

Rob interrupted, "When you renovated this family home of yours you got a special dispensation from the city council to keep that fourth story. It isn't legal with the city height restrictions. The Bayside Conservation Society is concerned about the preservation of the community feel. The Historical Society is concerned because of the many families who haven't been as fortunate. What are your thoughts on your special treatment? Does it have to do with your celebrity?"

Katherine had planted her hand on her hip impatiently. "This house was designated a historic site. There are specific responsibilities I'm held accountable for in its preservation."

"There have been complaints filed." Rob shifted his posture forward a little.

Now she'd raised her chin and visibly breathed deep. "As you all come in, I'm sure you'll agree the intricate presentation of this historic home for our community is an ideal complement to the history told in our exhibits."

Amber's camera showed Rob shake his head.

The very young woman could then be seen as she

moved to take advantage of the awkward silence and began waving her hand, risking the phone she was holding and causing a sleek, satin wristlet dangling below her hand to swing wildly. "Samantha Wagner, 'Purseblogging' reporter. Don't you miss the excitement of Rodeo Drive? Will you miss the excitement of Fashion Week?"

"Welcome Samantha. I enjoy your blog articles. I still design my brand, and I plan to be at Fashion Week, but that's months away. This project has been close to my heart. I'm especially proud to open it in my hometown and dedicate it to my incredible Great Grandmother Ellen Stedman. And I want to thank MJ and introduce her to all of you. She's been integral to the museum and I'm grateful for her talents and support."

Moonjava stepped into the video. "MJ?" Murmurs came from the paparazzi huddle.

"Katherine calls me MJ, I'm Moonjava." The video recorded how the rest of the group on the lawn glanced at each other, and then at the 1960's jeans clad vision standing next to Katherine.

Famous E Network reporter known by her first name alone, Adriana, lowered her hand from her mouth and was the lone voice. "Who are you wearing?"

MJ made her priority clear by ignoring that question. "I specialize in the history that's represented by the purse exhibits. I'm so glad to be part of Katherine's effort to give fashion a deeper meaning beyond artistry."

The group had refocused calling, "Katherine. Katherine."

Adriana jumped forward shouting, "Katherine, will

you give us a preview of your new design?"

Katherine had cleared her throat, and everyone seemed to hold their breath, everyone other than Rob Tomlinson and the Magnolia tree pacer. "The Bayside is my new limited edition. It will be revealed tonight at the end of our fashion show. Our mayor will pull the winning raffle ticket and present the winner with the first Bayside purse. In our fashion show we're featuring one iconic purse from each decade of the 1900's. Community leaders are each carrying a different purse in the show."

Rob could be seen making a statement into his phone recording, then fingering the screen and moving toward the porch stairs. He motioned to his photographer as if to indicate she should hang back and get some more outdoor shots first.

"Please come in. MJ will show you where to set up for the show. Welcome to Purse-onality." Katherine had turned aside as Rob walked up onto the porch and past her with just a glance, and on through the open door. The film showed Bayside's newest resident watching from the doorway, best-selling mystery author Anthony Marconi.

Katherine liked his intricate murder mysteries. Now she was intrigued that he'd watched her with the press.

Katherine stopped the video, rubbed her eyes, and faced the big window on the backyard. The storm had subsided. Although there was still a misting rain, the stiff breeze had stopped. At the end of the patio, against the rhododendron hedge, just for a moment had she seen something? A person there, facing the house? Was it her imagination? The motion detector hadn't turned on the outside light. She stepped toward the French doors and pressed her nose against the glass. Looking across the yard to the corner of the alleyway that ran along the property, she thought she'd seen something. Yes, a figure standing hunched over by the white picket fence. Something silver on top of the jacket just caught the distant streetlight.

Katherine ducked, and ran over to turn off the office lights. She pulled out her cell and called. "911, what's your emergency?"

"I'm Katherine Watson at the Purse-onality Museum. Someone's sneaking around my backyard. I don't know if it's Brenda Dirling's murderer. Please send someone. Hurry." Katherine waited for a reply. She'd put the speaker for her cell on and was holding it in front of her. The phone's lighted screen revealed the white splotches on her fingertips from the tense hold she had on it. She jumped when the voice broke through.

"There's an officer nearby. We'll alert him. Hold the line."

Katherine was worried by the operator's monotone. Did she understand the urgency? Katherine watched in disbelief as the shadow figure moved toward the shed attached to the waterwheel. Too late, she thought to get a picture after the person disappeared inside the shed.

"Oh no," Katherine muttered. She spoke into the phone, "Hurry. I think it's the killer, maybe looking for something left behind? Hello?" Had the operator hung up?

"Yes, the officer is on the way. Please stay on the line." The operator's voice now sounded bored.

A sharp ray of light from inside the shed cut

through the darkness. The light jumped around. Sweat collected on Katherine's upper lip as she imagined the killer looking through her things for something, maybe critical evidence. Fear gave way to irritation at the invasion. Irritation gave way to anger. Someone had to stop that killer from removing whatever incriminating thing was so critical it had driven a return to the scene of the crime. Katherine wanted to scream. Where were the police? Maybe MJ was right about them. She pressed against the French doors. The light in the shed went out. Her breath caught in her throat. The silhouette walked out of the shed toward the alley leading to the maze that burrowed throughout Bayside and beyond.

Katherine spoke gruffly and fast, "Hello. Where's your officer? The suspect is getting away."

"Ma'am, please stay calm and hang on the line. They're on the way."

Katherine unlocked the door to the yard and whispered to the 911 operator, "I'm in pursuit."

Chapter Five

Katherine used her toes through her loafers, feeling her way in the darkness. All was quiet except the patter of rain on leaves, as she picked her way toward the shed. She stopped in horror as the open shed door revealed a faint light moving around inside. The shadow had returned? She tiptoed forward, impatient and willing a fleet of police to arrive. With her next step she walked right into the wind chime hanging from the apple tree. With a loud clang, the light turned off in the shed. Katherine jumped behind the tree trunk, between her and the shed and quietly gasped for breath.

She faced the house as she struggled to control her panic. She didn't want this figure to escape. Had he come back from the alley into the shed again? She leaned with caution to her right so she could look around the tree in time to see a person running toward the alley. On instinct she followed. As she passed the shed, she forced herself to look in the open door, but there was nothing to see. She rushed toward the alley, but her pursuit was brought to an abrupt halt as she tripped over the rhododendron root and fell hard. A couple of tears later, she rolled over and sat up. She was rubbing her arm gently when breaking brush sounded from the direction the runner had taken. She heard growling directly behind her.

"Platz." A gruff voice commanded in what

sounded to Katherine like a foreign language. The menacing growl continued. Kat froze with the dual threat. "Hands up. Slow now."

Katherine raised both hands. "I called the police. They'll stop you."

A flashlight clicked on behind her. "Ms. Watson? Heir, Hobbs." The growls stopped with the command. The German Shepherd trotted over to the officer, who was looking at Katherine. "Are you all right then?"

Katherine staggered up out of the mud, trembling with fear and cold. She nodded and brushed her hair off her face. She groaned as she recognized the officer. Jason frowned. "Are you sure you're all right?"

"Yes. There was a light on in the shed just now—"

"That was me, 911 dispatched."

"There was also a flashlight, and someone ran—"

"Which direction did they go?"

Katherine pointed down the alley. "Down the—"

The officer grumbled a word Katherine didn't recognize. "Such, Hobbs." The dog raced past Kat, nose to the ground. Quickly following the dog's lead, Jason shouted back at her, "Get back in your house, now."

She rubbed her arm again and tried brushing some of the mud off, succeeding only in smearing the mud deeper into her turtleneck. She rubbed her hand on her jeans. Ignoring Jason's command to her, she walked straight back to the murder scene. What had this person been after? Her cringing toes confirmed that her loafers were soaked through.

She ducked under the police tape, as the intruder had done. She turned on the building light and shielded her eyes until she was used to the brightness. The place was a mess. Katherine wasn't sure if that was from the break in, police search, or murderer's return but no doubt she would be the one cleaning it up.

Open and overturned storage boxes lay scattered. Kneeling down, she set one of the boxes upright. There was a clink of shattered glass. "I don't even want to know." Katherine shook her head. The gardening tools hung along the front wall. She noticed a gap where the square faced shovel was missing. A loud creak from the door broke into her thoughts. Scared, she grabbed the hoe hanging on the wall and turned, ready to fight. Katherine waited, poised with hoe in hand. When nothing more happened Katherine moved further into the shed.

Her glance followed the additional, sagging crime tape inside. It zigzagged toward the dark, back of the shed. At that end was the door that led out to the water wheel. She leaned the hoe against the wall and stepped with care over the numbered triangles and chalk marks scattered on the floor. Kat was drawn to that door. She wanted to reconstruct her friend's last moments, yet she was repulsed by the cruel threshold. The muddled path through the shed was awkward to travel as she stumbled over a tangled hose. When she regained her footing, she picked up the hose and threw it out of the way, venting a little of her frustration. It hit a watering can that was on the ground and knocked it over. The can was empty except for a shape that bounced in the light and onto the floor. Katherine went over and stood up the watering can and picked up the rock. It was a small, mostly dirty round shape. Then there was a sound, a bang against the side of the shed. Katherine stuck the rock in her pocket and instinctively crouched down behind a wheelbarrow. When all was quiet again, she looked further. Her pace was slower now, she was fiercely scanning the floor for other evidence, and she was barely breathing.

Why would Brenda have come out to the shed that night? She hadn't mentioned she was headed outside when they'd both left the office. Did someone force her to leave the party? Or how did they trick her to come out here? Was she looking for something in the back of the shed? Or, was the front blocked by her murderer, so she moved to run out the back door?

Three plastic triangles, mystery markers on the ground to her left she guessed showed where evidence had been removed. Earlier, she'd seen and overheard from the officers what they'd found. There was a handkerchief, torn paper, and some torn material in the shape of a thumb of a glove. Was there a confrontation? Or did the murderer sneak up on Brenda, and brutally choke her with that chain strap? Katherine hesitated, solemn as she approached the door to the wheel. She twisted the knob open and gazed at the decorative flowerpots, broken now and scattered on the ground where they'd fallen off when the wheel had been turned on, when it wasn't supposed to be, when it hanged her friend Brenda to death.

"You shouldn't be here. You need to go."

It wasn't so much the commanding voice that freaked her out, as it was the hand grabbing her arm. Katherine screamed and jumped. Seeing the officer, and then his dog's intent stare at her, she took a breath. "You shouldn't sneak up on people."

"You're disturbing evidence. We haven't cleared this shed for entry yet."

Katherine bristled visibly at that declaration. "Well

it's my shed and I found something." Katherine's mind raced back to when he'd taken the note from her and refused to give it back. "I found out that tonight's trespasser disturbed it first." Katherine quickly added. Sticking her hand firmly in her pocket, fingers around the jewel, she moved to continue out the back door.

"No, go out this way," the officer instructed, pointing back to the front of the shed.

"Do you always speak in commands?" Katherine kept an eye on the dog, not convinced she could trust his controlled demeanor. She took a step and reached her hand out to the man. "Maybe we should start over again? I'm the owner of this place. I'm helping your investigation."

"I know who you are. Hobbs and I will walk you back to your house." He indicated she should keep walking.

She tilted her head curiously, with a small smile that she hoped appeared friendly. "Hi, Jason. It's nice to meet you. And your dog, what is his name?"

Jason commanded, "Fuss Hobbs." The dog stood up and heeled to Jason as he walked forward. Was that an odd dog name or another command? Katherine was deciding what she wanted to do next, when Jason stopped at the light switch, waiting for her. She walked outside as Jason turned out the light and moved through the door with the dog. They were back out on the lawn now and it seemed that the storm had moved through.

"His name is Hobbs." Jason firmly closed the shed door behind them.

"Hobbs. Hello Officer Hobbs. Is that dog language you speak to him?"

"Hobbs is trained in German, ma'am." At this

mention of his name, the dog gave all his attention to Jason.

"You really are a German Shepherd, Hobbs." Katherine laughed as the dog momentarily glanced toward her and then immediately back to his partner. They all started walking across the lawn toward the museum, but Katherine began to cut over toward the alley. "My grandparents live in that cottage across the alley. I need to check that they're okay."

"We'll go together then," Jason answered.

It was Katherine's grandfather who opened the door. It was no surprise to see concern in his dark brown eyes and wrinkled brow to have this odd trio knock on the door in the middle of this terrible night. "Is everything all right?"

Jason spoke up, "There was a disturbance, but I've searched the neighborhood, and all is clear. I don't expect any further problems. Ms. Watson wanted to check on you."

Katherine spoke up, "Are you and Gran all right?"

"Yes, she dozed off a while ago. I was just getting her things organized for tomorrow. Are you all right? Do you want to come in?"

Katherine gave him a hug and lowered her voice. "Oh no, I don't want to wake Gran."

"Just keep your doors and windows locked." Jason nodded. Then looking directly at Katherine, he added, "I'll just take you back to your place now."

The deadbolt slid into place behind them as they stepped toward Purse-onality. It was a quick, quiet walk to the back door and into the kitchen. As Katherine walked in, she clenched her two hands together, pressed them against her lips, and blew her breath on them. It

51

was more a reaction to her nerves rather than the weather. She turned on the overhead light. Jason and his dog stopped at the threshold to the kitchen. Hobbs sat down. The warmth of the house was a relief after traipsing around in pursuit. "Would you like some tea or water or something? For you or Hobbs?"

She caught him looking her over from hair to hands and down her legs, and his half grin appeared then vanished as he shook his head. Irritated, Katherine wiped her muddy hands on her jeans, and walked over to the sink. Now she was feeling warmer, not from the house, or the warm water as she washed her hands. She thought she felt his look all along her back, but when she turned to face him, he was looking toward the back door. She saw tracks across the floor from her shoes.

Jason jerked lightly on the leash and Hobbs stood up. "We're going back out to surveil the area. I just wanted to be sure you're in the house for the night. That's not a smart idea to go chasing someone who could be the murderer. You did the right thing to call 911, now leave it to us. If you see anything else, call 911 again."

Jason tapped the dog's collar and Katherine followed them as they walked back through the mud room and out the door. Closing the door behind them and watching through the window as they walked away, she put her hands on her hips, replaying in her mind what he'd said. Purrada wandered into the mud room, undoubtedly hoping for an unscheduled treat. Katherine reached over to the pet cupboard and muttered to herself, and the cat, "Not smart to go chasing . . . Leave it to us . . . What a jerk . . . Chance to catch that murderer and failed . . . Incompetent and mean."

She dropped a treat in the cat's dish and gave him a scratch on the ear. She fingered the rock in her pocket. She stood back up, walked over to the sink and washed off the rock to find what could be an interesting stone. Too tired to pursue it tonight, she tossed it into the catch all drawer. She pulled up her sleeve above her throbbing elbow. "Oh great, my arm's bruised." She glanced in the full-length mirror on the mudroom wall and now she could see the muddy mess she was from shoes all the way to streaks in her wet hair along with a big glob under her right eye. "Now my ego's bruised too." She turned out the light and headed for a hot shower mumbling, "Hobbs. Jason Holmes. If you can't solve this for Brenda, I will."

Chapter Six

Tears streaming down her cheeks woke her Saturday morning. Her friend was gone. They'd never talk or laugh together again. Her grief enraged her.

After a turbulent sleep, she shivered over her nightmare. Its focus had been on that waterwheel and how she had tried to run away from it, but Russ had grabbed her and pushed her onto the ground in front of it. He showed her his wedding picture as he cried. In the picture he was in his tux at the altar next to Brenda in her gown. Instead of her bouquet, Brenda was holding that chained, crossbody bag with warped crystals melting and a panel engraved 'until death do you part'. The waterwheel turned, groaning and creaking and taunting her. On every paddle there was a different council member, except on one paddle where The Bayside Tote sat. All the council members laughed at her. They threw rocks that they grabbed out of the watering cans they held.

She rubbed the tears from her face and the sleep out of her eyes, attempting to yawn the weariness from her soul, so she could face the day and what life would now be. The sun shone through her third-floor bedroom window. The transparent, billowing, pale pink curtains framed the irresistible view over Main Street and out to the Bay, with the rugged mountains of the Peninsula and Rainforest beyond. The window was accented by the royal blue of the sill, with the rest of the room a light, creamy white. She got up from her warm, big bed and walked barefoot on the walnut floors to her dresser. She paused to lean forward and linger over the scent of the colorful bouquet in the tall Waterford vase. These were the last of the summer flowers from the Farmer's Market.

Dragging on gray slacks to match her mood, a loose, dark blue sweater, and comfortable flat shoes, she ran a brush through her hair and made her way downstairs. She stopped at the bottom by the gift shop and looked out the window. Colored leaves hung like decorations from the trees, dangling to delight. Katherine dragged her feet along the polished floors toward her kitchen at the back of the house. Her grandmother was ensconced at the breakfast nook. Next to her on the long, farmhouse table was an open book. Katherine guessed it was the birding book she'd recently been reading, a new interest of hers.

Katherine had come to enjoy starting the days with her grandmother at breakfast. It was a distinct contrast from her life in L.A. on Rodeo Drive when her assistant would have her latte-to-go waiting at the studio, so she'd just dive straight into her hectic workday, sipping while working. Instead, now she started her days with family and conversation.

Katherine walked into the kitchen and glanced briefly at the grouping of family pictures with her great grandmother, her grandparents, with MJ, her sister Helen, and her twin sons the day they left for college. She smiled at her gran. "Good morning. How are you today?"

Gran was framed by the bay window overlooking

the back yard, the alley and her cottage. Love and sympathy shone from Gran's eyes. "I'm so sorry about this horrible murder, Katherine. What a terrible thing. Who could ever want to murder Brenda? I've known her since she was a child. She was a beautiful girl. You look terrible this morning."

Katherine shrugged her shoulders.

Her gran nodded. "I'm sad too. I heard that you stopped by last night with police? I have to chat with the police today. I might have a clue that could help them."

"I'm supposed to see Detective Grace today to drop off the blueprint of the museum." Something furry glided by her leg, with a couple of squeaks. There was Purrada, fluffing.

Katherine knelt down and petted her lush black fur. "Are you looking for attention or more likely something in your dish?" The cat rolled over onto her back on the beige linoleum. Katherine stepped over to the cupboard in the mud room. Anger surged through her and flushed her cheeks as she thought of her farewell to Jason in the middle of the night. She grabbed a can of tuna and used the electric can opener. The combination of familiar whirring with the undeniable whiff of fish grabbed Purrada's attention. She immediately came on the run and waited for her cat dish to be filled and put on the floor.

Katherine walked back into the kitchen. "Gran, have you had any breakfast? Can I tempt you with some scrambled eggs?"

"You could, if you throw in a nice cup of tea and a vanilla crème filled cookie."

"Why didn't I think of that? Coming up."

Katherine crossed the bright kitchen enjoying the sun rays streaming in from outside. A cup of tea sounded good to her too, maybe several cups of strong, black tea. She filled the electric kettle and got out the tea bags. She bustled around the kitchen grabbing food, plates, and utensils. Getting busy with everyday tasks, her gran near her, the purring cat, all these ingredients worked together to help with the dark cloud in her head.

Purrada strolled by as Katherine walked over to get the eggs out of the double door refrigerator. Katherine stopped herself from tripping over the cat in front of the fridge. Purrada paused, posed, and then continued her stroll, reminding Katherine of a model on the catwalk.

She grabbed eggs and cracked them in the bowl on the counter and stood by the sink scrambling them for the pan. Her gran had turned on the radio for some music and Katherine was enjoying the lively jazz strains. She was starting to feel a little hungry herself. She hadn't eaten much at all for the last couple of busy days. She grabbed a few of the vanilla crèmes out of the cookie jar and put them on a plate, while she munched on one.

She reviewed her tea choices and decided on the lavender laced Earl Grey. She got out the bags, and then she put a couple more on the counter, desperate for strong caffeine. Then she ended up putting the whole box on the counter. She surprised herself as she stared at the box and started laughing.

Her gran applauded. "Oh, please share your cheery thought."

Katherine turned back to her. "Adding more and more tea bags to keep up with my need for intense caffeine this morning made me think of a day Brenda and I got together. I was so tired. I mentioned to Brenda about Rebecca Minkoff's purse line called The Morning After Bags. Rebecca has a knack for naming some of her bag lines in very catchy ways. Brenda and I had a laugh about it. It's just a silly memory. Brenda made fun of it by using my brand line—'behind every woman is a fabulous bag, stuffed to overflowing the morning after'. I told her I'd pass along her sentiments to Reese Witherspoon, Jessica Alba and other fans of the Minkoff bag." Gran chuckled.

The front door shut followed by humming and MJ walked into the room. Katherine said, "I wasn't expecting to see you this morning"

"And I wasn't expecting to find you giggling this morning. I thought you might want to see a friendly face."

Katherine gave MJ a hug. "Thanks for that. So, are you going to tell me what's so funny?"

"Oh, it's just silly." Katherine lowered her voice. Her gran coaxed Purrada over to her.

Katherine took the cookie plate to her gran. MJ followed her. Katherine giggled again at how her gran's eyes lit up at the sight of the cookie treat.

Her gran chose a cookie and said, "You and Brenda were always so silly together, with your little jokes and such from the very start, even as toddlers." Katherine kissed her on the cheek and went back to the stove to finish the eggs. She looked at MJ. "Do you want some eggs?"

"No thanks, but I'd appreciate tea when it's ready."

MJ sat down at the table. "Hello Pam. I'm sure you're gathering yourself together. What's the plan today, ladies? Is it back to your whiteboard of suspects?"

Pam's interest revived. "We have a whiteboard of suspects? Where is it? I have a name in mind." She helped herself to another cookie, eager to listen and to indulge.

"Interesting. Well, Katherine thinks we can solve this case. I spent extra time this morning meditating about Brenda and meditating on today's daily mantra to center myself for the time ahead."

"What is today's thought? I feel I could use some centering." Pam shifted in her chair and leaned forward. Katherine rolled her eyes.

MJ paused as if to gather herself. She stood up, arms reaching forward with her thumbs and forefingers touching. She took a deep breath. Katherine and her grandmother exchanged patient glances, and Pam leaned back in her chair again. There was only the sound of the kettle heating up and the eggs scrambling. In her own good time MJ announced, "The only normal people are the ones that you don't know very well."

Katherine brought the plate of eggs over. Then Pam said, "Yes. I can see that. And I think people who know you well are best at hiding secrets from you. Live with your wits about you." Pam picked up the Tabasco and applied it liberally to her eggs before picking up her fork, and diving in.

MJ got comfortable at the table again, with her back to the wall between the kitchen and the mud room. She rubbed her hands together briefly and grinned. "Did you know you're featured in the online news this morning, Pam? Rob wrote a long feature article about his interview with you during the gala." MJ glanced at Katherine across the room. "Did you see it, Kat?"

Pam gushed, "I'm in the paper? Oh, Peggy and all my friends will want to hear this. What does the article say?"

"It starts with your picture. Take a look at the picture here on my phone." Pam reached for her reading glasses, and MJ put her big screen phone on the table for Pam to see. Katherine was mesmerized by what she was reading on her own phone, oblivious to the steaming kettle behind her.

MJ laughed and walked over to unplug the kettle. "Are you reading the article, Katherine?"

Katherine rolled her eyes and shook her head. "Oh, Gran really, did you have to bring up, you know, that?"

"What do you mean? Oh MJ, I like my picture."

"You know what I mean, Gran."

MJ was laughing so hard she had to stop pouring the water from the kettle into the pot. "Oh Katherine," MJ exaggerated the extra syllables in her name, "every child has a favorite something they carry and cuddle. Yours is just so primordial." MJ grinned.

Katherine washed the pan from the eggs and muttered, "I can tell, this isn't the last I'm going to hear about it. This trivia better remain as Bayside gossip and not end up in the syndicated press, or God help me in the tabloids."

MJ responded, "Maybe your grandmother is right. Maybe it's the people you think you know who can hide secrets from you the best. What else are you hiding from us, Kat?" MJ laughed.

Gran spoke up then, "Speaking of cats, the four-legged kind that is, I have a favor to ask please. Do you see those new bird and squirrel feeders I've set up outside the cottage across there? I put them out about a month ago and just look at all the animals enjoying them now."

Katherine walked over to the table to join everyone by the bay window. At the end of the path, in the front yard of the cottage she could see critter standing room only at the feeders, with others circling in flight patterns waiting to land and enjoy the bird treats. Squirrels were scurrying with nuts. Gran smiled, pleased with the attention for her wild animals. "I've joined the Bayside Birders and I've been learning a lot about all these. There are pigeons, crows—not ravens here in Seattle, stellar jays—those are the loud ones."

Katherine groaned. "Oh, those are the squawkers that wake me up early in the mornings, are they?"

Gran ignored her. "I fear for my critters from the neighborhood cats." She pointed at Purrada who yawned back at her. "I've seen cats lying along the yard watching my innocent animals that are just enjoying themselves and having a meal. Could you all please watch out for these predators?" Gran stared and shook her finger at Purrada who squeaked out a meow and started licking her front paw. "Please shoo them off when you see them?"

Katherine scratched Purrada's ear and said "No problem. I'll keep an eye out."

Gran shook her head, and seemed unconvinced until MJ added with emphasis, "That's outrageous. Live and let live. I'm pawsitive I can purrsuade the neighborhood cats to move along. I'll be on the watch."

Through their laughter a side door slammed. Was that Amber coming in through the gift shop's door on the side porch? She'd mentioned last night she planned to take a break from her studies, at the college library to stop by and do some inventory for the museum shop. She also wanted to spend a little time reviewing purse donations to the museum.

It had been Amber's idea for the museum to spearhead a donation drive collecting purses for the High School Homecoming. They would go along so well with the dress drive organized by Sharon at the Bayside Boutique. These purses would be available along with Sharon's donated dresses for the girls who needed help with the costs of Homecoming. At Amber's suggestion, Katherine had coordinated with Sharon.

Amber walked in the kitchen. "Hey, everyone. Oh, those cookies look good."

Katherine put her hand on her gran's shoulder. "Life goes on." Gran nodded.

Amber offered a smile. "I'm going to do some work in the shop. Plus, I brought by the donation box from the Coffee Corner, so I can sort through that for homecoming things. Maybe something will have potential for an exhibit."

Katherine smiled. "You never know. It was nice of them to let us collect at their café."

"It's a full box. The girls will love picking out a purse for Homecoming. It feels funny to be excited about it after losing Brenda, but I think she would understand," Amber said.

"It's exactly right. Brenda loved this community. She loved Bayside High. I have a box in the office too that you can look through. Going to the Homecoming deserves a little luxury and I'm glad we can do something to contribute. A nice accessory isn't something to be denied. Not when there's a community like Bayside happy to donate."

"I don't know all that much about the history of homecoming, but I do know about proms," MJ mentioned as she sat on the breakfast bench petting Purrada.

"I sense a history lesson coming on, Amber. I swear, the Moon knows the history of everything." Katherine laughed.

"Let's hear it, MJ." Amber sat down next to Pam and poured herself some tea.

Purrada watched everyone from her carpeted cat perch by the window. It looked like she was thoroughly enjoying the unexpected, warm October Pacific Northwest sun shining onto her spot.

MJ started her story. "It was 1900 and just a few colleges in the Northeast, for example Smith College, had a simple and homemade event created to teach etiquette to young people. At the girls' colleges, the boys were formally invited. The word prom is short for promenade, and they had a formal march of the attendees at the beginning of it. Everyone wore whatever was best in their closet, and the chaperones were ever vigilant, and there were no purses."

MJ offered Katherine a sympathetic look, who responded, "That sounds like a sin of omission to me."

With a tilt of the head MJ continued, "You know, my trust is in those seeking truth, not the ones who say they found it. Anyway, it took about twenty or thirty years, but parents of high schoolers liked this prom idea too, especially since it was heavily chaperoned. They started having their own events across the country in high school gyms with snacks and dance music under streaming paper decorations."

"It all sounds quaint, and kind of plain, and a lot of chaperoning," laughed Amber.

MJ smiled. "It was the 1950's, with an upbeat economy and the country's optimism, and the high school prom transformed. Gyms were abandoned for country clubs or hotels, and fancier clothes were worn to fit the fancier places. That started an industry of prom dresses, jewelry, and purses. By the end of the 1980's the prom became excessive displays with weekend long parties, hundreds of dollars for clothes, limousines, completely overboard and not at all inclusive."

Amber asked, "And what about in the '60's MJ?"

"Well, my Prom was long, straight hair and lots of rock and roll. I was dancing up on the stage because I was playing my guitar in the band. We thought we were wild, despite the patrolling, busy body chaperones. And they never did find out who spiked the punch." MJ gave Amber a sly, sideways look.

Katherine patted MJ on the shoulder. "Your secret's safe with us."

Amber giggled. "Well, I'll check out the donations so more kids can make history."

"Oh, wait a minute." Katherine got up and walked toward her office. "Let me get you the donation box I picked up from City Hall yesterday. I just had time to dump it in my office before the Gala."

Katherine brought out the box and Amber began digging into it. She tossed a couple of the purses onto the table. Purrada wasn't pleased with that at all. She got up, stretched with a bit of clawing, and turned her back on the group, sitting facing the window to watch any activity in the yard. She wasn't ready to give up her throne in the sunlight, but she certainly wasn't going to sit still for unidentified flying objects.

Katherine said, "I'll pick up the donation box that's at the library, so you can look through those Monday."

"I can guess lots of big totes and such coming from that group, all those books to carry, and Kindles, glasses cases, cloaks and daggers. Hopefully there are some smaller bags mixed in." Amber smiled.

"Cloak and dagger? What are you talking about?"

"I'm just kidding, but they're not all mild-mannered, quiet, library stereotypes. My friend Bonnie told me how her mother was fuming about losing the grant money they were expecting from the City Arts Commission for the library's new entryway to expand the Ongoing Book sale area. Bonnie's mom is head of the Book Sale Committee and she had recommended the architect, a close friend of hers. She was waiting to celebrate the final announcement when she was devastated to read an article in the paper about the new mosaic art walk along the beach at the scuba park."

Katherine asked, "Why? What does that have to do with it?"

Amber's eyebrows raised and she leaned forward. "Nothing for the library because instead the grant money all went to the scuba park, and her friend doesn't do mosaic, so he's out of it too. Bonnie's mom said it was all very suspicious. Apparently at the next library meeting she interrupted the agenda to tell the members it was an outrage and that they should demand answers. At the coffee hour she caused a big scene when she openly accused Brenda of swaying the Arts Commission's recommendation."

Katherine said, "Poor Brenda."

Amber added, "Apparently emotional topics get brought up all the time at meetings and between meetings, even over email. Maybe the donations box will prevent them from beating each other over the head with their extra purses and wallets."

Amber laughed and Katherine's thoughts churned. She needed to be sure to check out this group. "Cynthia had talked about having an event here for her Library staff at the Café. It could make sense to include this group. Maybe a delicious lunch would distract, and we can see how they all get along, and how they don't. And just in case, we might check their purses and wallets at the door," laughed Katherine, still processing this new information. She needed to be sure to check out this group. "What's Bonnie's mom's name?"

"Um, oh her name's Leslie."

"Right, I've met her. I've never seen her upset. Shouldn't be much of a risk having her here, I've only seen her carrying a fanny pack." Katherine smiled.

"Watch out for a full book bag though," Amber mischievously added.

Katherine's gran interjected, "Oh Leslie is lovely. She's in my Bayside Birders group. She's very knowledgeable from all her library reading."

Katherine held up a couple of purses on the top of the donation box that had been in her office. "I'll see if I can get Brenda's small collection that she set aside for the museum too. Brenda would have totally supported this idea. Donating a couple of her purses to the cause will be a way to make her a tangible part of it." The last time Katherine saw Russ, he'd shoved her away from his car. She remembered Jason's radio report at the front door, poor Russ arrested. Was Russ even home?

And if he was, would he answer the door to her?

Feeling a sense of purpose, Katherine paused to pour herself another cup of tea. "Would anyone else like more to drink? Or anything else?" The ladies all shook their heads. "In that case, I've got work that needs my attention."

Chapter Seven

Katherine wanted to spend more time thinking about her whiteboard line up. The large, standing whiteboard on a rolling frame was where she'd left it, against the far office wall. The side facing out to the room showed the current updates on the design for her new 'Summer at Sea' purse. The side facing the wall hid her suspects list. Katherine paused to admire her new 'Summer at Sea' waterproof accessory with a burst of that insatiable vitality that drove her passion to create.

Ever since she'd received that very first purse, young Kat had been perplexed that leather is not intrinsically waterproof. It can be stained and damaged by water, including just by foul weather. Even more ironic to her had been that purses made of crocodile skin were particularly susceptible to water damage. It had been a puzzle that Katherine had been determined to solve. And now she and her team had done it. They had a proprietary process that was extensively tested and worked.

The 'Summer at Sea' tote bag would be launched at New York Fashion Week as the epitome of waterproof fashion. A beautiful leather grain tote meant for the ladies who beach. If knocked overboard, it's fully submersible with no damage at all to the purse, or even its contents due to the seal closure. It's even manufactured to float with up to 10 pounds inside. The splash made by this new design would be immediately followed on the runway with her new weatherproof line. This process won't be revolutionary just for accessories; her approved patent would be useful for other things. And that had all started with her first crocodile bag as a child, along with her childhood friend Brenda who had wanted a container for her teenage things during swimming. Katherine thought of that first 'Handybag' she'd made up and sewed for Brenda. As a teen she'd been sure that it would work, until it shrank miserably.

She put the tea mug on her desk and pulled the whiteboard on its old wheels away from the wall. She turned it so she could look at the suspect list in progress, until she'd been interrupted by that mystery person lurking in her yard. The thought of the ensuing chase ending in only herself being caught by that K-9 partnership made Katherine blush, and then it made her clench her fists. She was glad that at the end of the night she'd left the whiteboard facing the wall to keep her secret theories from unwelcome attention.

When she reviewed the board, it struck Katherine that this content review was similar to planning for a fashion show. It was like walking down the model line and checking what everyone's carrying to be sure all's right. Now she would walk down this board and check clues to what each suspect carried to her gala, both literally and in their conscience.

The 'Rob' was printed in broad, heavy capital letters. The door creaked and Purrada padded into the room, tail waved high. She glanced at the board and headed toward her window to settle in for the afternoon.

Then the door opened further with a quick kick by MJ as she helped Pam into the room. "Take your time, Pam. We won't disturb you, Katherine. We'll just keep you company and help you think about how to handle the museum business, now that the gala is done. I know it's hard for you to think about business as you mourn for your friend."

The pair walked in and Katherine said, "I'm not thinking about the museum now. We'll get it open this week, but I'm going to figure out who Brenda's killer is so the police can make them pay. Whoever they are, I want them caught. They've forced us to feel the pain of a world without Brenda. I want them to feel pain. When they're caught it won't be enough, but it's something."

"We can help you figure out who did it," MJ said.

Pam had been looking at the whiteboard. She pointed. "Oh, and add my suspect name to your list. It's Anthony Marconi."

"The author? Okay well, let's get started then." Katherine stepped to the couch and fluffed a pillow for her gran to sit against. "We won't let a murderer hide in Bayside."

They helped Pam settle on the couch, and as she sat, she seemed to stretch her limbs as comfortably as Purrada had stretched on the window seat.

MJ stood next to her and the board, with hands on her hips. "You have four suspects."

Katherine nodded. "First I've listed our local, opinionated, hot-story seeking, rogue reporter, Rob."

Katherine's grandmother shook her head. "Rob grew up here. I've known him since a baby and he's a hardworking, honest young man. His writing is very good. Even on the college paper some articles he wrote were published outside of the college. His mother was very proud. MJ, what do you think of Rob?"

"He's an interesting writer, because although he carries the passion of youth on his sleeve, his journalistic technique is old style. He does his research and goes where the facts lead him. He's not looking for a story that isn't there." MJ smiled in appreciation of the young man. "And he supports causes. I don't see him as a fanatic. Besides, what cause would pit him against Brenda and make him want to murder her at a fashion-history gala? Honestly I don't think he was even interested in being there last night."

Katherine shook her head. "Brenda's murder may have been a way to serve two purposes for him, a big headline and a hidden motive. MJ, you pointed out the local online article he wrote about Gran."

Pam smiled. "He's really very nice, Katherine. He got me talking and he was so interested, so curious, I enjoyed the conversation. He wrote a lovely article."

Katherine paced in front of her desk. "Well, you gave him a good article, but maybe he gave himself what turned out to be his bold headline article - 'Murder at the Gala'. This is the first time he had a front-page headline, so that's a step up for him. Then he goes on to describe Brenda as a divisive community leader, and outlines her stand on emotionally charged issues, taking the opportunity to weave in his own social and political statements. He ends the article implying more information to come, and now Brenda will never get a chance to respond."

MJ shook her head. "Of course, there'd be an article about the murder. The other reporters covered it as well, but their names aren't on your board. Rob was doing his job."

"He also casts doubt about the worth of the museum in Bayside, and the fashion industry in general. That's his job?" Katherine pointedly added.

MJ slipped her shoes off. "Live and let live, you know. You're overly sensitive. You'll prove the worth of your museum and your styles, not that you should feel the need to prove anything to Rob or anyone else."

Katherine said, "That's not my point. There's something more. It wasn't other reporters who threatened Brenda personally. Rob did that."

"What?" MJ and Pam gasped. MJ sat down in the rocking chair next to her.

"Rob said Brenda had been collecting favors, and he threatened her personally, and keep in mind that the threatening letter was cut out words from what I think is his newspaper."

MJ said to Pam, "Maybe what you said is true, it's the people you think you know who can hide secrets from you best. Or can a person be driven to change this much from his childhood?" MJ glanced pointedly at Katherine who noticed it and met her stare evenly. MJ continued, "Some people change when they think they're a star or celebrity."

Katherine's stare down with MJ was broken when Pam tapped her cane loudly on the table. "People don't change at their core, and anyone can cut words out of a newspaper."

Katherine groaned and then applied all her attention intently into the notes she was making on the board under Rob's name. She added and underlined 'fame' and 'personal threat' 'ambition' and 'accused taking favors.' "I think we've got motive, and he certainly has the strength to attack Brenda. We'll have to study more details with the timeline to see if he had the opportunity. It's enough to keep him on the board."

MJ said, "You're looking at Judith Sanders? I know there was in-fighting between the mayor and the council members. Why do you single her out?"

Pam guessed, "Oh I think I know. Is it because she was the one who wanted to open her business in that building Russ owns but he gave the space to a different tenant?"

"I didn't know about that," MJ said.

Pam nodded and lifted her eyebrows in emphasis, pleased that she was adding new information. Clearing her throat as suspense built for the waiting audience, she smiled broadly. "That was the talk around town. Then Peggy's son mentioned it to her back when it happened and so Peggy confirmed it for the Round Table."

"You're talking about Peggy's son Graham? As Chamber of Commerce President, he would know." Katherine wrote 'Motive' under Judith's name and made the note.

MJ shook her head. "Come on, I don't think that's motive for murder."

"It's prime real estate. In retail location is everything. Her business has struggled." Katherine turned away from the board. "And here's more. On the council Judith has the most to gain. I read that she's automatically put in as Mayor Pro Tem now and her agenda on the issues facing the council are 180 degrees from Brenda's. I'm going to the meeting Tuesday." She quickly turned back to the board and printed the Pro Tem title.

"She did have opportunity." MJ took a deep breath. "Judith and Brenda were standing in the kitchen before the runway show. At the time I was thinking that Brenda was on her way to get the Bayside, the raffle prize purse, for the show. But as I checked on Sandy and her hors d'oeuvre trays, I remember now that the two of them moved into the mud room, and actually Judith was holding Brenda's purse, what ended up being her noose." Katherine added the information to the board.

Pam shifted on the couch. "If you're going to talk about people who disagree with Brenda, I'd say the number one suspect is that developer, what's his name again? He's so hungry to ruin our wonderful Bayside. He doesn't care because after he's done building on every inch of our town, he'll just take his money and move on."

MJ added thoughtfully, "I've noticed that he has a cloud of glumness surrounding him always. He has an extraordinarily long neck, and when he walks, he stretches it far out in front of him and lets his head hang down awkwardly along with his ponytail, gazing straight down at the ground in front of him as he walks. When he talks to people, as little as he does, he's often staring down at their shoes."

Katherine wrote down the name Tom Corey. No one contested his qualifications for the suspect list. Under motive she noted 'building restrictions' under opportunity 'stalked Brenda' and under means she wrote 'strength'.

Katherine pointed her pen at the women. "If we're going to talk about out-of-towners, we need to consider Michael Clarke. He walked in on Brenda and me when we were chatting in my office the night of the gala. Thinking back, it was as if he'd been listening to us. Maybe he wanted to hear our reaction when we discovered his death threat. He interrupted us with a lame excuse. We need to find out more about him. He was working odd jobs."

Pam interrupted, "Oh no, he's been working for Ida Hansen recently and he's renting a room from her." Katherine and MJ exchanged glances. Pam raised her hands, palms up. "What can I say? We Ladies of the Round Table keep well informed."

Katherine paused and thought about how Michael had knocked on the open door and then briskly walked in a couple of steps. He'd had a big grin on his face as he'd spoken up, "Um, Ida asked me to find you." He'd said she wanted to ask a last-minute question about the runway show. At the time she'd been concerned he might have heard how they'd made fun of his boss hysterical Ida.

Pam shook her head. "What would he possibly have against Brenda? Bayside is his new home. Ida's family is one of Bayside's founding families. She's the town historian for Heaven's sake. He's helping her run the Founders History Museum now. Why would he murder?"

Diligent Katherine finished adding notes to the whiteboard about opportunity and means. As she put the cap back on the marking pen, she thought about a note she'd made on her phone when the police were taking her guests' names and asking preliminary questions. "There may be someone more to add. It was something that was said to the police. Hang on. Let me check my phone notes." Katherine noticed MJ gazed at the ceiling and rocked in her chair, no doubt to the beat of some sixty's song. Pam closed her eyes.

The knocking on the window startled them all, including Purrada who squeaked loudly as she rolled off the bench and galloped out the door to the kitchen and beyond. Michael Clarke himself was outside looking in at the scene. He smiled and waved broadly. Katherine waved back and tried to roll the front of the whiteboard to face further away from the window's view, but it seemed to be stuck on something and wasn't budging. She pushed harder and it threatened to tip over. She steadied it. Amber was out on the porch with him now and had taken his hand in both of hers. Katherine frowned as she wrestled with the board.

Pam said, "Your suspect list is stuck on the rug, dear." Pointing out the window she added, "Are we seeing the first clues to a budding romance?"

Katherine adjusted the wheels and then turned the board to the wall. Worry etched lines into Katherine's face as she said, "Is it romance, or a clever young man covering his tracks?"

Chapter Eight

Amber smiled at the feel of Michael's rough, large hand intertwining around her fingers. She could tell that Michael liked the feel of her hand in his too by the way his thumb gently stroked the side of her forefinger. "It's great to see you. I think I almost gave your boss and her friends a heart attack when I knocked on the window. You should have seen them jump." He squeezed her hand, and her soul soared.

His big grin melted her heart and she raised his hand and twirled under it to the music in her heart. She laughed and teased, "You're lucky Katherine didn't throw a heavy purse out the window at your head."

Amber opened the door to the gift shop and led Michael off the porch. He closed the door behind them, and Amber walked to the large cardboard donation box on the counter. A pile of purses was scattered next to it. Michael walked toward her, hands in his pockets.

Amber picked a purse out of the pile. "I'll be done in a few minutes. I just want to finish checking these out and then we can take off for the Octoberfest."

"There's no hurry. Take your time. Those are the donations you said you were picking up this morning? You got a lot. That's good for the high schoolers, right? What do you have to do with them?"

Amber briefly thought how glad she was she'd worn the bare midriff top with her tight jeans, so she could feel his arm on her waist. "I'm looking through to see which are usable, which aren't, and what kind of cleaning or repair they need." From the top of the pile, Amber grabbed a brown, beaded bag that was firmly rectangular and began to inspect it. The beading was all tightly intact, and the little bag sparkled all over as she tipped it forward and side to side. No bare spots.

Pretending she was a high schooler ready for the Prom, she held the purse in her hand. It was comfortable next to her hip, resting in her cupped hand with just a couple of inches framing each side of her palm. What she liked most was that the dainty strap was beaded as well. It was just long enough to dangle the bag from your hand, not by any means a shoulder strap. There was a zipper that went all along the top of the bag and part way down the sides. The beading covered the zipper so well, it was almost invisible, except for the large, sparkling bead dangling on one side and acting as the zipper pull. The glorious bead was just large enough to grab between forefinger and thumb, which made it about twenty times larger than the rest of the beads. Amber gently pulled on the bead and the zipper rode smoothly to the other side, opening it wide so she could inspect the inside lining.

As the zipper moved, her peripheral vision caught Michael tentatively touching a couple of small, sequined bags on top of the pile. "Let's see what gets you women so crazy about purses." He dug deeper, into the middle of the pile and Amber glanced over to see that he'd grabbed onto something metal. When he pulled out this purse his eyebrows arched up and his mouth popped open.

He chuckled and nudged Amber's shoulder. "Hey

cool, I found a chainmail purse. Chainmail like the knights wore. Check it out." Dangling from his hand was a shimmer from a tiny, metallic purse with a painted art deco design. It did look like a very miniature version of the chainmail for a knight from Camelot. It was made out of very tiny little chains that appeared to have been hand painted with a faded but still colorful art deco design. Michael turned it front to back, and around again, then he shook it up and down and laughed. "I've never seen a purse like this, but that tiny metal is sick. It's so little. Look, the purse is barely bigger than my hand, and it's so flat. What would you carry in this?"

Amber smiled broadly with surprise as she gently tapped the bottom of the purse he was holding so she could see it shimmer again. "I guess it'd be like what we carry today in our wristlets, just the essentials. I didn't even notice this beauty when I dumped the donation box out. There are some like this in the 1920's exhibit. I wouldn't expect something like this to be donated. It's a collector's item."

"You said the 1920's? This is like a hundred years old? Cool. Here hold it." Amber took it and Michael grabbed his cell and shot a picture of her holding the purse up. "You look hot. Here, let's put it back on the counter so I can get close up shots front and back. I might be able to find some history on this at the Founders History museum when I'm back at work."

Amber laughed and leaned toward him. "What are you talking about? I mean, you can take all the pictures you want, but we have the history on these purses right here at Purse-onality. Hang on a minute. Come with me." Amber took Michael's arm and walked with him over to the 1920's room. She turned on the lights to the exhibit room.

It was a mini scene straight out of Gatsby. She hugged Michael closer to her. She led him over to the wall across from them, below a hanging sign that said Whiting and Davis. Beneath the sign was a large collection of metal purses and, mixed into the eclectic designs and shapes, were about half a dozen that were the same size and similar look to the donated find. Each of these had unique, hand painted designs.

She leaned against the exhibit's railing with an air of authority. She'd studied all about this decade of purses for the Gala, so she was well versed in the history. "Whiting and Davis was kind of a big deal a hundred years ago. They still exist today, still making purses and also jewelry, but these were truly their glory days with the shiny metal and the art deco. They complemented the shiny flapper dresses at the time. In the mid-twenties they were even stars of an Irving Berlin stage show called the New Music Box Revue. Women danced in silver and gold mesh dresses with a huge purse hanging in the background as the scenery."

"These things are so skinny; how would you carry fifty thousand dollars in it? What am I saying? Anyone with fifty thousand dollars would just buy a bigger purse." Michael laughed and Amber joined in.

Then Amber continued, "With World War II, the metal was all going to the War cause and there were shortages, so they got away from the mesh for a while. The company is still best known for their metal work but never to the same extent as in the roaring '20s."

Amber tried to open the clasp on the purse from the donations box. "This one looks like an El-Sah style. If I remember right this style was the top of the line at the time for Whiting and Davis. For this line they kept the flapper trim to a minimum. It looks like less than an inch compared to some of these others in the display. Instead, the focal point was a central jewel or a pattern of jeweled stones dotting the mesh and repeated in the bag chain. See, that's what the turquoise looking stones are, although it looks like a couple of the stones are missing."

Michael wrinkled his nose. "Hmm, El-Sah? Interesting that they gave some of their purses names? It's kind of weird too."

Amber grinned. "Designers name some of their bags now too. It's an industry thing. Katherine does it."

"Good to know so I don't offend her by accident. The little I've seen her, I don't think she likes me."

Amber continued to struggle with the clasp. "She's hard to get to know. I better have Katherine look at this donation and see if there's something special she wants to do with it. Maybe we could auction it for a fundraiser for the Homecoming or something. She'll have to find a way to get this thing open though. It seems stuck."

Michael's arm was around Amber again, and that thrill up her spine was back. His face hovered close to hers. She could feel his warm, minty breath along with the gentle scrape of his cheek, and now she picked up a musky soap or after shave scent. "Let me try it for you."

She let go and he struggled with the purse as he held it and Amber closely. He gave Amber a hug, and then took a pocketknife out of his jacket.

"Oh no, don't break it." Amber put her hand on his forearm.

"Don't worry, I won't break it. This will unstick it." He inserted the point of the knife into the crack at the top of the frame and wiggled it.

"Please be gentle," Amber said breathlessly, eyes wide.

Michael gave her that smile she couldn't resist. He held the little purse up for her to clearly see, and then leaned the knife edge fully to one side. He sliced the knife edge over to the other side, and the purse popped open.

Grateful Amber exhaled and clapped her hands together. "Nice job." Her cheek brushed his stubbled cheek as their heads drew together for a look into the narrow opening to see the golden silk lined interior. Michael continued to hold it open when Amber tentatively put a couple of her fingers inside and slid down one side of the purse. Amber whispered, "You never know. You might find something forgotten, maybe a lipstick holder or ladies' handkerchief. This looks empty though. I think it's so cool to get a peek into a person's history, even if you don't know who that person was."

Michael nodded. "That's what I like about working at the Founders History Museum even though Ida's such a drag. You learn a lot about people from their past. I also like the money." He grinned.

Amber had continued to work her fingers around the soft interior of the purse, and then she took it from Michael and rubbed back and forth along a spot a third of the way down one side. "It feels like there's a hole in the lining here." She held the purse up higher, closer to the light and peered in. "Oh yeah. I see it now. Katherine will need to repair that. It feels funny along there though, almost like there's something inside. I just need to drag my finger along it. Yeah, it feels like a rectangle shape. You can just hardly feel it. There, I think I've got it." She pulled a small, folded piece of fragile paper along the inside and then out of the bag. "Wow. Let's go back to the shop and check this out."

It was a quick walk back, and Amber laid the bag down on the counter, and then the paper next to it. She and Michael leaned over the paper as she began to unfold it with care. It was folded several times, and as she unraveled it Amber could see there was writing inside. Her trembling fingers began to work faster, impatient to see what it said. At the sound of a tiny paper tear, Amber caught her breath. Michael stood closer to her side and she paused, then she started unfolding again.

They huddled even closer together to make out the words from the faded ink. Michael began to read in his low voice.

My dearest love,

I treasure every moment we've shared and wish I could feel my arms around you once again, your lips on mine, our hearts entwined. I go to my death knowing that you love me, and you believe in my innocence. I only regret we have no more time together, and the pain I've caused you.

I love you, and our dear baby Francine. Please help little Frances grow to know I'm not the vile monster these people made me out as.

My darling, let today's visit be our last time together. I couldn't bear for you to be there when they, when I take my last breath.

Instead please take Frances to our favorite spot

and read to her from that wonderful Doctor Doolittle book you have. I'll think of my two beautiful girls there. That will be my dying vision through eternity. Will you do that for me? And know I'm there, with you both.

All my love,

Harry

When Michael finished reading Amber brushed away a tear. Michael put his arms around her in a gentle hug. "This is crazy. What's he talking about? Why can't they be together?" He rubbed Amber's back with his hand. She gave a feeble smile and he rubbed his cheek against hers again.

Amber examined the purse. "There's nothing else here. And this box combined donations from the school, some of the stores around town, City Hall, and from the library. I don't know how we can trace where it came from. Do you think we could look at some of the records at your Historic museum and find out something there?"

Michael put the letter back on the counter and smoothed it out. He focused his cell camera on it and took several shots, then another shot of the purse. "It's worth a try."

Chapter Nine

Sitting in her red, 1968, convertible Mustang car with the black leather interior, Katherine treated herself to a moment breathing in the view and sounds of the gorgeous Bayside Marina. In this amazing weather she enjoyed her drive with the top down. Beyond and across the beautiful waters, the forested Peninsula with its dramatic mountain peaks was just a ferry ride away. This neighborhood was among the priciest and most luxurious in the state of Washington. The houses were large and immaculate, with small yards and tremendous views. Like Brenda's house, many were equipped with solar panel roofs, defiant of the gray days the state is well known for.

She got out of the car and slid her hand along the sleek lines of the hood. She didn't know a lot about cars, but she did take pride in this classic, expensive vehicle that was in mint condition. She even enjoyed driving the manual transmission.

She walked up to the front door and her glance hesitated over the doorbell at the hand painted Home Sweet Home sign with Brenda's and Russ' names. Seasonal pumpkins and potted chrysanthemums greeted visitors to the home. When Katherine rang the bell Brenda's son Danny opened the front door of what used to be Brenda's home. He was in his high school team sweatshirt and jeans. His hair was a tousled mess,

Katherine wondered if this was from style or grief, then noticed that his eyes were red. Hopelessness hung heavily on him as his shoulders hunched over. He said nothing.

Katherine's prepared remarks vanished from her mind as she absorbed his anguished look. Her head began to ache in a sudden and painful avalanche of devastation that tumbled roughly across her shoulders and then rammed full force into her heart. She stepped forward and hugged him, dropping the parcel of Sandy's casserole and baked foods on the ground. "I'm so sorry, Danny. I'm so sorry."

He stepped back a foot, into the home's marble entry and squeezed her arms briefly. "I just can't believe it. Why would anyone?"

Katherine glanced up at the top of the tall, paired glass doors that had been customized with an intricate wrought iron casing. She shook her head, and the boy's eyes were on her. She said, "Your mother was such an incredible person. She was so proud of you and your sister. She loved you both more than anything. No one can ever steal that from you."

"I want to find whoever this is and beat them into the ground. They murdered my mom." He pounded the side of his right fist against the frame of the door, and as the door shook, he pounded it again.

Katherine was watching his eyes flashing now with a dark tension that seemed out of place in such a young man. She grabbed his hand and as a stray tear fell down her cheek, she shook her head. "It wouldn't bring her back, Danny. We'll do what we can to help the police catch this monster. It's justice that your mother would have wanted. As mayor she would have been the first to speak out against any more violence, and she certainly wouldn't have wanted any trouble for her beloved son."

Danny put his hands on his hips. "What my mother wanted was to come home last night."

Her heart gave a physical jolt, as Danny roughly wiped away a couple of escaped tears.

She couldn't think what to say other than, "I'm so sorry."

Danny looked away, then shifted his weight looking around and then down on the floor. "What's that?" He pointed at the sack at Katherine's feet.

She picked up Sandy's parcel. "Here's something for you all to eat. I know you don't think you feel like eating, but it's for when you do. This is good stuff from Sandy that she especially made and wanted me to bring over for you all."

Katherine had to reach for his arms to give it to Danny. He reluctantly hung onto it and managed a brief, "Thanks."

"Why don't I go see your dad and you can put that stuff in the kitchen?"

He nodded. "Dad's in the den." Danny walked away, none of the usual pep in his step. She took a deep breath of relief that Danny wouldn't be nearby when she walked into the den. Just in case there was a scene, she would at least spare the boy that. She didn't know if she was going to receive a welcome from Russ.

She paused, inhaling deeply, the breath catching suddenly in her throat as she recognized the rose scent from the unique aromatherapy and potpourri that Brenda had created just for her home. Brenda's laughter and spirit were tangible.

Katherine headed downstairs to the den. She

hesitated in front of the closed door at the foot of the stairs, wanting to run home, to run anywhere, to run away. Somehow, she found the strength to knock on the den door. When there was no answer she knocked again, and then she walked in.

Stiff and slow, Russ got up from the couch and walked away from the door. He stared out the window and after a lengthy silence he became a blur from her tearful eyes. She grabbed a Kleenex from her purse and wiped her eyes. Standing so still and quiet, she couldn't see anything in particular that he was looking at outside, only that he was looking away from her. All she wanted to do was to reach out to him and try to find some way to offer him some comfort. Instead she clasped her hands tightly together and stood still, absorbing the tension and despair in the room. She shivered, despite the heat of the room and the fire in the fireplace.

Russ was still in his shirt and pants from the gala, looking very much the worse for extended wear. His shoes were nowhere to be seen, tie and jacket also discarded. The effort to talk seemed to overwhelm him. "I can't look at you now Katherine. I know you were hiding a note from your office, Brenda told me last night that she was worried about you. You could have stopped this. I can't stand it. My dear Brenda got mixed up in your death threats." He stood his ground with his back turned to her.

It was the sudden silence that stung Katherine more painfully than the sharp words. They both just stood, saying nothing until she didn't think she could take it any longer. He faced her with a look she'd sadly describe as disgust and said, "You should have called the police. I should have called the police."

Katherine's vision blurred as her eyes filled with tears. "Oh, Russ if I'd thought Brenda could be hurt in any way, I would have closed Purse-onality. I'd have done anything to keep her safe. I thought I could handle it. I thought I could stop anything bad from happening."

Russ was pacing in front of Katherine now. His voice was loud and harsh. "Oh really? You thought you'd control it all and make it turn out just the way you wanted it to. Well this isn't some new design, or some fashion shoot. This is people's lives." He stopped pacing and she could see tears on his cheeks. She gasped, willing her feet to move but her body was rigid.

As Russ began talking again, he had his back to her, his head tilted as if looking at the ceiling, his arms folded, and his tone pathetic. "You can't feel what it's like to know, like I do, that I could have saved the love of my life from certain death, but I did nothing. I attended a party and let her suffer. When she died, I was watching a damn fashion show." Russ paused then. He put his hands on his hips. "You can't feel what it's like to be pulled away from your beloved wife's body at the morgue by the police who arrest and take you down to the station, stuff you in some tiny room, and question you for hours because they think you murdered your wife because you're caught in some fictional affair." Russ whirled around and his red face made her jump. He squinted in a way that Katherine thought screamed pain. "You don't know what it's like to call your lawyer, pay bail, and be told by a detective to stay available for further questions, to come home to cops taking things they call evidence from your home. You've never had to tell your kids that they'll never see their mother again because you didn't do something you should have."

Devastated, Katherine cried. There was nothing she could say to explain herself, or to make him feel better. It was obvious that of all people, she was not the one who could bring him any comfort. "Russ, I'm so sorry."

"Oh, you're sorry. Oh, well Brenda's so-called friend is sorry. Well that makes up for it all." Russ walked to the overstuffed, leather chair and collapsed into it, staring at the fireplace.

Dazed, Katherine backed out of the room and closed the door. She was leaning against it, feeling the beginnings of a headache's dull throbbing. She walked back up the stairs and heard Brenda's teenage daughter call her name. Katherine turned her head. "Oh Christine." Katherine wrapped her arms around Christine's ballerina body. She was in pajamas and a robe, but obviously had not slept at all. Tears streamed down her cheeks.

Christine led Katherine to her bedroom. "I'm lost without her. I know kids who can't get along with their parents, but I miss her so much already." Christine reached for another Kleenex out of a box on her bed that was surrounded by several used tissues. "Daddy's so devastated. Danny and I don't know what to do. It hurts. We hurt. How could someone do this to Mom, or anyone? You're Mom's friend. You know how great she is."

"I know, dear." Katherine sat on the bed and hugged her some more. "It's hard for me to understand this too. And whoever it is, they're still out there. I'm trying to find out clues that can help the police capture whoever it is and bring them to justice, for your mom."

"What kind of clues?"

"I'm not sure yet. There might be something on her cell? Your mother used her cell phones a lot, the city one and her personal one she kept in that wristlet I gave her. Is it here? I just wonder if there's something about it that would give us some information about where she'd been or who she talked with, anything that could lead to a real clue."

"The police haven't got her phone?"

"No, and I've been calling it and it first went to voicemail, but now it's battery is, um out, or someone has turned it off - maybe so it can't be tracked."

"Well, I got to your party late. I texted my mom to tell her I was on the way when I left school. I talked to her when I got there, just for a few minutes." Christine stared at Katherine and tears started as Christine spoke about the last time she'd ever talk with her mother.

It was an uncomfortable pause, and then Katherine awkwardly hugged Christine. "You know, the last moments I was with your mom, she was so happy and enjoying herself. We were talking about fun times together and laughing in my office."

"When I got there, I interrupted her talking with Mrs. Sanders."

"You mean Judith Sanders? Were they talking about city council work, or just chatting?"

Christine shook her head. "It sounded more like an argument about the building heights limits. It was coming up for a vote this week. Mom had been talking with most of the council members about it for the past month. Mom was calm as always, even though Mrs. Sanders seemed like she was hardly listening to her. As soon as I got there, she hardly said hello to me, and she said something about going over to catch up with her husband and walked away."

"Did you see where she went so fast?"

"It was funny, when I started talking with my mom, I noticed Mr. Sanders was standing over by the band, but Mrs. Sanders walked right past him and over into the hallway. She disappeared into one of the other exhibit rooms without even nodding to him or anything. Maybe she was just making an excuse so she could get away from Mom and her city council talk. Mom had told me last week that some of the council had been fighting her on issues coming up for vote. Maybe Mrs. Sanders was one and she was tired of arguing."

Katherine patted Christine's hand. "What did you and your mom talk about when Judith walked away?"

Christine hesitated. She stared away with a distant look and mechanically answered, "She asked how band practice went and if Sam was there."

"Sam?"

Christine started gesturing with both her hands. "We're sort of dating. It's been strange because of his dad and my mom. . ." "

Katherine nodded, now recognizing the name from a recent article in the news about the new construction in Bayside, and the profile of the family running the primary company involved. "Sam Corey. You're dating the son of the developer who is leading the fight for raising Bayside's building heights." She was momentarily curious why Brenda hadn't mentioned this to her.

"He's very cool. Not at all like his dad. Anyway, I told her band practice was good and yes, Sam was there. We're working on a new piece for the Idaho competition and I needed a lot more practice. I told her I needed to check with Amber about last minute updates for Homecoming. She said last she'd seen Amber was in the gift shop with Michael. I'm sure you know that they've been dating. Anyway, then I left to go talk with Amber."

"You don't remember if your mom had her phone with her?"

"If she did, it was probably in her purse."

"The police found her business phone in her purse but the other one hasn't turned up."

"Well, her phone isn't here, and when I texted her from school I texted to her phone, not the city phone. I don't know where my dad was when I came in. They weren't together. I didn't see Dad until the fashion show started. I didn't stay for the end of that. I headed home early. I didn't know . . . what happened . . . until my dad got home." Christine rubbed her eyes again.

"I'm here for you, dear. Anything you need. Call me anytime. I loved your mom very much. What can I do for you now? Are you all right?"

Christine nodded. "I texted Sam. He's coming over as soon as he's off work. I'm going to talk to Danny. We need each other. Dad needs us. I'm scared because the police questioned my dad. He loves mom. He'd never . . ."

Katherine held her hand and squeezed it gently. "Of course not. Don't even think about that. We're going to prove that. Thanks for talking with me. You've helped me start to piece together your mother's evening, who she talked with and what she was doing. That will help prove your dad is innocent and help us find who did it. I can't imagine what, or who could have made your mother think to go out to the shed during the gala, but we'll find out." Katherine gave Christine another hug and walked to the door.

Christine spoke again, "When I got out to the Gift Shop, Amber was with a customer. I waited for her to finish and noticed my mom talking with that author who lives in the beach house down in the Sunset Sands development."

"Anthony, the mystery writer. Yes, I met him. He's doing a reading and signing this week for his new book at Georgia's Bookshop. I think he's planning to do a library presentation too. Did they seem upset?"

"I don't think so. I didn't really watch them or anything, I just noticed him talking with her, then Amber tapped me on the shoulder, and I forgot about them." Christine gave a low sigh.

"Of course. I'll see you soon, Christine. Call or text me if you need anything, or if you think of anything else be sure to tell me or the police."

Katherine walked out and back to the main floor. She was certainly not going to talk to anyone about seeing Brenda's purse collection today.

Neither Danny nor Russ were in sight, so she let herself out the front door and hurried over to the solitude of her Mustang. As she opened her car door she paused to look back at Brenda's house. Now she could see Russ leaning against his fist on the den windowpane. From where she stood, she couldn't see the expression on his face, but she could imagine.

Katherine choked back the lump in her throat, got in her car and started the engine. She steered toward downtown Bayside, and Georgia's Bookshop. Her talk with Christine had surfaced new suspicions around a developer, and also a certain author already listed on her whiteboard.

Chapter Ten

Amber rushed to the high school with the last of the purse donations. Then she drove her practical Saturn Ion to the library to do some research. Later she'd meet Michael.

The first books she skimmed through weren't very useful. Then she ran into Cynthia in the stacks who thought she could help. She mentioned this had been a popular era with other people researching at the library in recent weeks. She found a couple of helpful books and got Amber started at one of the library computers on a very productive online track.

Amber walked by Judith Sanders to get to the library printer. Judith's computer screen displayed something like legal papers, and then a screen switch to blueprints. She printed the screen information she thought would be most helpful for Michael and checked out the two books. She walked past Leslie's Ongoing Book Sale area, near the door.

Amber drove the back alleys to get to Michael at the Founders Museum. She could slide right into the back-alley parking. The maze of alleys that crisscrossed throughout Bayside always delighted Amber. Not like dirty and dangerous places in some cities, Bayside's alleys were dirt drives that were well maintained by the people with homes or buildings looking out on them. Much of it was lined with potted flowers. Amber had learned that these alleys had started out as practical driveways to businesses and homes. During the once thriving smuggling ventures between Canada and the Seattle area they'd really grown as alternatives for moving merchandise from the water beaches and coves. Amber sometimes imagined stories of clandestine, romantic rendezvous along Romeo and Juliet balconies overlooking alleys here and there, or she'd sometimes daydream about daring adventure scenes.

Her business textbook was on the passenger seat next to her, with the old love letter gently pressed between pages for safe keeping. Inside her backpack was her laptop with the fascinating notes she'd made at the library. She couldn't wait to tell Michael what she'd found out.

Sharing this mystery with him was great, but what was ahead of them at Ida's Museum? She pulled her little coupe over to park next to the fence for McAllister's Sweets shop. It was just a couple of buildings down from the museum. She didn't want to attract any unnecessary attention for Michael having her car at the museum on a day it's closed, and she might stop in later to buy a treat and head back to her apartment anyway.

She grabbed her backpack and with the book with the letter under her arm she walked, texting Michael that she was there. He opened the back door for her. As usual, Amber's smile beamed. It was impossible for Amber to hide her delight when she was with him. He closed the door and took the book from under her arm, dropping it on one of the hallway shelves. She slipped off her coat and dropped it on the floor in sudden surprise as Michael pulled her to him. She wrapped her arms around his neck and his broad shoulders, now pulling him close to her. Their embrace quickly transformed into a deep and luxurious kiss. It was a few minutes until Amber was willing to interrupt and talk about her research. She drew back and whispered to Michael, playing her fingers along his shirt, over his shoulders and his chest. "I brought the letter with me. It's inside the book. And I've got some really interesting information I found out at the library." Amber gave a jump of joy with her announcement.

She nodded as Michael grinned at her. She always enjoyed seeing his spontaneous grin. It was natural, sincere, and so carefree. He took her hand and led her into the office. She sat at the desk and Michael pulled up a chair next to her as she turned on her laptop. "Wait until you hear this. I found out who Harry is and what happened."

Michael put his arm around her as she began reading. "In 1922, the first woman to run a political campaign in Seattle became mayor, Bertha Knight Landes. She ran for office because of political corruption. She wanted to stop illegal gambling and make a better police force. One of the first things she did on the city council was an ordinance to close Seattle's taxi dance halls. That's bars where women called "taxi dancers" would dance with men for money."

Michael chuckled. "Taxi dancers? Seattle's biggest problem was taxi dancers?"

Amber stopped reading to explain, "It was the corruption in the politics, government, police, businesses that was the core of the problem really. You'll see how that all wraps into the hanging of

Harry. Remember, in 1922 it was also Prohibition."

Michael nodded. "Okay you hooked me, what else?"

Amber continued, "Seattle was home to corrupt cops on the force that used Prohibition to make money. Look, what the *Argus* newspaper 1923 article said." Amber scrolled down the screen and started reading parts of the article. "Saloons, in the guise of soft drink places, started up on every hand. Lewd women rented apartments and did a big business selling booze...Seattle has become...so rotten that it stinks."

"Lewd women." Michael laughed.

"So, this Bertha Landes was sick of it. She put the mayor on the defensive. He argued that lax enforcement of prohibition, gambling, and prostitution laws were not his fault. He couldn't stop corrupt cops, and local laws kept him from firing them. When Landes became mayor, the number of annual arrests for alcohol violations more than doubled. Speakeasies disappeared across the Seattle city line into the rest of the County, where they could still get away with it. Here's what she said about that. 'Vice and lawlessness cannot be completely eradicated, but open, flagrant violations of law should not be tolerated for an instant.'"

Michael shifted in his seat. "She sounds like a fun time at a party. Okay, so I've learned a lot about what Seattle was like during the time of the letter, and it sounds like a real drag, but what does that have to do with poor Harry?"

"Harry Blakely was hanged during this time when the laws were being tightened, maybe as an example to others. He was found unconscious at a crime scene in the office of one of these dance halls. In the room with him was a dead cop. Harry had a gun they said he used to shoot the cop. They said in court that Harry had been bribing the corrupt cop so he could serve alcohol in the dance hall and allow other illegal activities. In court they said that Harry was the accountant for his employer, who didn't know about Harry's arrangements and illegal profits. According to the news, the employer was shocked to find out all this, including that Harry was a murderer. Guess who Harry's employer was."

Michael scratched the side of his head. Then he smiled. "I've got it. He worked for the mayor who was also a businessperson."

Amber slanted her head slightly to the right and laughed. "That would have been ironic. Good guess, but no. Harry worked for Theodore Hansen of Bayside Founding Family fame."

"I didn't see that coming. I haven't seen anything about that in any of the records here at Ida's Museum. I guess proud Ida doesn't want to tarnish her family name with mention of a murder in the family history. Nice work, Sherlock. This is good to know about my boss." Michael laughed as Amber frowned.

Michael gave her a kiss. Then he blurted out, "There are historical files and old film down in the basement. There might be something in there about it. Ida keeps me working just on the museum floors that are open to the public, but I've done some exploring downstairs. I pick pocketed the key to the basement door and got it copied. She never caught me."

"Michael, she's really going to be upset with you."

"I told you, I'm good. You never know what you may need, Amber. I'm telling you she's weird. Why hire an assistant and then restrict him from the source of the exhibits he's supposed to work on? At least, I'm guessing that's all that's down there. Let's go find out."

Amber thrilled when he put his arm around her waist and grinned at her. He magically made a large, sparkling silver key appear in his other hand. Amber pulled back and picked her coat up off the floor. "I don't want Ida to catch us snooping downstairs. I've seen her yell in a rage at someone, and I don't want that ever to happen to me. Let's go to the coffee shop, or my car, or something and just Google some information online."

"No worries, she's at a seminar in Seattle for the day about recording Veterans' War stories for the Library of Congress. She wants to start a whole program of recordings for Bayside Vets. She won't be back until tonight. We're all alone here, babe." Amber put her arms back around his neck and raised lightly up on her tiptoes to meet his lips again.

He smiled at her. "The elevator." He took Amber's hand and led her down the hall to a dark recess by the side of the elevator wall. At the end of the hallway they turned to the left and Michael pushed the down button on the wall. Amber thought how dingy the doors to the single elevator were, especially in the dim lighting here in the back of the closed museum. When the doors opened, Amber thought of Katherine and how her claustrophobia would probably stop her from getting in this small, old thing. She'd spend all her time searching for stairs. Amber sighed, glad she wasn't claustrophobic, and also glad that Purse-onality had been completely renovated, with a bright environment.

As the doors closed them in, Michael clicked in his counterfeit silver key in the panel, turned it and punched the 'B' button. The elevator noisily moved down one floor. Michael put the key in his pocket and stepped over to stand right next to her and hold her hand. She breathed in his faint scent of coconut oil that was so familiar to her. She asked him, "What if Ida comes back?"

The elevator doors opened, and they walked out. "We'll be out of here by then. The lights down here are really dim. I wish I'd brought a flashlight."

Amber opened her wristlet. "I've got the light that's attached to my key ring. It's just small but maybe it'll help." She popped it on, and the little beam traveled just a short distance in front of them. "Let's look along the walls and see if we can find the dimmer switch so we can turn it up." From a brief search they found a lights panel on the side of the wall housing the elevator.

Michael surveyed the area. "Good thing there's no windows. No one can see the light and wonder who's here."

Amber was less confident about not being discovered. There were piles of clutter amid the musty scent of the large room in front of them. Cabinets lined the walls and surrounded a couple of tables with just a few desk chairs. There was a desktop computer on one of the tables. Some of the others had papers lying on them. Some of those papers were in frames. There were a few old objects too. Amber noticed a couple of store signs, a totem pole, and one table had a lot of old children's toys scattered across it. Along the back wall were two large, filled bookcases. In the distance, were two doorways framing dark rooms.

She walked forward to a cabinet and pulled open a drawer. It was filled with paperwork, and books. She noticed the outside of the drawers were labeled. The one she'd opened read - Marina and was filled with ship manifests, freight manifests, and old photos too. "Michael, these files are organized in categories. Maybe we can find some court records or news articles drawers that have something on the hanging?"

They scanned the cabinets, sometimes opening drawers and shuffling through files. Michael cleared space on one of the tables and as each of them found folders or pages with potential, they read through them together at the table. Amber closed another file folder and put it back in the drawer where she found it. This was just the start of a couple of hours.

Amber took a break, checking her cell. Almost 3:00. She had a couple of emails from friends, and a text from her roommate reminding her about the dorm party tonight. Michael's broad shoulders and strong back enticed her. He'd spent the last hour searching the computer files on the museum database.

Her mind wandered back to when they'd met. She'd been on the ferry, traveling home from hiking on the Peninsula. What a beautiful day she'd had outdoors, with the whole summer stretching ahead of her. After a quick goodbye to her friend at the dock and promises to get together again soon Amber had boarded and walked upstairs on the ferry. When she sat down and opened her backpack, she accidentally spilled its contents. Suddenly he appeared, helping her, giving her that endearing grin. It had been amazing how immediate their passion had flamed, and steadily grown over these months.

"I've got it." Amber was startled out of her reverie with Michael's jubilant declaration. "I found Harry, and his wife is Anne."

"Harry and Anne." Amber repeated.

"Yeah, this is really tough. I'm saving it with some more stuff on my thumb drive."

Amber walked over and put her hand on his shoulder, reading part of the screen. "You have so many screens open, what's all this running in the background? Where did you find this write up? What is it?"

"I had to hack through her security system, but that didn't take long. She doesn't have much set up blocking access. There's a lot she's restricted from museum visitors and guest researchers. I just skimmed some, it's pretty interesting."

"Michael, what are you doing hacking systems? Isn't that illegal?"

"No worries, cutie. Okay, I've got it all saved. Let's get out of here and I'll show it to you later." Michael was shutting down the computer when the floorboards on the first floor creaked. Michael grabbed the thumb drive and they both rushed to the table where Amber's files were laying. Michael closed the file drawers and Amber gathered the files in her arms.

"Give me the flashlight." Michael held out his hand. When she gave it to him, he pointed to one of the doorways to the other rooms. "Go hide in the other room. I'll turn off the lights and get back to you."

Amber rushed over to the doorway. By the light of the main room she was able to see well enough that this was a room dedicated to books. She saw a big, covered bin against one wall. Its covered lid was locked or else it could have been a great place to hide inside. She wondered about the big, metal tube extending into it from up above on the outside wall. A lab was set up on the opposite wall, including test tubes and jars of chemicals next to papers and books and a steel sink. She decided to hide behind the bin. The light dimmed. Odd bumping sounded from the other room. Oh Michael, Amber trembled as she hoped he'd find her. There was mechanical clunking, and then the outline of the elevator doors lit up and opened.

She was startled when Michael grabbed her hand. He whispered, "Stay down." He guided her across the room, into a short hallway. He pushed his other hand along the wall, like he was looking for something. Suddenly doors opened onto the daylit parking lot. He pulled her forward whispering "Run!" and they both ran out without looking back.

Chapter Eleven

Katherine hurried down the back stairs to grab her purse and head out to meet Ida for Sunday brunch. As usual, she was late. First, she'd overslept. Then she'd been caught up in details about opening the museum for business on Tuesday. At the foot of the stairs her grandmother's endearing, crackling voice floated across the kitchen threshold.

"I just can't think what could possibly have brought murder to Bayside. I can't imagine anyone here could murder dear Brenda."

Katherine walked in as MJ put down her granola bar. "I try to believe only the best in people, I see the peace inside them, unless they show me otherwise. There are a lot of new people moving into Bayside. It's really been growing. That's what's caused some of the issues that have stirred up deep emotions among Brenda's city council. Has Bayside angered someone new to town? Or is a troubled person living nearby?"

"Morning ladies, I'm late for brunch with Ida."

"With Ida?" her gran commented eyes wide as she dropped her spoon in her bowl.

"I know. I was surprised when she called me yesterday. She wanted to see how I'm doing, and she said something about last minute collaborating on the history event we're hosting with her Founders Historical Society at our café Tuesday morning. I'm certainly interested to hear what she has to say about the Gala and her employee, Michael."

Her gran leaned forward. "You're going to interrogate her?"

"I'm just going to chat with her, but she may give me some new information about our suspects on the whiteboard, who knows. I just need to grab my purse and then I'm gone."

Katherine bent to kiss her gran on the cheek, anxious to quickly move toward her office. MJ stood up to pour herself more coffee. "You might want to absorb my meditation from this morning's yoga."

"Great MJ, if it's short." Katherine barely paused as she started across the room.

MJ put her cup down on the counter, reached her hands forward slightly, touched finger to thumb, and closed her eyes. "Life can only be understood backwards, but it must be lived forward."

Katherine nodded and gave a little wave over her shoulder to her gran. "Okay. Thanks."

MJ inhaled noisily and plunged forward, arms outstretched into what Katherine imagined was some kind of yoga pose. Katherine walked past her. She had the purse for today firmly in mind. She grabbed her large, organizer satchel. It was a golden yellow, with tan handles and base. The zippered close went in a horseshoe shape all along the full length of the bag and down its sides. The sectioned interior was large enough to carry any paperwork, along with personal items.

In her other hand she'd be carrying the one exception to her rule of exclusively carrying her own line. It's a Nicole Lee briefcase. These fun, colorful designs of women enjoying life were this designer's signature. Katherine's briefcase showed a young woman next to her bike with flowers all around and a few picnic items in the bike basket. She put her laptop and the bags she'd designed for the Bayside Library in the briefcase so she could surprise Cynthia with them after brunch. A dedicated managing librarian, Katherine was sure she'd be at work this afternoon. She ducked out the French doors, onto the porch, and toward Main Street.

Katherine missed yesterday's sun. Bayside was back to its rainy fall weather. When she got to the restaurant she blew in the door, startling an adorable, freckled toddler who had a pink bow in her red hair. She was standing by a tall man with a matching complexion.

Katherine put the briefcase on the ground as she gave the child a big smile. "Hello there."

The little girl stared at her with a quivering chin, and then she exploded in tears and cried, "Mommy!" She ran over to a woman on the other side of her father. Katherine immediately recognized Stacy, the greeter at Al's Café, the restaurant where Katherine's gran and her Ladies of the Round Table met and dined weekly. The little girl practically leaped into her mother's arms and Stacy held the child away from Katherine with an abrupt turn as she gently rubbed the child's back. "No worries dear, it's just Ms. Watson. She doesn't like the rain. It's all right." The mother shifted the toddler's weight and said, "Hello Katherine. Don't worry. The weather report is better for tomorrow."

"Hi Stacy." Katherine managed a grin. "If I know Bayside it won't be nice until mid-July. This is the Pacific Northwest after all." Katherine shook off her coat and hung it on the end of the restaurant's rack by the door. When she turned back around, the hostess had grabbed menus and was walking the family to a table. The toddler, no longer preoccupied with her scare was wobbling along next to her mother, holding hands. Stacy briefly turned her head and raised her other hand in a little wave back at Katherine.

Now Katherine could see the full extent of their family resemblance. Like mother and so like daughter, both were wearing cross body purses. The mother's was a white Coach with a flowing fringe all around it. The fringe style was a short-lived revival experiment by Coach. The little girl's was a white, furry looking poodle face. Katherine's unfortunate streak of snobbery reared its ugly head. She attempted to dismiss it, but then gave in. By her expertise she'd labeled the cross body as the most inelegant, awkward, and disfiguring of purses, only to be used in desperate situations. And here was a woman foisting that legacy onto her own child. Yet another generation doomed, unless, the young ones rebel.

The clatter of dishes and silverware mingled with the easygoing strains from the Kenny G Songbird recording that was playing over the speakers. The murmur of relaxed conversations floated over the dining area. Warm Italian scents spiced the air and reminded Katherine that she was hungry. The wait staff walked purposefully around the tables as they presented steaming dishes of lasagna, ravioli, and oven roasted vegetables. Katherine smiled and nodded at Ida who was waving from one of the tables by the glowing fireplace.

"Hi Ida. Nice to see you. Sorry I'm late."

"No problem. You're always late. I guess you're just so busy. But I'm glad you could get together today." Katherine set her briefcase on the floor and was fine for now to shrug off the stinging remark along with her purse which she hung on the back of the big chair. There were more important matters on her agenda. She smiled and looked at Ida as she sank into the cushioned chair and leaned back to maintain her composure.

Ida picked up her menu. "It's so hard for me to choose what to eat when I come here. There are so many good things on the menu. I hope you have an appetite. All that work on your purse place. It's so much responsibility. Thanks again for including me in your little fashion show. I enjoyed it all. And, you've had to deal with Brenda's murder. How are you doing?"

Katherine paled with the memory of how she and Brenda had laughed in her office about Ida, her excitement at being in the fashion show, and her general giddiness over the gala. She paused and drank water from her glass. Her eyes brimmed with tears, and as she spoke, she tried her best to smooth out the noticeable shake in her voice. "I'm so sad. And I'm shocked, and so sickened by the horror of how she . . . I'm sure you are too. It's so unbelievable, like a nightmare I can't wake up from. And this psychotic killer hasn't been caught."

Ida put her menu down. "Yes, I'm feeling the same, plus I'm tortured with my own guilt about what I did."

The pony-tailed waitress came to the table then and asked to take the ladies' orders. Eager to hear more about this guilt, Katherine wanted to tell her they needed more time and send her away, but Ida asked about the specials for the day. Ida debated the meal choices at length as Katherine sat in shocked silence. Her imagination took over. What was Ida going to confess? Some evidence she might have? Did she know who did this? Had she been threatened? Maybe it was even a confession about a conspiracy? Katherine grew aware of the heat from the fireplace that had seemed inviting when she first sat down. She fanned herself with her napkin in fast waves of her hand and tapped her toe under the table, fan and toe now in sync. She breathed a heavy, vocal sigh.

Ida was oblivious, smiled at the waitress and said, "I'll have the lobster ravioli."

Katherine jumped in to order the linguine with grilled chicken breast and hot tea. Ida asked for more coffee. The waitress smiled as she took the menus and hurried off to get the coffee. Ida leaned back in her chair. "I've always liked this restaurant. I like that it's dark and the tables are far enough apart for some privacy. I like the art on the . . ."

Anxiety overwhelming, Katherine pushed forward with her elbows on the table and her arms outstretched across it and blurted out in a raspy whisper, "Ida, you were saying something about feeling guilty about Brenda? What did you mean?"

The waitress popped up again with the tea and more coffee. It took so long to pour. Katherine tapped her fingers and thought she could count each drop individually. Finally left alone with Ida, Katherine was ready to burst. She made an effort to project only concern in her tone. "Ida, I can't imagine why you'd feel any guilt. Can I help?"

"Oh that. Yes, I guess I just feel bad. The light was

on in the shed when I was looking for Michael. I remember seeing it, right before the fashion show. I'd walked into the gift shop thinking that he was probably talking with Amber, but neither of them was there. As I glanced out the windows, I noticed how the shed stood out against the dark backyard because there was a flood of brightness on the ground outside the open door, and it lit up the trees. I didn't think much of it at the time. I just left to keep looking for Michael. Now I see that if I'd said something maybe the murder would have been stopped. Maybe then someone would have checked on the shed or even called the police earlier."

Katherine's shoulders sank. "That's it? You can't upset yourself about that. You had no way to know. You're thinking of it in hindsight, but at the time there wasn't any specific reason to be concerned. Did you tell the police about it later? I guess any information could help them."

Ida shifted in her chair and Katherine brightened as she decided to pursue this questioning. "Was there anything thing else you noticed, or anyone else you saw?"

Ida leaned her chin on the palm of her hand as she rested her elbow on the table. "No. Not anything that I can think of. The fashion show was starting so I rushed back to the café to get in the line. I didn't find Michael until much later."

"Did Michael ever tell you where he was? You know, earlier he came by my office and gave me the message you were looking for me."

Ida raised her voice, surprised. "He did? A message from me? I was never looking for you. Why would he say that? You know, just before Brenda was found, I was talking with Judith. She was saying how tiring the squabbles at the city council meetings have become. She said she's never seen it so divided. Now with Brenda murdered, I wonder how they'll carry on. I'm going to Tuesday night's meeting to see what happens."

"I'm planning to go to this one too. With Brenda gone, and a temporary mayor in place, I think they'll try to force big changes that could hurt our town, like trying to bulldoze through changes to the building height limits. Ida, as a historian you may want to preserve Bayside against high-rises too. There are so many reasons that over development could be bad for our citizens. Brenda never wanted that. She was an environmentalist. Are the city council members voting on this again, to reverse their decision with Brenda?"

The waitress put her tray on a stand next to their table and served their plates of colorful lunches. "Is there anything else I can get for you now?"

Both ladies shook their heads. Katherine said, "Thank you." The waitress folded and picked up her stand and tray and walked back to the kitchen.

Ida cleared her throat. "So, Katherine, you sound like you have strong feelings about the council meeting. I heard you're looking for the murderer, along with the police? It sounds like you think the murderer is on the council or may be connected with them somehow."

Katherine broke eye contact with Ida. She put her napkin in her lap. "I'm just concerned, like everyone else in Bayside."

"I don't know how you can recognize a real murderer. How does anyone truly know what's on a person's mind and what's in their heart? You really can't tell anything from what they project on the surface."

"Well, you'd be surprised about that. People drop clues."

"I know a person makes an impression, but that impression can be meant to hide what's inside. You understand about impressions and marketing. Your whole world is purses. You think everything is as simple as materials, designs, and what a woman wants to carry. But that doesn't tell anything about the woman."

Katherine's grip on her fork tightened and she focused on moving the steaming linguine around on her plate and gritted her teeth. She could feel Ida watching her. Challenging her.

Ida laughed. "You don't think you can tell important things about people, about their character and their motives from what they're carrying, or something. You don't, do you."

"Ida, you'd be surprised. You can tell things about a woman from the purse she carries."

"And what can you tell about someone who doesn't carry a purse?"

Katherine frowned. Some time ago Katherine couldn't help but notice that Ida rarely carried a purse or briefcase or anything. Like today, she'd wear coats or sweaters or jackets, and jeans or pants year-round that had many pockets where she stuffed whatever she needed.

"Like you Ida? Except I noticed you carried a beautiful antique purse to the gala."

"Yes, as part of my ensemble. The costume for your show, you know and to show off something of my family heritage. That was the wedding purse for my great grandmother Elizabeth Hansen. She married into our family when she married Theodore Hansen in 1928. It was an ornament for her wedding day."

"It's a beautiful antique piece." Katherine recognized she hadn't masked the wistful tone of her voice. She grabbed her fork and knife hard. "Maybe you're right Ida. Silly to think purses can indicate anything meaningful." Katherine dove into her linguine full force.

"Fun for some and something that draws crowds, you hope, but not a real display of serious history. That's why I'm happy that we've coordinated the Founders Historic breakfast event together. Now that will really be a success. Your purses and cafe can attract the crowds, and I can teach a lot of people some real history, and we can raise awareness and donations for Biographies for Boys and Girls all at the same time."

"Free books for kids of all ages, is a great cause. At Purse-onality we earnestly believe in learning from others, since we teach too. It's exciting that we have every table fully reserved for the event. We're looking forward to hosting Tuesday's event." Katherine noticed a small frown growing in the wrinkles on Ida's face, so she added another comment to smooth things over. "I'm so glad you thought to have your event at our café. All the details you planned are set."

Katherine smiled as Ida's frown was replaced with a regal nod. The humbled designer bit her tongue and tuned out the additional prattling as Ida went on to describe the wonders of her own Founders Historical Museum and future events she had in mind.

As she periodically nodded her head to the rhythm of Ida's voice, Katherine noticed Anthony Marconi sit down at a table with fashion blogger Samantha Wagner. She thought that seemed like an odd pair. What in the world did the two of them have in common? Yet their conversation seemed energetic and flirtatious. She made a mental note to stop by their table on the way out if they were still there, just to say hello and maybe satisfy her curiosity. Another mention in Samantha's broadly read blog would be a plus too. She briefly glanced at the blogger's Chloe bracelet purse resting from her arm on top of their table. It was a gray leather mini that could also convert with a shoulder strap. The hardware was a brightly polished gold color. The publicity might be worth gifting one of her own designs to Samantha so she could be seen with it.

Katherine tried to tune in to Ida again. She was rambling about the glories of her Bayside Founding Family relatives.

Chapter Twelve

Katherine stopped at the Bayside Library. The parking lot was crowded, but there were a few empty spaces scattered throughout as it looped around to the back of the building. Many locals parked at this convenient spot when they were downtown, whether they were stopping in the library or not. The storm seemed to be passing through and there were hints of blue skies and sun ahead. She jogged across the lot and up the steps to the double door and stepped inside.

Katherine headed to the Information desk and smiled at the tall, somewhat distinguished gentleman with his Richard nametag prominently pinned to his golden-brown sweater. He was talking on the phone. As she approached his desk, he motioned with his hand and a smiling nod for her to wait just a moment. She put down her briefcase with the package of new, custom library tote bags and waited to find out where she could find Cynthia, the managing librarian. She was anxious to get on with her to-do list and then resume her murder investigation.

About to shoot off another text to her team on Rodeo Drive about a New York order, Katherine stepped aside as a thirty-something woman in jeans, sweatshirt and a backpack passed her. She held the hand of a miniature, matching blonde haired, little girl skipping alongside. In her other hand was the leash for a beautifully groomed miniature collie. Stopping to take in her surroundings, the woman and her entourage walked past the people who were grouped along the side wall tables working on computers and reading books. She noticed the woman pass assorted people who were roaming the rows of shelves with books and DVD's and other items for check out. Straining on her tiptoes, Katherine could just see a group of children sitting on the floor next to dogs. She smiled at Richard, left her briefcase on top of his desk in his sight, and moved toward the dogs. As she approached, she heard the children reading aloud.

The dogs were all shapes and sizes, just like the elementary age kids. They were dressed in a variety of play clothes, and sneakers or boots, including some a bit on the muddy side as if pulled in haste from the playground or sports field. They were paired with dogs of assorted breeds from tiny Chihuahua to even one Great Dane, and some adorable unknowns.

Some pairs were sitting, and some were lying down. One young girl with auburn hair who read with her arm around a cocker spaniel especially caught Katherine's eye. Her book was a Nancy Drew adventure, and she was mispronouncing several of the words, but the dog didn't mind at all and even encouraged her with an enthusiastic lick of her face now and then. The little girl laughed at the licks, and always resumed, pointing to the page as if pointing out the evidence to her furry friend. Katherine smiled as she tilted her head to the right and thought fondly of her own childhood bookshelf. The Nancy Drew collection had been a staple for Katherine growing up. It had been hard for her to share the collection with her little sister, who she'd felt never appreciated Nancy's courage. Her sister Helen was such a frilly dancer, never sitting still long enough to analyze. You can't solve a mystery when you get impatient and skip pages between pirouettes.

Katherine had always loved puzzling out the details to solve mysteries. On the ground next to the Nancy Drew adventurer was a small purse in the shape of a soccer ball. Hovering nearby was a watchful mother, holding a Starbucks coffee and checking her watch. Apparently, the reading was just one of several Sunday morning stops mother and daughter had planned.

A spaniel was listening to a young boy with blonde hair and lots of freckles. It sounded like the boy was just learning to read, and his four-legged friend listened with patience to Dr. Seuss, offering little tail wags at appealing points.

Katherine thought back to fun Sunday mornings with her sons when they were young and excited to visit the library, but even more excited to throw themselves at the playground on the grounds. Maybe if they'd had dog time then, her young boys could have sat still too. She started back to Richard when her eye focused with curiosity on the next child and dog pair sprawled on the floor. She walked just a couple of steps closer, and then paused by a post and large fish aquarium that defined the entrance to the children's section.

Funny, she thought she actually recognized that dog. The young boy who had a severe stutter and kept his face very near the book struggled to read. At the end of a page he checked with his canine companion. The big German Shepherd wagged his tail and barked. The boy laughed revealing a gap in his front teeth and petted the dog. The man sitting on the floor next to them had his back to Katherine and was clapping. He said in a loud whisper to the boy, "Oh wow, what did Clifford do next?" Grinning at him, the boy put his face back in the book with wide eyes focused on each word as he stuttered his way forward. The dog lay down again but watched as if following the story. The man leaned back as he nodded his head to the boy. He also gave the dog's ear a tender scratch and then a few gentle pets along his back.

She could see it now of course, even without the K-9 bullet proof vest she could recognize off-duty Hobbs and his partner, Deputy Do-Right. Katherine's jaw dropped and she put her free hand across her mouth. Eyes wide and brain in full gear, yes, she knew that was Jason. How embarrassing after that fiasco when he stumbled on her fumbling around in the dark and mud in her yard. She slinked quickly to the other side of the library post so that it concealed her from their view. This was one of the last places Katherine ever thought she'd see these two.

She peeked around the post. There was Jason pointing to the page in the book, smiling at the young reader. Could Jason have some compassion after all? He always acted so harsh, seemed so mean. He ordered everyone around as if they're just another of his grizzly K-9's. He's actually petting his dog here. And he and the dog like kids. Who is this man? No, wait; this is probably some police department Public Relations required assignment.

"Hobbs, look here. Look at Clifford." The little boy held his open book up toward the dog, but the dog was sitting up now and he was staring directly at her. Oh no.

She dashed over behind the aquarium and realized of course that the clear plastic to see the fish through wasn't the best cover. She ducked behind the wooden cabinets that had the aquarium on top. She really wasn't interested in seeing, or being seen, by Jason Holmes today. She acted as though she was looking for something she'd dropped on the floor.

A girl in pigtails and jeans wandered over. "Are you okay, lady?"

Katherine nodded and smiled.

"Are you sure you're okay? I can help you." the well-meaning little girl insisted.

Katherine put her finger to her lips and whispered, "I'm fine. Everything's fine. Thank you." Katherine stood up with her back to the children's area. She gathered a semblance of dignity around her aura, as she thought MJ would have said, and she walked back to the information desk.

This time she was greeted with a "hello," from Richard. "I'm sorry to keep you waiting. What can I do for you?"

Katherine just wanted to get out of sight as quickly as possible, before the dog reading group finished and they all headed out the door, right past her. "Oh, that's all right. I wanted to give new book totes to Cynthia. Is she here?"

"Sure, she's sorting books from this morning's delivery from Regional hold requests. Let me go get her for you."

Katherine picked up her briefcase again. "Thank you. I like your reading group over there by the way. Looks like fun." Katherine nodded toward the children.

Richard picked up a bookmark from a pile on his

desk and handed it to Katherine. "Our Ruff and Ready Readers. It builds confidence with the kids, and it's a fun time for them. I think the dogs like the attention too. The volunteers bring their dogs in every Sunday."

The bookmark had a picture of a retriever looking over the shoulder of a girl reading *Where the Wild Things Are.* Underneath was information about the program. Katherine glanced at it and slid it in her purse. "Thanks."

Richard walked away from the desk. Katherine gave a quick look toward Hobbs, who was sitting up and shaking hands with his reader. She hoped Cynthia came out before Bayside's finest walked by. She grabbed one of the books on the sorting cart and buried her face in it, with her back to the Ruff Readers. She didn't turn around until she heard Cynthia's voice next to her.

"Hello there. I'm so glad to see you." Cynthia pushed her glasses back along her nose and greeted Katherine. Pointing to the book Katherine was holding she asked, "Haven't you read this mystery before?"

Katherine looked at the cover. "*Rebecca.* Oh yeah, a classic." She put it back on the cart.

Cynthia said, "I think you've read every mystery written."

"If only I could say I'd solved them all." Katherine smiled. "Cynthia, I stopped by with a surprise for your library."

"Now I'm intrigued. Let's go sit at the tables by the windows, next to the Ongoing Book Sale Corner, and we can chat. Do you have time? I wanted to ask your advice about something." Katherine nodded and was relieved when Cynthia led her away from the Ruff

Readers. They sat at a table next to piles of boxes labeled Friends of the Bayside Library.

At Katherine's puzzled look, Cynthia explained, "The volunteer group is behind with sorting the book donations for sale." Katherine laid her briefcase between them on the table.

"How's the purse business, Katherine? Working on exciting new designs?"

Katherine nodded with a smile. "Always. I enjoy the artistry of matching design to women's needs for functionality and lifestyle. A design for every personality."

"Women like different styles, but you think their purse matches their personality in some way?"

Katherine slid her fingers smoothly along the edge of her briefcase as she answered, "Yes. If you think about it, you can read clues about a person when you look at what she's carrying."

Cynthia laughed and teased Katherine to prove her skills in purse and personality matching. "Okay, you're on. Read a purse for me here at the library. Tell me what the purse says about the person."

"Okay. Let me look around, but I don't want to be too obvious." Katherine, enthusiastic to play grabbed a book and moved closer to Cynthia. She held the book up as if pointing out a paragraph. She gave a furtive glance at nearby library patrons. "I'll start with the purses on the table by the corner window. I did notice a couple of interesting bags."

Cynthia whispered, "You mean Joanne and her daughter Jennifer?"

"They're carrying mother and daughter Chanels. The mother is hanging onto the golden age luxury and celebrity, and Joanne is a very spoilt teenager."

"I don't know if you learned about purses and purse-onality, or if you just know them well. I have to agree with you on both counts." Both ladies giggled, drawing glances from other tables, and Joanne. They both gave her what Katherine hoped had been friendly nods.

Katherine looked across the aisle, a couple of tables down. "Take a look at Chelly's bag. She's got a huge Vera Bradley. It's all fabric, vivid patterns. The colors on hers look faded, and the shoulder strap worn. This purse tells me that she's a quilter, or sewer herself, or some kind of tactile artisan so she recognizes and appreciates the quilted workmanship in this brand. She's carrying a lot in the bag because she's very active, but it's all well-organized. I'm betting she's got a complete matching set of quilted accessories inside so she can grab what she needs fast including wallet, maybe cell phone case, maybe camera case, laptop case. She's very loyal to this purse and brand. This is someone who sticks with what or who she loves no matter what and nothing will convince her to switch. No, she's not switching purses out. She doesn't have a lot of purses, because she loves the one she has."

"I'm impressed with your details." Cynthia glanced sideways again. "Look, she's taking out a matching case with her phone now. You're right. I bet there are all kinds of accessories in there. What do you say about Teresa over there, with her little clutch?"

Katherine dove in. "She's a girly type, fancy girl, and the Queen of Organization. She plans her day ahead in detail to be sure she has everything she needs in that small bag, and nothing more. She has to keep it clutter free. Of course, planning her day isn't all that hard since she doesn't have all that much going on. She's got plenty of time for a long lunch with her friends, or her business acquaintances, I guess. She's a bit of a fashionista: flirty dresses and skirts, high heels and so on. Appearances mean everything to her. She always wants to look right, have lots of friends, be in control and have all the attention on her. That's what she always tries for."

"Well, she's very dressed up for the library today." Cynthia lowered her voice again to a whisper. "Teresa was Brenda's personal assistant for how long? Did that start before she was elected mayor?"

"Yes, all through her election campaign as well."

"Rumor has it Teresa and Russ are having an affair. Is that a love Teresa would murder for?"

Katherine felt a small furnace of rage light in her heart. Disgusted, she folded her arms and admonished Cynthia, "Don't be ridiculous. A bunch of nasty rumors based on nothing. None of it true."

"I don't know why people talk like that," Cynthia stammered.

Katherine breathed deep and relaxed her grip she just noticed had tightened on the table edge. She forced a calm tone and said, "What I find so interesting is how the young gals now carry just little wristlets for every day. Like Amber in my gift shop. When she's carrying anything at all, it's just a wristlet with a few dollars, phone, keys, id, that's about it. I think it's a societal shift with the younger generation that doesn't want the burdens of previous generations. They want to be unencumbered, the freedom of youth finally being expressed."

"Katherine, you may end up seeing the end of the purse in your lifetime."

"You mean like Ida? I just came from a brunch with her and I noticed again, she rarely carries a purse. Not for me. The purse won't die for me. It will only continue to evolve."

"What about women who don't carry a purse? What do you think that indicates?"

"That person carries a lot of secrets instead. Everything is hidden away in pockets or left at home away from public view. That person wants to dictate society norms." Katherine nodded her head toward one of the computer tables. "Look at Linda over there with her boss."

"I didn't know she worked for Tom Corey. She's project managing in the construction world, but I didn't know it was right here in Bayside."

Tom Corey was subdued, speaking on his phone as he looked at what Linda was pointing to on the screen. Next to his chair, Tom's bag seemed like a mismatch for a businessman, who would carry an organized leather messenger bag to control daily chaos from non-stop phone calls, emails, and texts, and keeping information handy for impromptu questions and meetings. This sack was illustrative of mid-aged Tom Corey with his hair styled ponytail and this hipster bag. It was almost bohemian, artsy, brightly blue dyed khaki material. The bag's style with its young, wild, and free look only seemed to accentuate this developer's paunch.

Speaking again to Cynthia, Katherine focused on Linda. "She's carrying her huge leather tote, as if it was a workday. Career woman and mother of two, she has to be prepared for anything and for work on weekends. She carries files, kid things, and her own essentials. I've even seen her search through it for her wallet under a change of clothes to wear later that evening. Sometimes I worry about Linda. It's an exciting time in her life with so much going on, but I hope she takes time to smell the roses and take care of herself sometimes. It's beautiful leather though. She does have nice taste."

"You know more about people's purses than you do about them. I think you recognize who someone is, not by their face but by their purse." Cynthia giggled.

"Well I certainly recognize Linda's finicky taste in material. She'd never carry anything like those cheap canvas totes you often see. Lots of times those canvas ones are free. I thought of ordering some to give away for the museum, and immediately slapped myself. I mean, they're useful, but I see them as for students and interns and others who are tightwads. You know, there's the champagne purse-onality and then there's the ugly canvas totes 2-for-1 drinkers."

Katherine opened her briefcase with a smile. "I have something for you and the library. I've designed and made a sample batch of champagne totes for your library. I felt like I hurt your feelings when we talked before about the ones you use now. Wait until you see these. I think you'll want to order for your sale. I may even make some similar for Purse-onality."

Cynthia picked up the tote on top. She bounced in her chair and gave a delighted scream. Katherine couldn't help but laugh at her antics and blush with satisfaction at the flutter of attention from other tables. She whispered, "You like them?"

"These will be very popular. This is so much more

than a grab bag, Katherine. You got creative with this." Cynthia held up one of the fabric totes and with a hand on each side twirled it in the air. "The pale blue color is so cheery, and the material is smooth and shimmery to touch."

Cynthia pulled open the side snaps. They easily gave way to elongate the tote when desired, long enough so that it could easily carry tall coffee table books. The beribboned top of the bag had a zipper close, and in the front, a convenient outside pocket for easy access. On the outside pocket was Katherine's new signature cat, looking up at dark blue lettering - 'Booked at the Bayside Library'.

"Take a peek into the outside pocket." Katherine nodded and smiled with mischief.

"You've built in a card holder on the inside. Oh, you've done that for the library card haven't you? Nice. Katherine, you've outdone yourself. This material is so silky." Cynthia slid the bag across her arm. "Just wait until Leslie sees these. Yes, I want to order some once we talk pricing. Leslie's volunteer fundraising will spike. Her latest wish is to fund expansion of our very successful Ruff and Ready reading program. So, your bags with the cat silhouette may end up raising money that goes to the dogs." Cynthia laughed.

"That group reading in the children's area? I was surprised to see the police officer, Jason, there with his search dog. I met him the other night." Katherine ended her sentence on a low tone, trying to sound casual on the subject. She pretended to be looking for something in her purse.

"Jason and Hobbs are dedicated to the program. He loves spending time with kids, and I think he likes spending his time off the job with his dog. He really loves that dog. You know, he lost the dog that was his partner on his tour in Afghanistan. He doesn't talk about it much, but I think he misses his Army dog very much. When he came home, they reassigned the dog he was with. I know he's tried to find that one but hasn't had any luck yet."

"I don't know any details about his service." Katherine was struggling to hide her surprise at all this new information. "That's sweet that he feels such loyalty to his Army dog."

"Oh yes, he says he wants to give the dog a well-earned, beautiful retirement."

"Interesting. I wish I could help with that. It sounds so worthwhile. I don't know much about Army dogs."

"Well, I don't know all that much either. You could talk with Jason about what he's found out so far. He's reserved about his private life, but he warms up as you chat with him, at least he did with me. He came to Bayside after graduating from the Police Academy, where he went when he left the Army."

Cynthia laid the tote on the table. "You know, Leslie's going to love these. She's not here today, but I'll be sure to show them to her as soon as I see her this week. She's been depressed, ever since she applied for the grant money for her Ongoing Book Sale. She lost out when the grant went to the Scuba Diving Park instead. Leslie was quite devastated, sort of overreacted if you ask me, but I understand because she is such a passionate volunteer. She'd written and presented the grant application to Brenda and the city council and she just couldn't believe it when the mayor cast the deciding vote to award it to the Diving Park instead.

She's been moping around here ever since."

"Well, I'm sure there will be other grants in the future. I can see how the Scuba Diving Park could be a worthy organization as well. As mayor, Brenda had a lot of tough decisions to make about equally deserving but competing causes."

"It's so sad about poor Brenda. Actually Katherine, since you're here I wanted to ask your advice about something. I have to admit I'm in a situation, and I wonder if you might be able to help."

"Of course." Katherine was surprised at Cynthia's sudden change in demeanor. Only real trouble ever made a smile vanish from her sunny face. Katherine leaned forward in her chair. "You suddenly sound worried."

"I am. I got a threatening note in my employee mailbox here at the library. It wasn't mailed. Someone just stuck the envelope in the cubby. It has to do with not keeping precious historical information private. It's threatening. I told the police about it and they're coming to take a look at it."

Cynthia took a folded paper out of her pocket. "The news reported there was a death threat against Brenda that you received at the gala. I got this Friday afternoon. Do you think they're from the same person?" Cynthia held out the note.

Katherine abruptly stood up, almost knocking her chair over and startling those nearby. She grabbed for her purse and struggled to find a tissue or anything else in her bag. "Oh, you shouldn't be touching it Cynthia, fingerprints and forensics and so on can get messed up." Katherine was nervous at the thought of another note that could be from the killer. She accidentally dropped her bag and most of its contents ended up scattered on the floor.

Katherine sprawled on the floor putting her things back into her purse and Cynthia frowned and squinted as if calculating how to somehow hold the paper without touching it.

Katherine suggested, "Put it on the table." She sat down again with her bag and they both hovered over the note. Katherine had already noticed that the paper was different from the other one, but the lettering was also from newsprint. Instead of half size notepaper this was on plain, bright white, full sheet office paper. The words were just as disturbing:

Cynthia, Bad librarian. You don't protect info or library money. You will get yours. Protect the past. Don't tell secrets. When you see a book, remember this.

As she read the paper, Katherine's head tilted to the right, her eyes squinted and when she was done, she shook her head as she straightened up in her chair. "What in the world is this? Protect secrets? No wonder you're upset."

"Is it like the note you got, the night of the gala?"

"Well, they're both threatening, and made from words cut out of newsprint, but they're on different paper. This one is definitely meant for you; it's addressed to you and it was in your mailbox. The one I found wasn't addressed to anyone in particular, but it was found in the purse I was raffling away at the gala. Good thing you'll have the police look at this. They have the other note too so they can do some comparisons. I took a picture of the one I found. Do you mind if I take a picture of yours, in case I think of something about it later?"

"Go ahead."

Katherine grabbed her cell out of the inside, slide slip in her purse. She noticed she'd received several texts but didn't take the time to read them. She focused her cell camera on the paper on the table and took a couple of shots. "Do you want to see my picture of the gala note?"

Cynthia nodded and looked at the screen on her phone. Cynthia handed the phone back. "How sad."

Richard walked up and motioned to Cynthia. She walked over and he had a brief word before walking away again. Cynthia came back to the table and took the note and the tote bags. "Katherine thanks again so much for the bags, and for listening. I've got a visitor from the regional office that I need to attend to. I'll let you know later what the police say. Can you email me a price for a bag order?"

"Will do. I'm running some errands now, but I'll email later today. Please take extra care. Be careful. Let me know if there's anything I can do to help."

"Thanks. Just keep it all in confidence Katherine. I don't want the staff unnecessarily concerned." Cynthia reached out and patted Katherine's arm.

Katherine walked out past the front desk and glanced toward the children's area. Her shoulders relaxed and her stomach settled down in relief that the Ruff and Ready Readers had disappeared.

She got to the exit and walked into sunshine. The air was even warm. She walked toward her car and reached into her purse for keys. There was a small plastic bag under her windshield wiper. Strange, since this was a legitimate parking place and she'd been inside such a short time. Katherine grabbed the bag, unlocked the door, put her briefcase on the floor in the backseat and got inside. It wasn't a ticket. Oh no, not another death note? Could it be? How did the killer know she was here? Was she being followed? How close had the killer got to her?

Katherine got out of the car and scanned the parking lot for anyone suspicious. There were few people outside, and none of them were paying her any attention at all. Then she saw Rob standing behind another car, a gray four door, and he was staring at her.

Chapter Thirteen

He walked toward her, his glance never straying from her face. Katherine stared right back at him, squaring her shoulders, and secretly fingering the pepper spray she always kept handy, in hidden pockets of her purses. She held the plastic bag with the note in plain sight in her other hand, along with her keys. He never looked at it.

When he stopped at the trunk of her car, there was a lengthy pause and then he smiled. "I've been avoiding you ever since you came back. I figured you wanted to avoid me. When I got the assignment for your gala, I was happy to have the excuse to see you. You look good. You look happy. You've really made a fascinating life for yourself. You always were on the lookout for adventure. I wish we could have talked more at the gala."

Katherine shifted her weight forward on her right foot with her hand on her hip. "Oh, you wanted to talk more, after accusing me of breaking the building heights law? Did you want to talk about other misdemeanors you've decided I've committed? Or did you want to move on to felonies? I'm fine, Rob. At least, I was fine until my friend Brenda was murdered. What are you doing here today, Rob? Why did you walk over here? Did it have to do with this?" She held out the plastic bag with the note inside.

Rob put his hand on the trunk of her car and leaned forward. "What's that? I'm downtown on an assignment, waiting for my photographer. You know, you still have a temper problem. I was just talking at the gala. No harm stirring up a story for the locals."

He took a few steps toward her. Katherine tightened her grasp on the spray but held her ground as he shook a finger at her and started talking again. "You know Katherine, it's not normal to carry a grudge your whole life based on childish disagreements Why can't you put it all in the past where it belongs? We're both back in Bayside for now. Why can't we get to know each other as adults? Are you afraid that you might like me?"

"I'm not afraid of anything when it comes to you."

"Good, because I want to talk to you about Brenda's murder. I'm not getting anywhere with the police. I think they're clueless on this case. I can tell you're sleuthing it on your own. I don't blame you, since it all happened at your place. It could cause problems for your museum, or even for your bigger business. I was thinking that we could combine forces, share information. We both want to find Brenda's killer."

Katherine stared at him, and then she started laughing. When she stopped, he shook his head with a frown. "I'm serious Katherine. I think we'd work well together."

"I do just fine on my own. I can't imagine you've turned up any information that would be useful to me."

"You'd be surprised at the access a reporter gets."

Katherine paused at that. Maybe this would be a helpful ally, if he's not the murderer. And if he is the murderer, why would he want to work together? Is he trying to pin his murder on someone else? Or just keep tabs on all the investigators? Katherine started to feel dizzy at the many different ideas flash flooding her brain. What she needed was caffeine. "Well, maybe we should chat. Do you have time now? I'm headed over to Sandy's Bakery to go over catering orders and get some coffee."

"Let me text my photographer to go ahead and start without me, and I'll catch up with him later. Do you want me to drive?" Rob pulled out his phone and started texting.

Katherine opened her car door. "I'll meet you there." She sat down and put the note in her purse. Odd that he never commented on it. Did someone else leave it on the windshield? She started the engine and put it in reverse. She turned to look behind the car and he was still standing there with his phone. She took her foot off the brake and let the Mustang roll slowly. She suddenly braked so the car wouldn't hit him. Their eyes met.

He walked toward her open window. "My photographer's already in place. I have to finish the interview first, and then file it. Coffee tomorrow morning instead?"

Waiting a day appealed to her, and so did a decision to discuss this mystery closer to home. "Tomorrow morning sounds good, say 10:00? And, why don't you come by Purse-onality instead. We can talk in the privacy of my office."

"Okay. See you then. Don't run me down now, or you'll never find out what I know." Rob smiled as he put his phone back in his pocket. He walked across the back of Katherine's car, waving at her in her rear-view mirror.

Katherine backed the Mustang out of the space and turned the steering wheel to move it toward the street as she switched from reverse to drive. Something caught her attention out of the corner of her eye when she drove forward toward the exit.

Jason was standing in one of the parking spaces next to a motorcycle that was gleaming metal. He gestured to his big dog Hobbs, who then jumped into the attached side car and sat up tall. When he patted Hobbs, Jason waved, and ran the few steps toward her. Startled, Katherine gave a tentative wave back and slipped her foot off the brake.

Jason tapped on her car window. "Glad to see you here."

Katherine dragged her foot over onto the brake again when he started walking alongside the car. She lowered her window as a warm feeling rose in her cheeks. "Oh hi."

He leaned down to look at her. "I was going to stop by your place. I feel like we got off on the wrong foot. I'm sorry for the loss of your friend. She was a good person."

Katherine struggled to keep her jaw from dropping at his apparent sincerity. "Well, thank you."

Jason glanced back at Hobbs, who was watching from his seat in the side car. "I was wondering if you'd like to get together and talk sometime. I'm not working Thursday night, if you're available."

This time there was no preventing her jaw from dropping, although she tried to recover fast. They were both distracted when a car horn blasted. Katherine looked in her mirror to see Rob's car inching toward her rear bumper. Jason stood up but gave no indication he would leave without an answer. What was going on with the male population in Bayside, so interested in conversation all of a sudden? She searched for a polite way out of a commitment. "Oh, I don't know about Thursday. . ."

Rob leaned on his horn again, a bit longer this time. Jason placed his right hand onto the Mustang door. "I don't want to delay you, and I don't want to listen to this guy back here anymore, but I would like to take you out for dinner. Are you really too busy for that? I mean, you have to eat sometime, right?"

Katherine put the car in drive and pulled it back into a parking space to give herself a moment to think. She parked and got out, waving to Rob to go ahead.

Rob pulled forward and clearly shouted to her through his open passenger window, "I'll see you tomorrow then, at your place." As Rob turned out of the parking lot, she thought what harm could come from getting together with Jason once. It might not even be a waste of time. She was willing to check out what information Rob had. Maybe Jason could give her real police information to help her own investigation. "Right. Okay, Thursday sounds good. Thanks for the invitation."

"I'll pick you up at 18:30." They stood in an awkward moment. Jason broke the silence. "Oh, I mean 6:30." He started to walk away, then stopped and said, "If you have a minute, maybe you'd like to meet Hobbs again under calmer times."

"Hobbs?"

Jason pointed at his K-9 partner. "Yeah, Hobbs. He's very tame and playful when he's not on duty, like a pet. He's different when he's working. Come on over and say hello. Here's a hint, he likes it when his friends pet him behind the ears."

Katherine laughed. "Sure."

The German Shepherd's ears perked up and a gleam that appeared to be interest brightened his eyes as they approached. Jason made a fast hand gesture and the dog jumped out of the motorcycle's sidecar and ran to sit down at his side. Petting the dog's head, Jason crouched next to the dog and they both stared up at Katherine who was smiling broadly. "Hobbs, meet Katherine Watson." Jason nudged the dog's front paw so that Hobbs would hold it up.

Katherine laughed and took his paw in her hand to shake it. "I'm delighted to make your acquaintance again Hobbs. I confess I'm a cat person, but I won't hold that against you if you don't hold it against me." She put his paw down on the ground.

"Oh Hobbs, show her what we think of cat people." And with a slight movement of Jason's hand Hobbs was sitting up with both front paws out begging. "That's his plea that you reconsider your pet position."

Katherine laughed and petted the dog with both hands as he stood up on all fours now. She scratched behind an ear. "Well, you are irresistible, if you truly represent those of your ilk. I have a cat at home that would disagree though."

"Oh well, Hobbs likes cat people, but what do you think about cats, Hobbs?" At Jason's subtle command the dog lay down on the ground and covered his head with both his front paws and started whimpering.

Katherine knelt down and scratched the back of the dog's head until he rolled over on his back and she switched to rubbing his tummy. One of his hind legs started twitching. "That's very funny. You two should take your act on the road."

Jason was smiling as he crouched down next to them. "You have a very nice smile."

"Thanks. So do you." And Katherine was surprised that she meant it. They stayed and played with the dog for a while and chatted about friendly things. When they said goodbye, Jason said, "I'll see you Thursday then. Pick you up at uh, 6:30. Come on Hobbs."

By the time Katherine walked back to the Mustang the motorcycle engine revved. Jason gave her a wave as he drove to the exit. She waved back and watched him, and Hobbs lean into a left turn onto the street. He got stuck behind a slow-moving landscaping truck. Jason was intent on his forward view, but Hobbs was looking all around with great interest. When Hobbs looked at Katherine, her eyes met his just as a hard grip and tug pulled against her upper body.

Someone had their arms around her, and she couldn't scream because they were tightly holding a big, white handkerchief over and in her mouth. It was also over her nose and she could feel that it was wet and sweet all at the same time, like a chemical. She struggled, kicking back with her feet and trying to get her arms free, but those were tightly held down. Katherine was in a panic and all her muscles seemed to seize up as she fought. Her last conscious thought was of a huge, black, furry growling beast jumping up at her shoulder height, knocking the person holding her away as she fell hard on the ground.

Chapter Fourteen

Warmth wafted over Katherine's cheek. She blinked and the darkness receded. She focused her gaze to see Jason's face so close, his breath fanned her skin. Wrinkles creased his forehead and the bridge of his nose. His hand caressed her cheek and he was kneeling next to her on the ground. The sharp pain first pierced her forehead and then radiated across the full front half of her head like nothing she'd ever experienced. She groaned in protest.

"Katherine? Katherine? Can you hear me? Just take it easy, nod if you can hear me."

She put her left hand up to her forehead in vain. "I hear you. I'm okay."

Jason took her left hand in his and held it just away from her face. "That was a bad fall you took. Just take it easy for a minute. Do you know who I am? Is your head hurting?"

"Yes, Jason. I just need an aspirin. Can you help me up?"

"Let's just try sitting up at first, nothing too ambitious." Jason helped her into a sitting position and stayed close by with a watchful eye. She could hear a horn honking and then a faint siren somewhere.

Katherine was unsteady and tried smiling to distract attention from her wobbling. "What happened? I remember someone grabbed me and I was fighting to get away, then nothing. Who? Why?" Could it have been Brenda's killer?

Now dizzy, Katherine leaned against Jason. He turned his head back and forth, and then whistled sharply. Hobbs bounded over to them and lay down next to Jason. "You must have made a big impression on Hobbs. We'd driven away, but next thing I know he's jumped out of the sidecar and racing to you. Someone ran away from the dog, but they were covered in baggy clothes and a hood up over the head. They had a good head start on Hobbs or got in a vehicle because Hobbs lost the scent. I'm worried about you hitting the curb and lying unconscious. When we get you to the ER, then I'll take Hobbs searching to see if we can pick up the scent again or uncover hidden evidence."

"Wait. What? I'm fine. I don't need to waste my time at the ER. I just need a couple of aspirin and maybe a nap this afternoon." Katherine tried to stand up. There was hesitation in Jason's hands as he held her steady, then he supported her as she stood. He opened her car door and guided her into the driver's seat with her feet on the ground. She reached for the wheel.

Jason shook his head. "No. You're just sitting here for now. You're not driving in this condition. Did the person say or yell anything at you? Do you remember anything about them?"

"No, nothing. Well, wait. Um, there was a big, white handkerchief. They held it tight over my mouth. It had something on it. It was on thick. I could feel the material was very wet."

Jason wrinkled his forehead. "Perfume or after shave?"

"It was a sweet smell, chemical. If it was perfume

it was very cheap."

"Maybe chloroform?" Jason muttered.

Katherine felt herself fading. "I have to go." Katherine didn't see her purse. "Oh great. Where's my stuff." The background siren wail became ear shattering. The ambulance drove fast up the street with lights fully engaged.

The sound cut off in an instant as the vehicle turned into the parking lot. Katherine grimaced. "Oh no, I don't need all that."

Jason stood up. "It's protocol. They need to check that you're all right and see about possible concussion. I'll check on you later. Hobbs and I are going to hunt for that attacker, or the handkerchief, or any evidence."

Katherine's protests fell on deaf ears as the paramedics ran to her and started checking her vitals. Jason handed her purse to the ambulance driver. He signaled to Hobbs and they both walked out across the lawn.

The paramedics interrupted her with questions about how she was feeling, and then continued their tests. She gazed back into the distance and saw Hobbs stop and bark at a bush. She tried to crane her neck, but she couldn't bend around her attendants that far. She could see Jason run over to see what his dog had found.

Chapter Fifteen

Monday morning dawned. On Tuesday the museum doors would open wide for the first time to guests and even to a school tour. Katherine squinted against the sunshine and took some more pain reliever for the headache. The doctor yesterday afternoon had given her a sheet of instructions about her concussion then let her leave the hospital. MJ had picked her up, made a fuss over her, left her in her grandparents' care, and walked over to drive the Mustang home.

Katherine groaned. Her head ached, her to-do list remained full, and her cell phone showed far too many unanswered texts and emails. Between the museum and managing her corporate operations virtually, Katherine had her hands and calendar full, but her mind was obsessed with catching a killer. Now it wasn't only about justice for Brenda. The killer may be coming for her.

She sat at her desk with a London Fog steaming in the café cup MJ had brought in for her along with her meditation for Monday—"You can't reach for anything new if your hands are still full of yesterday's junk." Katherine was just thankful for the tea. She petted Purrada who was lying on the desk. Her green eyes were steady, gazing off into the distance and her purr resonated. Katherine's dark brown eyes were focused on the note that had been on her windshield. She finally got to read it this morning.

Stay out of this or history will repeat

Determination growing, Katherine looked at more video from the gala that she had shot herself. It started outside the gift shop. Katherine remembered that at the time she'd been looking for Ida, trying to find her because Michael had made a point about Ida looking for her.

Katherine sipped her flavorful tea and leaned back in her chair to watch the screen. With some amusement, she noticed the dance of the guests as they stepped together along the wall of exhibits, almost to the tempo of the high school musicians.

The camera moved 180 degrees showing the gift shop. There was Amber attentive, listening to Michael whispering close to her ear. Then they gazed at each other. Michael spoke again, and it didn't look like it had anything to do with the inventory. Sitting behind her desk, Katherine frowned at the loving scene and put her hot tea down next to the keyboard. Conversations scattered throughout the crowd on the video made the couple's voices difficult to distinguish.

The camera was off the two young lovebirds now and past the few people standing in the alcove and continued forward into the main room. Katherine could hear herself greeting guests. On the video Brenda had joined Russ at a display. Ahead of them council members, including Judith Sanders whispered together and cast furtive glances at their mayor.

A motion out of sync drew Katherine's eye. The video showed Tom Corey, the eager developer, gesture toward Brenda and then speak rapidly to the man sitting next to him. Katherine zoomed forward on the screen for a better look. He was talking to Rob Tomlinson. She could see how tense Tom's expression was, and Rob was nodding and writing notes. He gestured in Brenda's direction. Was he complaining again about Brenda's efforts to form a coalition to maintain Bayside's building height limits? It wouldn't have been the first time, but perhaps the first time he'd talked to the press.

The camera bumped at this point, in the blur Katherine could see a few media people brush past. MJ was herding them toward the runway platform which was set up in the café at the back of the main room, separated by curtained French doors. The camera showed MJ open the doors and usher the group through to cover the show and the raffle winner. More people followed them. The camera jostled and ended up with a look back over to Tom Corey and Rob. That scene was calmer now, the men joined by two smiling women and all were chatting.

The camera turned back as one voice rose above all, "Pam, that's your mother." Peggy pointed at an enlarged photo of Katherine's great grandmother as a British plane spotter on the Welsh coast during WWII. It was hanging in the hallway across from the café entry, next to a closed door sporting a sign "Coming Attractions, the 1940's".

Katherine's gran beamed as she said to her friends, "Surprise."

The Ladies of the Round Table fussed about her and acted appropriately impressed. Katherine couldn't understand why they made such a big deal about it when the exhibit wasn't even completed yet.

"Oh Pam, how wonderful!" Peggy said. The other ladies were cheering, and Margaret described the photo to blind Winifred, holding her hand up to it so she could feel the size and texture of the walnut frame.

In the photo was a beautiful twenty-year-old with dark, short hair with loose curls framing her face. The rare black and white photo from that time, showed her sitting on the hillside on a cloudy day, smiling for the camera and holding her long range binoculars and handheld transceiver next to her on a large blanket of Welsh tapestry. Next to her was a leather, olive-drab colored satchel with a fold over flap and long wide strap. Prominent was a British Mark VII logo.

Rob walked into the video now, voice first. "Excuse me, Mrs. Watson? Do you remember me? Rob Tomlinson."

"Well yes, of course I do. You and Katherine were in school together. How are you, and your parents?" Katherine's gran on the screen smiled at Rob. Katherine cringed at this man she'd loathed her childhood years, and then she groaned as she remembered she's meeting him later today. She refocused her attention on the video. Rob was talking to her gran.

"We're all fine. I'm a reporter with the news. I know our readers would be interested in hearing about how you feel about this gala, and especially the story behind this beautiful picture." Rob held his index finger up as he backed into the café, grabbed a chair and offered it to Pam so she could sit down next to the picture. He and several people nearby took pictures of Pam together with the picture. "Will you tell me about your mother's picture? Where was it taken? What is she doing?"

Her gran wore a pleased expression. Pam cleared her throat and the corners of her mouth turned up.

"That's Carlton Hill just a five mile walk from her home in Brighton, England. During the Blitz, bombing of London in The War, she was one of Mr. Churchill's plane spotters."

The other Ladies of the Round Table all nodded. A few other guests paused to listen. Rob shook his head and asked, "Plane Spotters?" He shifted feet and glanced down at his phone to make sure it was recording.

Katherine sighed and noticed she was tapping her foot. If she had a dollar for every time this story was told, but the attention that night confirmed it was going to make a great display with the museum's expansion. Katherine had already imagined how she wanted to set it up. She stared at MJ in the video. She was nodding and smiling and encouraging Gran, as if she needed any encouragement at this point. Katherine considered skipping ahead, but she didn't want to miss any clues.

Pam nodded once and resumed her story. "There were many volunteers, along the coastline in particular. They'd radio about any German plane sightings, how many, which direction they were heading, what type of planes, and any other information. Good weather or bad, my mother could be there for hours, battling to stay awake and searching for enemy planes. Often there was nothing to report. Bravo for that. But sometimes there was. German planes would fly over on their way to London or to factory locations. They didn't always drop bombs on predictable locations either. My mother told me she saw enough planes that she could recognize the different types just by the sound."

Rob stopped the recording on his phone and said, "I bet the radioed warnings gave people time to get into bomb shelters and saved lives. Are you designing the new exhibit?"

In the video the group of Founders Historical Society members had stopped talking and was huddled right in the middle of the entry from the other room to hear the end of the story. Katherine noted that Ida wasn't there. They applauded Pam, giving rise to a blush in her cheeks.

Katherine was surprised she didn't see Ida orchestrating the group, directing them when to take notes and commenting on their remarks. She was usually the center of their attention. Some of the members glanced sideways at Tom Corey and some even frowned. No surprise. Historians had little use for Developers. Ida spearheaded that open antagonism. Where was Ida anyway? Was she backstage preparing for her grand runway appearance?

Some young children running headlong through the hallway for the main room crashed into her video. They burst in, surprising people including Brenda and Russ who stood behind the string quartet, about to enter the 1930's room. The kids were laughing and jumping, carrying the children's history books that MJ had suggested to give away. Their excitement was palpable as they ran up to their parents eager to show the gift they'd been given. Brenda and a few others stopped in the doorway to watch the children and to applaud the young high school musicians who had just finished a song.

Stopping the video, Katherine rubbed her temples. There was a knock on her office door and Amber popped in. "Good morning. MJ told me what happened. How are you feeling?"

"I'm doing all right, a little low on energy this morning but I'm fine."

"Don't overdo it. That reporter is here from the paper and wants to see you. Should I tell him to come back another day? Or I can give him a tour and answer any questions if it's for an article on the museum."

"He's early for a 10:00 meeting we had. I might as well get it over with. Please let him in."

Katherine had just turned off her large screen and taken another pain reliever tablet when Rob's voice preceded him into the room. "Katherine I've been thinking about my article on the investigation, and I just need corroboration from you and a look at that note. I have a few questions for you that I want on the record too." Rob sat down with his phone on the desk between them.

She leaned forward and perched her head on her hands. "Don't turn your recorder on. I have a few questions for you first. We're talking to each other, but don't start thinking we're friends. We still need to clear the air. I heard you threaten Brenda at the gala. You said it was personal. What was your grievance against her?"

Rob paled, and she felt like the momentum had swung her way. He put his phone back in his pocket. "I don't know what you're talking about."

Katherine played the video of the dramatic encounter on her large screen for him to see. At the end he stroked his chin and stared back at her. "That's not what it looks like. And even if it was, what are you accusing me of? You really think that little of me? You're nuts. I don't kill people that I have disagreements with. Don't you know, the pen is mightier than the sword? I'm telling you, her policies played favorites with Bayside's elitists. I was going to expose her to the voters during the upcoming election, so she'd be stopped. It's a personal vendetta because her politics drove my mother out of her business. My war against Brenda was waged in my paper and my blog, not in your shed. I spent the gala working. Ask my photographer."

Katherine was taken back with his vigorous defense, and for the first time in this case she doubted herself. She made a mental note to check with that photographer. "I'm just asking you about it, Rob. How would I know you worked during the gala? You never published an article about the museum itself. All your press coverage is sensationalism on the murder."

"That's your complaint? You didn't get your press release? You'll get it when my editor decides. It's news, but not top news now. I want to ask you some questions about the husband out on bail. He was having an affair according to some of my sources. Can you corroborate?"

"No!"

"What about that note then? Can I get a look at that?"

Katherine wasn't ready to trust Rob with the new note, so instead she showed him the picture she'd taken of the gala note. She didn't want to subject Cynthia to Rob either, so she kept the picture of her note hidden. His expression turned puzzled, and she was surprised to see him speechless. She tamped down her impatience watching Purrada and counting her constant tail waves as she sprawled across the conference table. Rob interrupted her count. "That's weird it's made from cut out letters from a newspaper. Easy for the killer to get their hands on I guess but old school and a computer printed note is much handier."

Rob reached over and made the image larger and studied it. "You know, this print looks like it might be the jumble puzzle letters font. I wonder. Can you text this to me?"

"Will you let me know what you find out?"

"Text me and I'll tell you what I find." Rob got up from his chair and leaned on the desk. "You know, I don't have anything against you Katherine, despite how you've treated me over the years, but I do have my limits. Don't ever accuse me of murder and then ask about your museum's press, not if you want to stay on my good side." And with that Rob walked out of her office.

Chapter Sixteen

The last thing Katherine wanted to do this Monday night was sit at the Bayside Bookshop and listen to the local celebrity talk about writing. She was on a double dose of pain reliever. The store owner Georgia had fully supported her museum opening and for Katherine, as she shifted uncomfortably in the metal chair that was wedged in with about thirty others, this was her thank you.

Every chair was filled, plus standing room quickly disappearing. Katherine had exchanged greetings with the ladies sitting next to her. She noticed it was already five minutes past the announced start time. She fingered the luxurious midnight blue pebble leather at the top of her swagger style KW purse. As she thought about the time to design these smart organizing compartments and hidden pockets, Georgia's unique, snorting laugh simmered up to overflowing from the back of the store. Katherine turned her head to see between bodies standing behind her. Anthony Marconi and Georgia walked together to stand in front of the group. Georgia wore a frilly black dress showing off her petite figure and contrasting with her golden blonde hair. Her gaze lingered dreamily on Anthony's face and then she addressed the audience. Katherine couldn't remember Georgia ever wearing a dress to work before.

"I'm so honored to have this special event and I

hope you all enjoy yourselves this evening. Our special speaker is renowned, New York Times Bestselling mystery author Anthony Marconi…" She was interrupted by a twittering of applause, giggles and some sighs. Katherine had woken up from her laconic daze now and examined the crowd. It was a fully female audience, and a couple more women walking in the door. When it quieted down in the room, Georgia continued with the introduction no one was interested to hear. The audience was energized and on the edges of their chairs. Anthony stood just to the side, gazing out at his adoring fans with a charming smile. His black, wavy hair was shiny in the overhead lighting. His broad shoulders were accentuated in the navy blue, pullover shirt with its four buttons open from the loose neckline, hinting at a tan chest and toned abs. He gave a strong waving movement with his large right hand that was appreciated by the crowd. Katherine leaned back and thought, oh for Heaven's sake.

Coy Georgia stepped aside to sit in a chair just to the side of her speaker. Anticipation heated the room. The author stepped forward with a wink and a nod. "Georgia, you've knocked me out with such a nice introduction." He gestured with a hand to his audience. "And your co-conspirators here are killing me with the kindness of their welcome.

"Let me tell you about my new thriller, titled *Murder in High Places*. This new mystery in my Jack Hart PI series, he's hired undercover by the mayor of Los Angeles to check into his suspicions of corruption in the city government, and report back to the mayor directly. Their relationship takes on a dimension beyond business, as they begin a romantic rendezvous.

Jack is going to deliver his preliminary findings on the corruption, when the mayor is found murdered. The power struggle that follows is dangerous for city officials, citizens, and the killer targets Jack, knowing he is part of the mayor's investigation. Jack is reeling. . ." His pause enhanced the full impact of his statement on his audience. "That's right. He'd fallen in love with the mayor and vowed to avenge her."

Katherine dove deep into thought. Are these similarities to our real-life tragedy? Was there a real background behind this plot? How well had Brenda known Anthony? But, no, Brenda and Russ the happiest of couples were dedicated to each other. Brenda could never be interested in anything like this man. Could she? He's an author. He must be exaggerating, imagining, fictionalizing. Katherine couldn't imagine that Brenda wouldn't have told her if there had been something between them. She needed to find out more about this man, more about where he was and when at the gala.

He answered questions from the audience now. Diana, assistant baker at Sandy's shop stood up with enthusiasm and batted her eyelashes. "How do you like living here in Bayside? Do you ever miss New York?"

The author leaned back casually against the desk. He smiled, engaging his audience as the group leaned further forward almost in unison. "I have great affection for my adopted town of Bayside and its charming residents. New York is a vague memory, and pales in comparison to a sweet harbor town like this in the Pacific Northwest where I'm able to see and speak with such lovely people as all of you every day. Am I right? I mean, am I right? I'm a lucky guy." The crowd murmured their agreement. Diana blushed when Anthony winked at her as she sat down.

Georgia stood and waved her arm in the air to get everyone's attention. "Mr. Marconi is nice enough to stay and sign book copies if you'd like to form a line. Thank you so much Anthony." Georgia began the applause and the eager crowd joined in. People rushed forward to form a line. Katherine hadn't planned to buy a book, until she found out about the plot. Now she thought she should study this mystery, and also make some notes on her whiteboard about suspect Anthony Marconi.

It took some time for her to get to the front of the line since she was at the end of the rush, and everyone took extra time chatting with the author during their turn with him. Katherine tapped her fingers on the back of her book copy, then noticing her impatience she mentally scolded herself to get her emotions under control despite her tiredness, which she blamed on the concussion. As she got closer to the author a few of the single young women slipped a piece of paper clumsily into the author's hand when he handed them back their signed copy. Katherine rolled her eyes as she presumed the papers had their phone number or other contact information. Finally, she stood in front of the author. A handful of ladies were chatting with Georgia at the front door.

"Well hello, thank you for buying my book, and also for the invitation to your gala the other night. I'm so sorry it ended in tragedy. Let me introduce myself, it's so nice to meet you Katherine, I'm Anthony."

"It's nice to meet you. I was sorry I wasn't able to chat with you the other night. Your book sounds thrilling. I notice parts of your plot parallel what we're going through in Bayside. It's an odd coincidence."

"Yes. I wouldn't have expected something like this to ever happen in Bayside, and to such a lovely lady as Brenda. Of course, book writing and publishing takes a great deal of time, a couple of years even. Yes, a strange coincidence it was all published just as this tragedy happened."

"I didn't realize you and Brenda were, friends."

"Like you and she were. Perhaps you'd like to get together for coffee or dinner sometime? We can talk about old friends, and new ones?"

Katherine was surprised at the invitation but welcomed the opportunity. Extra help analyzing this man could come from the Ladies of the Round Table. "That sounds nice. You know, some big fans of yours get together for dinner at Al's Café on Wednesday evening, early and I'm planning to be there. They'd be very excited to see you. Would you like to join us? We can go there together from Purse-onality."

"Let's plan on it. Here's your signed book, and I'll come by your museum about 6:00 Wednesday, if that works."

"Great, I'll see you then. Thanks for signing the book." As Katherine walked out the door, she said good night to Georgia and congratulated her on a very successful event. As she looked back, she saw Anthony wipe his forehead with a white handkerchief edged in red thread.

Chapter Seventeen

At the beach the wind was just strong enough to push around the clouds, but not enough to paint whitecaps on the bay. Katherine instinctively went to pull her jacket tighter around her, but it was a warm breeze for fall in Bayside. Feeling her toes in the sand, she let the enormity of the place sink in. She was at home in this spot having spent time and adventures here with Brenda over the years. This beach had been the setting for many soul-searching talks between the two of them.

This wide expanse of white sand, the far-reaching bay a seamless entry into the Puget Sound and further out the Pacific Ocean. Even tonight this spot was comforting. The bright moonlight cast a silhouette of the mountains on the distant peninsula. She'd lived in the shadow of those guardians for years.

She wrestled with her list of suspects in the recesses of her mind and maneuvered in the moist sand along the edge of the water, through sinking pockets. She noticed the tide was far out now. Under her breath, Katherine breathed a silent wish that the breeze carried over the gray depths.

Her Two-Pocket-Swagger styled bag was an everyday bouncy, light style on her shoulder, and she'd accessorized it with lots of fun, shiny charms that glinted in the full moonlight. The center section of the purse had a secure zipper close for items she needed fastened in, so she was confident she wouldn't lose anything on the beach. But on either side were equally large open sections for easy access to phone or glasses or other necessities with just a flip of a finger between hidden magnets. Such a practical purse for every day that she'd designed in leather with chiseled designs of historic women profiles. Tonight, she carried Helen Keller. It occurred to her that she should include a design with Rachel Carson's profile. Brenda would have agreed. From her left shoulder, the purse strap fell down her arm from her shoulder. Katherine pulled the strap up, and then hung on with both hands.

She looked back over the water. A couple of fishing boats rode the small waves, bright lights outlining their shape to prevent other boats accidentally plowing into them. The ferry was also well lit as it chugged close to its pier. Ship attendants walked out toward the end to direct traffic off and on the boat. The captain played the deep, resonating horn, formally announcing the arrival. The tiny waves slurping onto shore grew bigger with the ferry's wake and ventured further up the sand. Katherine sighed to herself. "Brenda would have loved this scene."

She walked with purpose now toward her objective. Further from the ferry dock, she pulled the flashlight out of her Swagger pocket and used it to light the way to the cave. Following the water's edge, she arrived at the big boulders against the hillside that supported the railroad tracks. She put her shoes back on and climbed the jagged surface of the big rocks. On the other side was the cave entrance she and Brenda had discovered as kids. Her flashlight lit the cave a few feet ahead of her. She hesitated, then quelled her fears. No reason to think anyone else would be here. She'd be in and out very quickly. If Brenda had some kind of secret, she might have left something about it here. There hadn't been anything found elsewhere, and no one else knew about this spot.

Inside and at the back of the cave, she stooped down and moved the mound of rocks covering the hole that was as wide as a loaf of bread and as deep as her arm. She shone the light at something she saw at the back, or was she just imagining it? Katherine reached in and her thumb scraped metal, definitely not a part of the rock. She pulled on it and her light showed a familiar, dull gray initial. She flipped it with her thumb and instantly recognized the interlaced KW, her Rodeo Drive signature brand. Katherine's breath was shallow as she tugged on the emblem. Yes, it was attached to a zipper. It was her recent gift to Brenda.

At the time it was Katherine's mocking nudge to modernize. "Brenda, when you're handshaking with the public you don't need a bulky bag in the way. Use a wristlet for your phone, cash, and credit cards. Then slip the wristlet in your big K. Watson Tote bag later when you're carrying files to the office." She'd slipped it over Brenda's hand. Remembered echoes of their laughter mixed with tonight's sound of waves rushing onto the beach.

Katherine unzipped the wristlet. Tucked in the slip pocket was her original gift note to Brenda, a Starbucks card, and a tiny camera. Turning on the camera, she saw pictures of Tom and Judith on the sidewalk outside City Hall, by the Founding Pioneers statue. They were talking to each other with intense expressions, oblivious to all around them. There was a picture of Anthony at a cozy restaurant or maybe a bar, looking relaxed. There were pictures of paperwork, but on the camera, Katherine wasn't able to zoom in enough to determine what the papers said.

Katherine paused at Brenda's selfie with Russ who had his arms around her. Last were a couple of pictures of pink tinged fluffy clouds touched by the sunrise over a dark and quiet beach. Katherine imagined Brenda at her last sunrise dive. Brenda rarely missed a sunrise dive in this underwater park. Katherine's mind whirled. Why hide this camera in this place? What was the importance of any of these photos? Why did she take them? Did any of this have to do with why she was murdered? The questions flowed and crashed through her heart.

Katherine put the camera back in the wristlet and turned to walk out of the cave. She wanted to get home to her suspect board. She focused the light forward to the cave entrance. As she started walking her light caught a stream of sand falling over the top of the entrance. She turned off her light and pulled herself back against the wall of the cave and squatted down. Maybe someone followed her? She waited in silence.

As her patience ran out, Katherine put the wristlet in her swagger's inner, hidden zipper pocket. She grabbed the mace that was in the convenient outside pocket and held it up, ready. Leaving the light off, she sidled along toward the only exit. She thought she was alone. In a burst of adrenaline, she walked out, climbed over the rocks and ran onto the beach.

At the water's edge, the cold waves slid over her feet and the hem of her pants. She noted a couple of people standing on the beach with their dog. The ferry honked as it moved out from the dock. Someone standing on the dock and staring down the beach caught her attention. Anthony Marconi was looking right at her. How long had he been standing there? And why?

As Katherine approached, Anthony waved at her with his left hand. She waved back and turned in the direction of the path that led up to the dock. She wasn't sure what to say, but she was curious.

"Well hello there." He took her hand to help her up. "I didn't expect to run into you here. Were you digging for shells in the dark?"

"Hi. That would have been fun. No, I was walking and thinking. Thinking of Brenda."

"You miss her. It's hard."

"Hard to believe. What are you doing here?"

"I'm looking for inspiration for the next novel, and procrastinating writing tonight." Anthony chuckled.

"What will happen with your beleaguered PI in the next book? It must be hard for him to come back from losing the love of his life and being accused of her murder." Katherine asked.

"Oh, he's in a quandary, of course. His new case takes him on a wild ride. His primary suspect seems to be a bust. He's staking out other suspects. His brother-in-law can't get out of his way. But his love life is looking up again. I left him setting his sights on a new prospect."

"Can't wait to hear what happens next. And I can't wait to read the one I bought at your signing. I'm curious how he shifts the blame onto someone else."

He said, "You like mysteries? At Wednesday's dinner you can let me know if you like what you've read by then. Is it in your purse? Can I personalize my signature for you?"

Katherine made no move to open her purse with the wristlet inside. "That's nice of you. I'll be busy the next couple of days with Purse-onality's first day open and events at the café, but I'll make some time to read your book. I'm very interested. I may have questions for you."

"It's a busy time for you."

"Yes, I'm in a rush to get back now and work on some last-minute things."

"Well, I'll see you Wednesday then." Anthony gave her a close hug. His rough cheek was against hers, and then his warm breath whispered in her ear, "Ciao"

As he let her go, he smiled at her with all his charm. She smiled back. "Good night." She started walking back toward town, conscious of him watching her. She walked past the well-lit public parking lot and recognized Ida sitting in one of the few parked cars. Katherine didn't see anyone else in the car with her. From what she could tell with covert glimpses, Katherine thought Ida was staring down the beach, muttering to herself.

Chapter Eighteen

Sunshine and warm weather poured through the windows and open doors as the catering truck from Sandy's Bakery arrived Tuesday morning. The unseasonable fall filled Katherine with joy, until she walked past her office and remembered her late-night session with the suspect board. Her forehead furrowed as she looked at the puzzle pieces. They refused to fall neat and tidy into place. There was an increased urgency now that Russ was charged with the murder. She vowed to reanalyze her clues at the end of this busy day. Maybe she'd learn more from the people attending this Founders Historical Society breakfast.

Just a handful of women visited the exhibits that morning. She and MJ had greeted them, by the front door, inviting them to sign the guest book. Next to the guest book was an antique scale under a sign asking guests to weigh their purses to see how much they're packing, a measure of their strength.

Tuesday's first guests included Anne Schilling, President of the Moms of Bayside group, with some of the other mom's and their young children. Katherine greeted them all and recognized Anne's little boy who she'd seen at the library reading to Hobbs. They took turns signing the guest book and weighing their purses. Darleen Warren giggled holding her baby. "I wonder if my purse or sweet, little Melissa will weigh more?"

"My bet is if you weigh your baby bag it will break the scale." MJ had joined them. The small group laughed, and a couple of the moms nodded.

Katherine said, "I think you all know Moonjava. MJ is an omniscient free spirit."

The ladies greeted MJ and Anne asked, "Good to see you again. How are you on this exciting day?"

MJ breathed in and out with deliberation, then smiled. "Today's mantra is—to be great, feel great, act great. I'm meditating on that."

Amidst the ladies oh's and ah's Katherine said, "MJ chooses her focus each day randomly."

"As it comes to me from the Universe ladies, that's how I absorb life."

After their tour, the visitors all seemed quite happy with what they'd seen. They'd made some purchases in the shop and had vowed to recommend to their friends. Now Katherine's mind filled with last minute event details. She went into the café with a sign stating private party. That's where she ran into Ida with Michael in tow. She'd arrived early and was checking the room.

"How are you today? Ida, is everything how you expected?"

"Yes, I think it looks fine. Michael brought over a couple of boxes of my new biography, *The Hansens of Bayside*. I'm just wondering where to display them?"

Katherine paused to think. "How about displaying a few books here at your main table? Each smaller table has the book cover pictures already incorporated in their centerpiece. Amber has a nice display spot ready in the front of the gift shop too. It's right by the front door if you want to take the boxes with the rest of the books there, Michael."

Ida nodded. "That sounds all right. Michael, please be sure that Amber sets up the display so that the children's versions are separate from the teen versions, and both are separate from the adult books."

Katherine took a few books out of one of the boxes. Michael put one box on top of the other. "No problem. Afterward I'll head back and catalog those Veterans' interviews in the computer and prep them to submit to the Library of Congress."

"Yes, we need to finish that. Take great care you don't skip any required steps for the recordings or with the precious items they've donated. Use the checklist I gave you. It's important that Bayside's Veterans are represented and that their stories are told nationally for now and for generations to come."

Michael picked up the boxes. "I'm on it."

Ida gestured at her watch. "Hurry. They'll start arriving any time now. The books should be there as they walk in."

Katherine arranged books on the main table. "Ida, I'm impressed you wrote and published these books. It's a nice way to start the fundraising for the Biographies for Boys and Girls organization."

"Oh Katherine, this has been a long project that's a labor of love for me. The Hansen family history is very important. Of course, I'm proud of my family's contributions to society, but all of Bayside can be proud of their founding family. It's the least I can do to provide that story. I am in the history business, after all."

Katherine tried to stifle her sigh. "You should talk with Georgia about doing a book signing. Anthony

Marconi was there last night, standing room only. You could make even more sales. Marconi is an interesting speaker, although I found his new book to be a bit odd."

Ida shook her head. "I don't know that I need to do anything at Georgia's. I'll be selling them at the Founders History Museum. What about his new book?"

"It's extra chilling that the plot is about the murder of a mayor. I talked with him about that and he said it's a coincidence. He did seem upset about Brenda. It makes me wonder though, how long has he been developing the idea, and what sparked the plot for the book. Is art influencing life?"

"Yes, well I'm not a big mystery fan. He certainly seemed to enjoy Brenda's company ever since he first rented the old Johnson place down by the water though. Maybe she was his muse or something." Ida walked over to stand right next to Katherine and she said in a hoarse whisper, "I wouldn't say this to anyone else because I'm fond of Michael. He's a good worker and I thought he was a good kid, but ever since that gala and the murder, he's been acting different."

"He seemed the usual today."

Ida motioned her hand to quiet Katherine. "You know he rents the third floor at my house. He's saving money for his own place. He snoops around about the police investigation all the time, asking me questions and talking about it with people who come into the Founders Historical Museum. It's interfering with his work. He's also spending a lot of time over here. Don't you find that strange?"

Ida moved even closer to Katherine. "Is he covering his tracks and recovering evidence? I mean, I'm not a mystery investigator but I do wonder about him. And I wonder about my own safety with him in my house. I'm nervous. What do you think, Katherine?"

Katherine didn't want to reveal that Michael was one of her own suspects. She found some of what Ida said interesting. Katherine remembered to whisper. "The one answer I can give you is that he's here more these days because he and Amber are dating."

"You know, I was thinking about what you said Sunday, that during the gala he had interrupted you and Brenda saying that I wanted to see you. I never told him that, and I wasn't trying to find you. Was he trying to get her alone because he had some grudge against her?"

MJ walked into the room. "I'm going to the front now so I can tour people through the exhibits. Then I'll bring them here. Just letting you know."

Ida fluffed her hair and straightened her dress. "Thank you. Please don't dawdle with them on the way in. I want to be sure they have time for a nice breakfast, and I want to be sure there's enough time for my remarks about history, my books, my new charity Biographies for Boys and Girls, and I want to share some new anecdotes about Bayside's Founding Family."

MJ left for the front door. Katherine was unable to stifle her sigh. She walked out the side door to the kitchen to let Sandy know all was ready, and so she could count to ten.

She helped Sandy arrange the food and watched her carry the last of the plates into the café. Katherine went down the hall to check for any latecomers. There was no one in the alcove, but she stopped short as she heard Michael and Amber in the shop.

"Michael, what did she say to you? Did she know we were there?"

"No. Our secret's safe, but maybe not her secrets. My USB with the family genealogy connections is hidden in my room."

"What about the letter and the hanging?"

"Shhh, not now. Too many people around here. I've gotta go anyway. Give me a kiss and I'll see you later."

Chapter Nineteen

Museum guests, Ida's speech, WebEx meetings with Rodeo Drive, and clue review had kept her busy, but Katherine was determined to make it to the Tuesday night council meeting. It was the first without Brenda, and important that her legacy is preserved.

The first surprise was the security guard standing at the door. Jason was searching all bags at the entry. Behind him the city council meeting chambers gleamed bright from the new, LED, solar ceiling lights. As the many observers entered through security, they squinted like underground moles emerging into a shiny, summer day. Some of them even reached out to slide a hand along the rich, wood paneling to guide themselves as their eyes adjusted. The administrative assistant was beaming as she greeted everyone. She handed each person an agenda, answered comments about the new lights, and assured others that the meeting was expected to start on time.

Katherine and Jason greeted each other. Tonight, Katherine had elected for an understated, all business look, embodied in a flat, cream-colored suede clutch that was shaped just like an envelope. It was large enough to carry a few papers, and some essentials like her cell and skinny wallet. It opened just like an envelope too, with a hidden zipper underneath to keep all contents secure. She faced Jason squarely. "You don't need to look through my purse. You know there's nothing diabolical inside."

Jason grinned briefly then held his hand out and said, "It's my job to check all bags going into the council room. You don't want to hold up the line."

There was a small crowd behind her. She groaned and handed her purse to him. He checked it and handed it back. "Enjoy the meeting." He motioned her through the doors into chambers.

There were a dozen rows of very long, straight backed benches, divided by a middle aisle and facing a raised platform where there was a long, semi-circular wooden desk with name tags displayed every couple of feet for seven council members.

Katherine settled in the middle of the front bench directly across from the name plate "Mayor Pro Tem". No stickers added to the nameplate like the butterflies, whales, dolphins, scuba divers, that Brenda had decorated hers with when she was mayor. Katherine realized that besides proclamations, speeches, and votes, there were lots of subtle ways Brenda had made her priorities known. Now Judith would sit there.

Katherine didn't want to miss a chance to speak. She checked the agenda to be sure building height limits was still included. Yes, buried between stray pet enforcement, and adjournment. It promised to be a long night. Katherine shifted on the rigid bench and glanced at the other people sitting along it. Rob gave her a brief wave. She assumed he was covering the meeting for the Bayside Herald. She smiled at him. Out of the corner of her eye a tie dye abstract pattern moved toward her. "Oh," Katherine let out an involuntary gasp as Moonjava homed in on the spot next to her. Katherine smiled to greet her. "What are you doing here?"

Moonjava took Katherine's hand, as she looked straight in her eyes. "I wouldn't let you go through this alone. It could get rough. I think this would be better if we had a group of people marching up and down on the sidewalk in front of those windows with signs protesting change to the building height restrictions. A demonstration would have been perfect on TV as you speak to the council. It's power to the people, in living color."

Katherine shook her head. "Well, I hope it won't come to that. I expect the council will do the right thing and defer this until a new mayor is voted in."

"Glad you're hopeful. I say, be prepared. 'Never doubt that a small group of thoughtful, committed individuals can change the world, indeed it's the only thing that ever has.' Margaret Meade said that. And Abbie Hoffman said, 'a modern revolutionary group heads for the TV station.' We should have protestors for emphasis." MJ paused. "And nowadays we need to show the protest on social media."

Katherine cleared her throat. "Here comes the council. It could be awhile from what I see on the agenda. I can text you and let you know what happens."

"Let me see that." MJ snatched Katherine's agenda. "There may be other things I'd like to have a say on."

The council members sat down. As expected, Judith had been promoted to temporary mayor and she was all smiles as she began. "Welcome everyone. Please rise for the Pledge of Allegiance, and then we'll get started on tonight's agenda."

As everyone sat down again, Katherine noticed that

Jason stood tall inside, by the door watching all activity in the room. Judith was fidgeting back and forth from one foot to the other in the front. She clasped her hands together and gave each council member a solemn expression. "This is our first meeting since the tragic death of our dear mayor. Brenda loved this town of Bayside and worked tirelessly with this council to do the best for our residents. I am humbled to take up the mantle and lead us forward. Please join me in a moment of silence in remembrance of Brenda Dirling."

Judith bowed her head, almost immediately sat down, hit her gavel on the table, and said, "Now, onto the agenda." Katherine sneered at Judith who stared back at her with a Cheshire grin.

The meeting continued, and the heater roared on despite the tepid night. The temperature in the room increased exponentially. At one point, Judith took off her jacket, glared at the assistant, and interrupted the proceedings with a hit of the gavel. "Monica, can you finally do something about this heat? We're all baking."

The council's dedicated assistant up to now had been engaged, not in the meeting topics but in casting dreamy looks toward Jason, who seemed to be enjoying the attention, from what Katherine had noticed. At the sound of her name, flustered Monica jumped out of her daze and with a red face cleared her throat. "I'm sorry mayor, did you need something?"

"Are you comfortable, Monica? Cool and content? The rest of us are baking in this heat. Fix it?"

There was a murmur of light chuckles, and a few groans. council members behind name tags Carl Sutter and Erica Tandy shifted in their seats and seemed sympathetic to Monica. She was now sitting forward in her chair shuffling papers. "I'm sorry mayor, I've tried adjusting the wall thermostat, but it seems to just get hotter. I can try to contact Maintenance Department?"

"Yes, try that."

Council member Tracy Elliot encouraged Monica in a softened tone and with a smile. "Please Monica, we appreciate any effort you can make."

"Of course." The Assistant got busy on her phone. Later as Katherine fanned herself with her agenda, she saw Monica fully distracted gazing at Jason again.

The evening and Judith droned on. Many in the audience, and a couple of council members were startled awake by a very loud ring tone of the Aladdin soundtrack song *A Whole New World*. The room's attention turned once again on Monica. She fumbled with her cell phone, her complexion reddening. Finally, she answered. Her eyeballs in frantic movement side to side; she was intent on the call. The room rustled with the paper people used as impromptu fans. Monica put the phone down and spoke to Judith. "The heat problem is being worked on."

Loud complaints scattered throughout the room. Judith's was the loudest as she hit the gavel on the desk. She nodded to Carl Sutter who had been speaking. "Go on."

People were grateful to leave the steamy room as soon as their agenda topics finished. Katherine stared at the wall clock and stole furtive glances at MJ with her tablet creating constant posts on social media. Was she strategizing a campaign protesting all city government? Was she mobilizing a flash mob on Main Street?

When the last agenda item came up, Katherine noticed all that was left was a contingent of developers, media, MJ and a few newcomers who had wandered in, perhaps curious from social media? Judith looked at the developers and said, "We can go ahead now and vote on raising the building height restrictions. I'm sure we're all tired. Is the Recorder ready to document the vote?"

"Excuse me," Katherine said and stood up.

Judith's elongated frown and icy cold stare pierced Katherine. Without blinking Judith said, "Recorder?"

Katherine spoke up, "It's in the protocol that the council must allow discussion on a topic prior to a vote. I'm part of the community, and I want to discuss." MJ started applauding in rhythm and turned with a determined stare to look directly at Rob. Rob's earlier bored expression had been replaced with a smirk as he sat up straighter and started taking pictures. MJ reached into her backpack and pulled out a sign that read "Save Bayside Views for the People". She held it high, aimed at the public TV camera.

Judith did not waste energy on the pretense of a smile. "Of course." She leaned back in her chair and furiously fanned herself with her agenda.

Katherine pushed MJ's sign down and walked to the microphone attached to a podium next to the wall of windows and the assistant's desk. Monica gave instructions, "You have three minutes. When your time is up a buzzer will sound and I'll turn the microphone off from here. And that camera over there mounted on that other wall, is recording what you say live for the local government TV channel. Thank you."

"Okay," Katherine said.

Monica pointed her finger at the podium. "Go."

Looking away from Monica, Katherine saw MJ's

and Rob's tablets both held high and aimed at her, a video record of her every word. She thought, oh great, all my years of purse designs and this small-town meeting is my fifteen minutes of fame.

Katherine cleared her throat. Not all council members were looking at her. Next to each other, Parker Brady and Joe Ortega were leaning close together and weren't even trying to hide their whispers. Whatever they were talking about captured their full interest. She cleared her throat again and tapped the microphone. The device screeched loudly, and whispers abruptly stopped. Katherine gathered her thoughts. She didn't want to lose their attention. Despite her determination to appear before the council on Brenda's behalf, she did not have a specific plan for what to say. Poised on the verge of speaking, her eyes caught Judith's nasty glare taunting her from what had been Brenda's chair.

MJ motioned to start talking. Her expression showed concern and impatience. Katherine leaned into the microphone. "Hello everyone. Thank you for this opportunity. I'd like to speak on behalf of the interests that were held so dear to our late mayor and to so many in the town of Bayside who appreciated her leadership on many specific issues to improve our quality of life."

Few of those left in this room at this late hour would count themselves Brenda's friends. These weren't the people who elected her and believed in her. So, Katherine faced squarely the camera mounted on the wall across from her and spoke to the many who she hoped were watching from home.

"Bayside is not a suburb of Seattle. We are a community with our own unique character and history that deserves to be preserved. We are so lucky with our beautiful environment and we need to protect that for ourselves and for our future generations. Our friend and Mayor Brenda Dirling understood this and worked hard to strike a harmony between growth and our gifts from nature. She fought hard against this change in the building heights code that would allow high rises in our downtown core. She had good reason to fight this and now with her sad, untimely death we all are the ones who need to carry on her fight to keep our town in harmony with its environment."

Katherine could hear her voice quiver at this emotional plea. She was passionate about taking up Brenda's cause and finishing it for her, but was she also starting to care about the fate of this silly town? As she stepped back from the podium to regain her composure, Judith leaned forward and signaled to Monica to cut Katherine off. Monica's attention was on Jason. Most of the audience was frowning. In the audience, Tom Corey was shaking his head. She stepped forward again, this time scanning the dais of council members as she spoke.

"I implore you to think past your treasury, past your wallets, and onto something that once it's gone won't come back. Vote no on this change in the building heights. Leave the beauty of the Bay and the mountains visible from all over our town for us and generations to come. Embrace the beauty that surrounds us and keep a…" Katherine was startled by a buzzer sound and a small vibration of the podium. Her microphone was cut off.

Judith immediately hit the gavel on the desk. "Thank you, Katherine Watson. I'm sure the members are moved by your words. You are just a visitor from Hollywood, but we appreciate hearing how impressed you are with our scenery."

Katherine clenched her fists on the podium and raised her voice. "I'm not a visitor, Judith. I grew up here. My family lives here."

Judith smiled. "Thank you but your three minutes are up. Sit down. Let's not have a scene." Judith then motioned to the back of the room. Katherine stood her ground until Monica gave an animated squeal of delight. Following Monica's gaze, Katherine saw Jason move from the door toward her.

Katherine sighed. "Oh, for Heaven's sake." She walked back to her seat where MJ was looking at her with a big thumb's up. MJ spoke to her immediately in a loud voice all the council members could hear, "I taped the whole thing. I got everything including when they cut you off and wouldn't let you speak for the people. I'm posting it all over social media right now." MJ started tapping on her tablet.

Judith shook her head. "No other speakers then. The council is ready to vote. All in favor of the new building heights raised as stated in the proposal before the board vote yes now."

Four raised their hands plus Judith. After she was sure the Secretary had recorded the vote, Judith smiled and brushed her hair aside. "Any opposed?" Carl and Erica raised their hands. Judith slammed the gavel on the desk with enthusiasm and announced, "The resolution passes. This council meeting is adjourned."

Chapter Twenty

Katherine was numb with initial shock at the sudden decision of the Council. She skirted MJ who tried to start a protest chant with the exiting audience. She brushed past Rob and his request for comment. As Katherine walked out MJ was shouting over and over, "People before buildings!" Katherine decided to get to her car and watch for Judith's exit from the building so she could follow her. She moved her Mustang to a dark spot in the lot and turned her engine off. She slouched in her seat hoping no one would notice her. Katherine stared at the door.

There was Judith now. Katherine noted her broad smile, and the brazen way she strolled out the door with Parker and Erica. They got in their cars and drove off.

Katherine waited a moment. What was she thinking following Judith like some kind of Katherine Drew or something? Then Katherine started her car and drove out of the lot. The new mayor's Lexus was easily seen on the empty streets. Katherine hung back since her red Mustang could be conspicuous.

After turning down a residential street, the Lexus disappeared through an automatic garage door. It was disappointing that Judith had just headed home for the night. Katherine turned her headlights off as she slowed down and parked the Mustang a few houses down. She turned off the engine and slouched in her seat. She wanted to check her cell phone to see if there were any messages, but she didn't want anything to light up her car on this quiet street. The houses all seemed to be curtained and no one was on the sidewalk or in the yards, but she wanted to be cautious.

Almost an hour later, Katherine was daydreaming about a potential new design for next year's fall line. In her side mirror a vehicle turned the corner. She slouched down further. Her whole body tensed as she saw the car slide behind her and park.

The engine turned off and there was complete silence. Katherine waited, looking around inside her car for anything she could use in self-defense if she needed to. She was startled when a dog started barking. She checked through the window across from her if there was a dog in the yard or something. The car door closed and in her side mirror Jason walked toward her.

"Oh no." Katherine put her hand up to her forehead and sweated, an uncomfortable searing heat spread over her face. The tap on her window was like the explosion of a crowd on black Friday when store doors open. She stayed still. There was the insistent tap again. She rolled her eyes. "Oh, for Heaven's sake." She sat up and stared straight ahead as she rolled down the window. "Hi Jason. I was just . . ."

"When dispatch sent me to the mayor's house about a disturbance, I wondered if I might see you here. How's your head from the concussion?"

"Oh, it's fine. I'm okay. I was just checking on the case. Judith has motive. You saw her at the council meeting. I followed her from—"

"The accused on that case is Russ. He's out on bail. Yes, I know you followed her. She called and reported that she was followed, and the perp is watching her house."

"The perp? And Russ is innocent. Wait. Judith knew she was followed? How? I was so careful. I kept my distance."

Jason crouched down to lean to her in the window. "Citizens don't surveil fellow citizens of Bayside regardless of suspicions or cases they think they're working on. Katherine you'll have to drive off now. Let it go. You should rest that concussion too. I'm not going to report anything if you drive away now. I can say the car drove off and leave it at that. Please."

Katherine shook her hair back and tilted her nose up in the air toward the windshield. "Of course." She reached for the key in the ignition then stopped and touched his arm with her hand instead. "Jason, on Sunday when I got attacked, I know that wasn't Russ. You and Hobbs found something on the ground. What was it?"

"We found the handkerchief the perp held over your mouth. The Lab is testing to see what's on it."

Katherine smiled up at him and said, "Thank you for telling me." She paused. "Was it a white handkerchief?" He looked at her with a blank expression. She could see that getting more information would be difficult.

She smiled at him again. "It had red trim on it, I think. And something else . . . Jason, I was the victim of the attack. I should be kept informed."

"The officer assigned told you about the edging? And the monogram?"

Katherine muffled her excitement. "Yes, the embroidered letter. It was a, let me think, oh this concussion . . ."

Jason groaned, then gave a chuckle and said, "Your acting skills are terrible, but the word 'persistence' fits you to a T. No need to stake out the Police Chief's house now." He patted her hand and stood up adding, "Have a good night. Get some rest."

Katherine nodded. She watched in her mirror as he walked back to his car. Then it dawned on her what he'd said. An embroidered T had nothing to do with Russ. She was about to jump out of her car to tell Jason, then she remembered the rumors of Russ' affair with Teresa.

Katherine drove to the end of the street and turned toward downtown. She was restless and thought about driving to her favorite latte place for a sweet nightcap. It might help the headache she couldn't seem to shake. She was surprised to see Tom Corey's truck with all his ugly business ads. It crossed at the four way stop ahead of her. Interesting.

Without hesitation she steered into a right turn at the stop sign and followed the truck at a distance. Katherine had her suspicions where he was headed at this late hour. She didn't want to pull onto Judith's street in case Jason was still there, and she didn't want Judith to see her. She parked her car a block away and walked to the corner. There was the developer's truck parked where she'd parked earlier.

She jogged down the street to see what she could find out. She slowed down when she got to the house careful not to trigger the motion lights. She stood at the side of the house and peeked around the corner of it to see the front door and window. The curtains were pulled tight. She crouched on the ground, prepared to wait despite her aching head. She prayed a silent thank you for the dry, warm night.

The sound of the front door opening, and the surge of bright floodlights woke her. Katherine was confused where she was and why she was on the ground. The familiar voices in the night reminded her. She stayed still on the ground listening to Tom.

"You've got the paperwork now. Sign it and let's get this done. That's what makes it all worthwhile, at least to me."

There was Judith's voice then. "I have just as much to gain as you. I told you it would work out. The only issue is that stupid Katherine nosing around. She was pathetic tonight. I don't want her stirring things up with people. I don't want her—"

Tom interrupted her. "If she tries to get in my way a concussion will be the least of her worries."

Chapter Twenty-One

Wednesday dawned and all Katherine wanted was to isolate herself in her office, design purses and review clues and suspects. That would have to wait though, because she'd promised her gran, she'd give her Bayside Birders a personal tour of the exhibits, followed by lunch in the café. The weather was nice again today and her gran suggested lunch on the patio among the backyard birds.

It was a group of twenty including six men interested in talking birds and history, and they seemed to appreciate a new perspective on purses as artwork. One of the men even joked to Katherine that she recognized the make and model of purses like he distinguished cars.

The early century purses and their painted bird designs on metal seemed to hold the biggest fascination for this group. In particular the Vintage Mandalian Scenic Mesh Purse Birds of Paradise Handbag delighted. They lingered over an Antique Beaded Birds purse with its very colorful bluebirds and red robins designed in the beading on both front and back. There was an audible gush in the room when they clustered around the 1920 Vintage Peacock bead art clutch purse. Pictures flashed. Their enthusiasm restored Katherine's energy, and she enjoyed chatting about the history, and learned about the start of the Audubon Society to protect birds from the growing trade in feathers in the United States in the late 1800's. The Bayside Birders voiced their pride in their 1965 charter which they said seemed a long time ago. Katherine thought, not when you're around MJ.

Everyone settled onto the patio tables and chairs for lunch. It was all beautifully decorated by MJ and Sandy, whose bakery benefited from increased catering at Purse-onality Café. The yellow and orange tablecloths on the half dozen card tables brightened the covered patio area and accented the potted chrysanthemums centerpieces. Katherine noticed the added touch of small, feathered toy birds next to each flower basket.

Katherine brought out the last of the sandwiches and placed them at her grandmother's table. She was sitting with Tom Corey's wife Janet, Judith taking time off from mayoral duties, and Leslie who was reciting bird lore from one of her favorite library books.

Her gran beamed up at Katherine. "Pull up a chair and join us dear. Enjoy this view of my feeders and birdbath. You need lunch too."

Katherine hesitated as she glanced at Judith but couldn't resist. This could be an interesting group to chat with. MJ brought iced tea to the table. As Katherine thanked her, she whispered, "Today's meditation - only your real friends tell you when your face is dirty. By the way, your mascara is smudged all along your left eye."

Katherine groaned over her makeup. She started to get up from the table when Gran patted her hand. "Leslie's been delighting us with tales about birds around Bayside, and beyond. Look at that group of pigeons, there must be a dozen of them feeding like crazy. And I just love those hummingbirds. Leslie says my feeder is attracting the type called Anna's hummingbirds."

"Katherine your gran is so nice. I enjoy sharing what I learn from my reading, and birds are one of my passions. Volunteering at the Library, I realize the extensive resources at hand. I'm always working to identify ways to reach out to the community, so everyone benefits."

Katherine noticed Judith shift in her chair, look away from her, and then check her phone frenetically. Katherine couldn't resist speaking up, "Leslie, I remember a presentation you did in front of the City Council recently with creative ideas for doing just that with grant money. Are you moving forward with that now?"

There was an instant transformation in Leslie's expression. Her eyes squinted, her lips turned into her chin, and her fists gripped the arms of her chair. Perspiration even beaded on her forehead as her face turned deep red and she barked out her words. "The mayor gave grant money that should have been mine to her Scuba Park."

Leslie glared at Judith, who laughed. When she stopped laughing, she said with a grin, "Leslie's right."

Katherine and her gran exchanged curious glances. Katherine said, "I'm sorry Leslie." Gran pushed the iced tea pitcher toward Leslie. "Have some more cool tea, dear. Oh, look over at that flock of pigeons swoop back down for more seed. That's a calming scene."

Leslie refilled her glass. She took in a deep breath and let it out in a measured cadence. "Sorry everyone, it just makes me so upset to see the blatant favoritism. I go crazy. The library is such a worthy cause."

Katherine ignored that gauntlet laid on the table. She'd never convince Leslie of anything different, but she did find her over-the-top reaction interesting. She needed to track her movements at the gala. For now, she took advantage of Judith being at the table. "Well Judith, council decisions are tough. The recent grant debate, and last night the contentious vote over building heights."

"I don't know what you're talking about. It was a close vote, but it passed according to all the rules."

"You know it wouldn't have passed if Brenda was still alive." Katherine bit her lip.

"Life goes on. The growth will be good for Bayside. The council members who voted for it see that. You'll be back in California by the time building starts, I'm sure." Judith crossed her arms.

"Developers will be happy and will make lots of money. I just don't understand why you pushed so hard for it right after Brenda's . . . I mean this was the very first meeting without her on what has been such a controversial topic. What's in it for you?"

Judith leaned forward and pointed her finger at Katherine as she replied, "You talk about Brenda as if she's some kind of saint. She was a regular woman who put her bra on the same way the rest of us do."

They were interrupted by a sudden blur from the sky landing amidst the dozen feeding pigeons that immediately took flight to escape attack, amidst a chorus of screaming crows circling above. One pigeon was too slow. The incoming hawk had the pigeon in its clutches. Blood dripped from its broken neck onto the lawn as the hawk messily grabbed it more securely. The hawk flew away with his prize. The lunching bird watchers were stunned.

Gran said, "Oh my."

Leslie responded, "Well, you're feeding all the birds now, Pam."

The scene put most of the guests off their food, and they began to gather their things to leave. Katherine helped her gran stand up to say her goodbyes. Pam said to her, "I was so concerned about the cats in the neighborhood, when I should have been watching out for predatory birds. You're looking one way and the killer swoops in from the other direction."

Chapter Twenty-Two

The last person Katherine expected to see Wednesday outside her front door, and about to knock again, was Jason Holmes. He was starched and polished, in uniform. Hobbs sat on the porch next to him, looking in expectation up at his partner, ready to act upon his next command.

Katherine opened the door wider; glad she'd fixed her makeup. "Jason. Hi, how are you? I didn't remember you were coming over today. Has something happened in the investigation?"

Jason relaxed his stance. "No. I mean, I don't know. Hobbs and I are working other incidents now. We don't have the latest information about the mayor's."

Katherine squinted, puzzled to see them here. She crouched down in front of Hobbs with her hand extended. He had a gleam in his eyes, and she could hear the swish of his tail on the porch floor as he wagged it and maintained his sit/stay position. She petted his head a few times, and then scratched behind his ears. He lolled his head back a little and his tongue hung out of the side of his mouth. "Oh yes Hobbs, hello to you too."

Katherine looked up and said, "You're not here to arrest me because of my stakeout, are you?"

"I'm glad you got home safely last night." Jason

189

glanced at Hobbs. "We're just on our way to work. We're on duty tonight. I wanted to stop by and check how you're feeling. I mean, with your concussion. Are you getting over it okay? Headaches still? That was a nasty fall Sunday."

Katherine lost her balance as she stood up again, instinctively reaching out to steady herself Jason steadied her with both hands and helped her straighten up. Katherine was conscious of the delicate scent of her Prada perfume and how very close she was to Jason's lips. She hesitated to say anything at all as she enjoyed the blissful energy between them, the touch of his hands covering hers, the nearness to him. He leaned in and she relaxed as she started to close her eyes, only opening them at the sound from behind her, in the house. The voice grew louder as Anthony walked closer to them from where he'd been sitting in the kitchen. "Katherine, I don't want to interrupt but we should get going. We don't want to be late."

Katherine slipped her hand away from Jason's. "Sorry. Clumsy of me."

Jason put his hands in his pockets. "You want to be careful about trying to do too much while you're recovering from that concussion. Don't overdo it."

Anthony joined them on the porch. "I don't think we've met. I'm Anthony." Anthony held out his hand to Jason.

Jason looked at Anthony briefly, then directly back at Katherine who blushed then and continued absently petting Hobbs on the top of his head. Jason shook Anthony's hand. "Nice to meet you. I'm _—"

Anthony interrupted him, "You're Jason Holmes." Jason frowned as Anthony continued. "Yes, your name's pinned below your badge there. Are you here to update Katherine about the case?"

"Something like that."

Anthony lightly rested his arm around Katherine's shoulder then and said, "Well, maybe we should change our dinner plans then?"

Katherine shifted her feet. "Oh, I think we're done for now, aren't we Jason?"

Jason stared at Katherine and she thrilled at his intensity. "Oh yeah, I think we're done." Jason reached into his pocket and handed her a small bottle of pain reliever. "For the headaches." He signaled to Hobbs and they turned and walked down the porch stairs.

Jason stopped and looked back at them. With one hand on his hip he said, "I'll pick you up for dinner tomorrow at 6:30 like we planned. Get ready for some fun." Jason nodded.

Katherine laughed. "I'll be ready. Fun and the dog too?"

Jason grinned and shook his head. "Nice meeting you Anthony." He signaled to Hobbs again and they got in the patrol car at the curb.

Anthony was looking at Katherine. "What do you think, Katherine? Are you ready for tonight's dining adventure? Who knows what mysteries we may discover?"

She gave him a mischievous grin. "With Gran and her Ladies of the Round Table friends, we could hear anything. Let me grab my purse and I'm ready to go. I'm looking forward to watching our resident bestselling mystery author in action at the dinner table. Just please, can you wait to accuse any suspects until dessert is served?"

He laughed back at her. "I'll be sure to wait. That's one way to be sure everyone gets their just desserts."

Katherine ran into her office to grab what she called in her line the City Knot. This had always been a favorite bag, and always a fun attention getter. The nappa leather was layered with gold chains crossed back and forth within the leather and it was inset with metal studs. The feel was rich, and the look was playful. It was her fashion nod to the classic designs of Bottega Veneta. She put the small pain reliever container in her purse and thought about how nice it was that Jason had stopped by. She was glad not to be covered in mud this time.

She'd dressed up for dinner with Anthony, long hair draped in place over her shoulders and looking almost flirty. She'd chosen to wear her sleeveless, silky, casual black Evan Picone dress splashed dramatically with a design within the material of small flowers in bright pastels. It had an empire waist, always most flattering for Katherine, and flared out at the bottom just above her knees with a full and flouncy finish. She caught herself smiling at Jason's flustered exit. It's funny how someone so gruff and tiresome can also have redeeming moments.

Then she thought maybe Jason didn't realize that her date with Anthony was dinner with Gran and the other ladies who are fans of his books. Was that why the silliness about tomorrow night? Oh no, she shook her head, tomorrow night isn't a date. Certainly, he didn't see it that way either. They could be friends, maybe. They didn't have a romantic future. There was that moment when she stumbled, and he held her hand. Yes, he did have appeal, but she didn't want any entanglements in Bayside, for Heaven's sake.

She reached to turn off her laptop and paused on the screen about CMD's. She'd come a long way in a short time in her knowledge about Certified Military Dogs. What would Jason think about her looking for his Army partner? Would he be upset thinking she was meddling in his private business? Or would he be happy? Well, she was making progress, and she was hopeful she might be able to reunite them. The German Shepherd's name was Robby, and it appeared he did return to the United States somewhere. She was glad he hadn't been left in the battlefield. Some research indicated most of the dogs are euthanized at the end of their service. Katherine hoped she wasn't too late to find Robby.

She turned off the laptop and glanced at the whiteboard where this morning she'd added Leslie as her new suspect, with her library knowledge and her passionate outbursts about Brenda. She hid the list, pushing the whiteboard against the wall and walked out to rejoin Anthony on the porch. They got in his car, an impressive Mercedes-Benz S550. MJ had dropped Gran off for the dinner and they were going to give her a ride home, if all went according to plan. Gran would be the one at the table who was not an Anthony Marconi fan. They headed down Main Street to the restaurant, on their non-date.

Chapter Twenty-Three

"Well here it is, Al's Café. Brace yourself." Katherine cautioned playfully. Her steps were light, and she was surprised how happy she felt in Anthony's company. She walked up to the door and paused outside smiling up at Anthony. "You've never been to a dinner like this. No Bayside stone unturned, no person immune. You're sure you want to subject yourself? You may learn more than you want to know about this town."

Anthony returned a grin of his own that broadly displayed the deep dimple in his cheek as if to say that he was not to be denied. "Bring it on. You say they meet every week? Sounds like they know where all the bodies are buried."

"That's truly spoken as a bestselling mystery author, but actually I wouldn't put it past them." Katherine brandished her broad smile. "You can't miss their table. It's the big round one in the middle of the room, unofficially reserved by the owner, sweet Al Perez." Katherine embellished what they were about to walk in on, waving her arms in emphasis. "They see all coming and going, and they're poised for reaction. The Ladies of the Round Table's deliberations are varied, and opinions are vehement."

Anthony pulled open the door for Katherine who added, "Into the lions' den we go to eat, or possibly, to be swallowed whole." Her words masked her concerns about potential opinions her gran could boldly express. Her grandmother's pointed remarks in private left no doubt that she did not like and did not trust Anthony. She had been very unhappy about the interest he seemed to show to her granddaughter. Although Katherine had seen endearing times at the Round Table, discomfort accompanied other occasions. The evening was unpredictable, and she had no idea how it would look through an outsider's eyes.

As Katherine slid through the door, she could see at the center table conversation was breezily in process. All eyes moved to see who was arriving. She was impressed by the high attendance, almost a full court. Not pains, nor arthritis, nor gloom of night had kept any of them from their self-appointed Round. The waiters were on the move, and Katherine indulged in the sizzling spiciness with a few deep breaths. Plates were clattering and there was chatter and laughter all around, other than the crying baby being comforted by a very tired looking lady in jeans and a sweatshirt.

Pam cleared her throat. "Kat, so glad you made it."

Katherine ignored the nickname and noted how her gran had pointedly left Anthony out of her greeting—here we go. She gave her a kiss on the cheek and then a wave to the group. "Hi everyone. You all remember Anthony Marconi from the Gala?" There were nods, and Katherine noticed the beaming smile from Margaret who she knew loved his books, and the slight cooing sound from Peggy who without doubt loved his looks.

"Ladies, I'm honored. Thank you for letting me crash your dinner party."

The busboy added two chairs and place settings to the table. Peggy tapped the empty chair next to her. "Anthony we're delighted. Please, sit down. I'm saving this seat for you, dear."

The author and the designer sat at the table, with their backs to the door. It seemed as if they were on naked display for the ladies, but Anthony seemed quite at ease. Katherine's guard was up seeing that Anthony had ended up flanked by Peggy, and her gran, but she had no control now. He's a big boy; he can take care of himself. Katherine always enjoyed chatting with Margaret and Winifred, who were on her other side. Conscious of Winifred's blindness Katherine said as she sat down, "Winifred, I'm next to Margaret. Is Amanda picking you up later?"

Winifred smiled and leaned in Katherine's direction. "Yes, she gave me a ride, and she'll be back to drive me home. I've been listening to Judy and Liz talk about their recent adventures globetrotting in Russia. So exciting. And now you and your author friend are here. This is a special night."

"That's odd." Peggy leaned over Anthony to Pam. "Amanda's usually here desperate to hang on every word we say. I swear she's a spy or something and someday she'll turn us all in to our government, or someone else's."

Anthony straightened his silverware, checking that the base of the knife, fork and spoon were aligned. He used his napkin to line it all up before folding it and placing it in his lap. Katherine noticed that her gran was studying Anthony, following his every movement with her serious eyes, barely masking her contempt with a thin smile as she appeared to be oblivious to Peggy's comments.

"This is a festive gathering." Liz spoke in a light tone.

Katherine pulled out her purse hook. It was an elegant, sterling silver barred gadget that slid onto the top of the table and then dropped below the edge with a hook for a purse handle to hang from. This one that her company manufactured included her Purse-onality SophistiKAT brand emblem of the black cat with the long tail so that it glowed from the top of the table for all to see.

She started making the hooks when she read that Queen Elizabeth used a ruby jeweled purse hook. In fact, her staff stayed on the alert, as to the Queen's use of the hook. When she spurned it and put her purse instead on the ground, she was signaling that she wanted an interruption. The staff should then deliver an urgent message or any reasonable excuse for her to get away. Katherine loved this story of a purse hook with purpose. She noted with amusement the emblems all the way around the top of the round table with purses dangling. Either everyone enjoyed her little gift, or they were all guarding against the saying she'd told them, that a purse on the floor invites bad luck and lost money. The Queen of England is daring.

"Anthony, I'm Margaret by the way, your books are so intriguing. I've read them all. I was particularly taken with your thriller *Dead West of Los Angeles.* The way you describe the murderous drowning and her desperation when there was no escape for her. It was as if you'd experienced it all, the planning, setting the trap, and then springing it. It was so touching and sad reading your description of her death in the book."

"Thanks, Margaret. That's nice of you to say." Anthony sat up straighter and relaxed his shoulders at finding an ardent fan in the group. "I do a lot of research for my books. I do try to act out some of the scenes as well so that I can really feel the perspectives of each of the characters. I have to know that moment of desperation, as if I have experienced watching her panicked last breaths." Katherine reminded herself to start reading his book. She'd like to know more about him, in person and through his work.

Margaret said, "Well I'm a retired schoolteacher from Bayside elementary. Reading is my favorite sport. I find that characters illustrate so much about human nature. I'm fascinated with the insights you have in the mind of your characters who murder. Your latest, Dirk is devious with the murder in your latest book. Will you tell us how you create characters?"

"I've known some ruthless people, and some generous people, and all sorts. My characters combine personalities of people I've met, and my imagination."

"And something of you perhaps?" Gran asked.

"Sometimes." Anthony raised his water glass and took a long drink.

Peggy leaned forward toward Anthony. "You say that some are people you've met? What about your next book? Will you be including anyone from Bayside in your new mystery? Perhaps a sophisticated, older lady as a love interest would add joie de vivre to the story?"

Anthony responded, "Did you have someone in particular in mind?"

Peggy cast a coy look at him. "Well . . ."

Margaret laughed, rocking back and forth and gently slapping the table. She could barely catch her breath long enough to respond. "Peggy, you would make a better target for the killer than as the love interest."

Katherine was charmed to watch Anthony flash his brilliant smile and his deep brown eyes. "My imagination soars with all possibilities."

Peggy glared at Margaret who was contending with hiccups after her laughing fit. She gestured to Anthony. "He means that as a compliment. I give him ideas. You may be reading about me in his next thriller."

"Well, good thing you can swim," Gran chimed in. There was a wave of chuckles around the table. Gran grew serious. "Is it true you're helping Kat solve our murder? Our dear Brenda?"

Loose lips are inevitable when the story is good, and Katherine didn't want this story getting passed around town. There would be consequences if word got back to grumpy Jason about disobeying his ridiculous demands for her to stay out of the investigation. Or even worse, what if Detective Grace got wind of amateur investigations of her case? Katherine spoke up, "Just to clear any confusion, I'm not investigating the murder. That's for the police. I'm just Brenda's friend helping however I can. I do want this murderer stopped, and I want Bayside to remember how wonderful Brenda was."

Anthony added, "I'm not a police investigator. But I do have skills following clues. I didn't know Brenda long, but I'm sorry for her death. I'd like to help if I can."

"Not her death, her murder," Gran corrected. "Let's call it what it was."

Stacy came over to take everyone's order but

hesitated hearing Gran's blunt words. She stepped back and juggled her notepad and pen with a visible shake to her fingers.

"Let's order. What's everyone having tonight?" Gran motioned to Stacy with one hand. "Would you write us separate checks please?"

"Please, ladies I'd like this to be my treat. Order whatever you'd like." Anthony opened the menu in front of him.

Gran nodded with a curiously stiff half-smile at Anthony. Katherine choked on her water. Leaning forward she ignored Katherine and added, "Lovely. You're so generous, Anthony." She nodded at Stacy.

"Yes ma'am, what would you like to order?"

"Oh, Stacy you're always so sweet. I'd like the Grande Grilled Chile Salmon, Veggies with Queso side dish, and a salad. Oh, and a glass of your cabernet, or should we order a bottle for the table?" Around the table Gran faced gaping mouths, puzzled looks, and a glare from her granddaughter regarding the unexpected expense.

Margaret said, "That's not your usual, Pam. I'm surprised. Are we trying new things tonight?"

Peggy put her menu on the table and raised her voice, "Ridiculous. Why you won't be able to eat even half of that."

Katherine's blush deepened when her gran motioned her hand for Peggy to lower her voice. "Stop kicking me under the table, Peggy." Then her gran said to Margaret in a lighter tone, "Yes, let's all try new things tonight. We need to live it up."

Winifred said, "Peggy, what are you having? Why don't you read out loud some things to choose from on the menu that are new to me?"

Everyone ordered, and Katherine silently vowed to contribute to the bill. The waitress left the ordered drinks on the table. Gran fingered her wine glass and gave Katherine her full attention. "Dear, you have a list of suspects, but you never accused Russ. We all know he didn't do it. Why the police are treating him the way they are I'll never know."

As she finished speaking her lips pursed and Katherine could see that she was getting worked up now. Gran gestured to Peggy, who in turn gave a pointed stare at Liz with a sharp nod. Liz jumped in, "The husband is always a suspect. Russ did have opportunity and means. Isn't that what reveals the murderer, Anthony?"

Margaret joined in. "Motive, Liz! There also has to be motive. What motive could Russ possibly have?"

"Well, I heard…" Peggy paused as the door opened and Tom Corey walked in with his business partner. Conscious of her surroundings again, Peggy lowered her voice. "I heard that Russ was spending a lot of time with Teresa."

"Teresa?" asked Winifred. "Brenda's assistant? I'm sure that was for scheduling events and such. That's perfectly natural. There's nothing to be insinuated there."

"Evenings and weekends without Brenda are odd times for scheduling, and good times for other activities. I'm just saying what I've heard." Peggy tapped her fingers on the table and mused with wide eyes at Anthony.

"If I was writing this in a book, I'd look into Russ' cell phone records. Did he try to find his wife that night on his cell when he couldn't find her? I'd ask why would he kill her in such a public way? He had nothing to gain by creating a spectacle. Most cheating husbands wanting out of a marriage by murder are secretive and calculated in their planning. In contrast, this appears to be a crime of passion."

Peggy nodded her head and with a smile gazed at Anthony. "I'm very impressed." She held up her wine glass. "Cheers."

Margaret lowered her voice, and everyone leaned in. "Well, if you ask me a better fit for motive, means and opportunity is that awful Mr. Corey who just sat at that window table with some man I don't know. He and Brenda had terrible arguments at the city council over the building height restrictions. I've read all about them in the news coverage. Brenda certainly made her views known about preserving the views and environment of Bayside."

Katherine cleared her throat and whispered, "I was at the council meeting last night and the heights restrictions were raised."

Margaret gasped in surprise and shook her head. "Oh no. That's telling. I wonder if he's here celebrating."

"Not everything hinges on politics. Brenda had a full life outside of the mayor's office," noted Peggy.

Theories were interrupted by oohs and aahs over the dinners Stacy placed on the table and everyone started eating. Katherine glanced in Tom Corey's direction, remembering her stake out. He began sneezing and pulled out a white handkerchief with a design in the corner, but she couldn't tell what it was and then he put it in his pocket.

After a delectable pause, Judy said to Peggy, "What about Brenda's work on the Library Board? I can't imagine anything controversial there. What about her scuba diving at the underwater park? What do you think about why she was out by that waterwheel that night? What could lure her away from the Gala?"

Peggy paused to be sure she had everyone's attention, for full effect. "I think she was tricked somehow. Maybe Russ got her out there? Maybe it was Teresa."

"Peggy, I think their marriage was as strong as ever. I don't believe there was any affair," Margaret declared.

But Katherine detected a slight quiver in Margaret's voice. She found herself speaking out loud the personal thoughts that she would normally keep locked inside. "Affairs happen. Spouses cheat. You can't tell anything from what you see on the outside of a relationship. But I don't believe that between Brenda and Russ."

Winifred put her silverware down on her plate with a clatter and suddenly announced, "What if the wrong person was murdered? What if it was someone else the murderer expected to kill?"

There was a silence at the table for the first time that evening. Then Judy asked, "Who was supposed to be the victim?"

"Katherine. It was her gala. Katherine, your gran said the note was found in your purse."

Katherine answered, "It was in the prize purse Brenda was going to award to the raffle winner."

"But would the killer know all that?"

"I guess that would depend on who the killer is."

Katherine gathered and creased her napkin into a perfect trifold and put it back on the table.

"It opens up the list of suspects, doesn't it, Katherine?" Peggy nodded with enthusiasm and then gave a gasp. "Katherine, that means the killer could strike again. At you. You have to be careful. You should have police protection or something. Has anything suspicious happened?"

Her gran spoke up then. "She was attacked at the library. She was shoved down and has a concussion. We're lucky she's alive, thanks to that policeman and his dog. They scared away the attacker. Maybe it was the murderer."

Winifred spoke first. "Katherine. Are you feeling all right?" Then all the ladies chimed in with their concerns.

Katherine assured everyone she was feeling much better. "Let's not get all worked up ladies. It's a theory. There's no one coming for me."

Anthony broke the tension. "The Bayside police may have some other reason for how they're handling the case. They may be watching several suspects until Russ' court date. We can certainly let the police know that Katherine may be in danger though. Right, Katherine?"

Katherine's enthusiasm for Anthony and his ideas took an immediate dive as she thought about her current standing with the Bayside police. The restaurant door opened, and Judy announced, "Winifred, here's Amanda." Judy nodded and smiled. "Join us for a coffee?"

As Amanda introduced herself to Anthony and declared what a fan she is, the waitress squeezed through to hand him the dinner bill. He thanked Amanda and she followed him as he walked over to the cashier. Katherine walked over and crouched by her gran. "Are you ready for a ride home? I've got a very nice car outside waiting for you."

Gran pulled Katherine closer and lowered her voice to a faint whisper, "I'm ready whenever you want, dear. It seemed like you and your author are having a good time. Is his company right now in your best interests, dear? I see your look when the two of you are together, and the banter. You may be flirting with disaster. I just want you to be aware and be smart. Think about what Winifred said, and what little you know about this author."

"Well, no one ever wants to hear that their friend was murdered instead of them, but I'm on my guard. I know you have your suspicions."

"Sometimes Winifred sees things very clearly. Then again, although she's my friend I admit she sometimes sees things through a fog." Gran patted Katherine's hand. The busboy reached in to clear the mess of scattered, used plates and silverware.

Katherine sighed. "It's not like it never crossed my mind that I could be a target. It's overwhelming to think through it all. Where do I go from here?"

"Chin up Katherine, you're going to figure out who that killer is and we're going to do what we can to protect you. Is it time to go back to your suspect board? Think it through. I'll think it through with you."

Katherine gave her a hug, leaning her cheek against her shoulder. "Thanks Gran, I do have theories. We'll have another meeting at the white board. I can't think what else to do to draw the right suspect into the open."

Her gran gave her a loving smile and patted Katherine's hand again whispering, "All your life you've loved reading mysteries. What have you learned? What would Miss Marple do, my dear? Maybe dangle your own clue, like a purse on a hook and we'll see who grabs for it?"

Gran. She's always practical, enthusiastic and vague.

Katherine jumped when Anthony put his arm around her shoulders and said, "Can I accompany you ladies home safe?" From his friendly expression it appeared he hadn't heard her conversation or noticed how lost in thought she'd been. Katherine nodded with a smile.

"Let me help you with your coat." He reached over to her chair to grab her coat.

Pam pulled on Katherine's arm and whispered to her, "Just be careful about dangling that bait. Be smart. Right now, we don't know who it is. The killer could be almost anyone."

Chapter Twenty-Four

There's a first time for everything, Katherine thought as she grabbed a small drawstring bag from her closet. She had dressed down in a plain aqua dress with a scoop neck and short sleeves, tightly gathered through the waist and then full, flouncy skirt to just above her knee. It was paired with low heeled shoes and her exciting, newly designed drawstring wristlet. She was thinking about the possibility of having a civil night with Jason. He's showed he could be nice, but would he be? Could they enjoy each other's company? Could tonight actually be fun?

She still had her doubts about the sincerity of his dinner invitation. Would it have been better to meet him for coffee, so she could leave if things turned ugly? She thought about his incredible blue eyes, then turned out the light and went downstairs to entertain herself with new designs in her office until he arrived.

At the bottom of the stairs she stopped and watched the last of the day's museum guests leave. A lump formed in her throat. It was library evangelist Leslie standing in the gift shop entrance. She released her tightened grip on the banister and hoped Leslie wasn't going to fly into one of her odd emotional rants. As she tiptoed along the hallway, she heard rummaging noises along with murmurs and as she neared the entrance, she recognized Amber's quiet humming of *As Time Goes*

By. Katherine frowned, she's been watching *Casablanca* again and she's in a mood. Hopefully not mooning over Michael, but no doubt she was.

Katherine put on a smile. "Hello, Leslie. I hope you enjoyed your visit today."

"Oh yes. I told my sister about lunch here, and of course the gala opening and she wanted to experience it herself. So, we stopped by this afternoon. Julie, this is Katherine Watson, Purse-onality's owner."

The tall, gray-haired woman wearing a colorful pantsuit and carrying a Katherine Watson satchel in her left hand stepped forward with her other hand extended to shake. "It's so nice to meet you. I'm a big fan of your accessories and I'm positively giddy over this delightful exhibition."

"I'm glad you enjoyed yourself. I can see that you two are sisters, with such a very strong family resemblance. Do you live near Bayside?"

"Not far, just over in Langton. I came up for a nice, long weekend visit."

"And you've met Amber."

"Yes, she looks so beautiful. She was telling us that she's a volunteer chaperone at the High School Homecoming tonight. In that dress you look like you're attending as a guest."

"Thank you."

Katherine gazed at her transformed, young friend. The young woman's thick, black hair was swept back behind her shoulders and meandered down in loose, wavy curls to almost waist length. The lacy bodice of her light blue dress clung easily to her small waist and came up to an off the shoulder neckline. The skirt of the dress draped in chiffon to a perfect point above the knees. The darker blue pump heels set off the outfit and a sleek wristlet of a complimentary shade had a dangling silver heart.

Leslie smiled and hugged her sister's arm. "Amber was about to give us a sneak peek at disco bags that just arrived for sale."

Amber tapped the top of a box sitting on the countertop. "Surprise! Your '70's disco bags are here! Look at these cute replicas. I think Darleen did a nice job on them." Amber held up one of them by the very long strap. "They look just like your original—a sparkly, thick oven mitt stuck on a braided strap.

Katherine laughed and fingered the sample. "She really did it." Julie stepped forward with a burst of applause. "I feel like I'm back under the disco ball. Back then women were striving to look professional and pragmatic. We all carried big, heavy, leather, flap over the front shoulder bags during the day. It was great to leave them at home for these light bags that went flying along with our twirls and whirls on the dance floor." Tapping her sister on the arm she demonstrated a classic disco dance move and Leslie joined in.

Amber covered her smile with her hand. "Your moves look great. I really mean that."

Julie held her hand out. "It's fun. Come on, pretend you're a different generation and follow my lead." Amber stumbled and giggled through an imitation of disco moves.

As they all wound down Leslie said, "Disco is unique." She gently fingered the disco shoulder bag again. "Look at that intricate, beautiful weaving. And see the knots on the woven strap, and that fuzzy tassel. A girl didn't want much on the disco floor, just a lipstick, some cash, id, and keys."

Katherine chimed in, "That's right, in my research there were no cell phone pockets, and no cells back then. Don't look concerned Amber, I made the concession so that these replicas are big enough for a cell to fit in. I think our customers will like the simplicity for a change of pace, and some of them will enjoy the nostalgia. Anyway, we'll see how sales go."

Amber moved the rest of the small inventory onto a shelf. "Thank goodness my generation solved all this by liking wristlets. But these are a piece of history and since all tastes are different, I'm planning to hang these on the rack over there with a miniature disco ball hanging over the display. The light on the ball will also pick up some sparkle from the tiny beads on the purses as well. It might look groovy."

Leslie groaned. "Oh no, groovy is a different era. Too bad you don't have the shoes."

Amber asked, "The shoes?"

Leslie laughed. "I still harbor one regret from the era. I could never afford those amazing platform shoes with the lights that flashed on the dance floor every time your heel hit the ground. Talk about groundbreaking! At the time this was the most amazing new novelty of technology, and I coveted them. Of course, the cost of these flashing shoe lights went way down years later and became favorites in children's tennis shoes. Both my kids got those shoes. Ah well, c'est la vie."

Julie pointed to Katherine's bag. "What's that cute bag you're carrying tonight?"

"It's a Capezio Nanette drawstring that I'm using as an out on the town bag. I love Capezio accessories, but most of the bags are really big for carrying around all the dancer's accessories. I just want the suggestion of dance tonight."

"That's cool. Is this one really a purse, or converted from something else?"

"Okay, I admit, it's for carrying ballet toe shoes. But I admire a master craftsman like Salvatore Capezio. He started out making the best theater shoes in the 1880's. By the 1950's devoted fans included Gene Kelly, Fred Astaire, and later Debbie Allen and Ben Vereen, and now Katy Perry and Lady Gaga love Capezio, it's art for the ages. I wish they made more purses. Until they do, I have to use my imagination."

Julie politely asked if she could feel the silky material. "Beautiful. It's been so nice to meet you both. Leslie, we really should get going." All the ladies said their goodbyes and the sisters walked out the front door.

Amber locked up the cash register and asked Katherine, "You're going out tonight too? Have a fun time. If you want a hot place to go, try the new Leehans over by Market. My friends are jamming there tonight, and their music is really good. You're going out with Anthony, right?"

"No, with Jason." Katherine fidgeted with the string clasp on her purse, finding her fingers unusually awkward. "We're not really going out. We're just talking about the case where there's some music with a band he knows. I just want to get some new information about the investigation, and maybe I'll do some sleuthing afterwards."

Amber leaned forward on the counter and tried to catch Katherine's eye. "Jason? I didn't expect to hear that name. You look very nice. You must have buried that hatchet pretty deep. You look overdressed for sleuthing, but you look very nice for a date."

"What?" Katherine cleared her throat. "It's not a date. See, my shoes have hardly any heel, and with this long strap I can carry my bag out of the way as a crossbody if I'm in a sleuthing situation. No reason not to be friends with a cop, and I'm thinking Jason may have information I don't have about Brenda's case."

Amber nodded with a grin. "Oh yeah, I can see that. Although, you sound like the woman doth protest too much."

"Taking a Shakespeare elective? Study harder. Without further ado, a better quote would be "Good company, good wine, good welcome, can make good people" from Henry VIII."

Amber frowned. "Of course, you'd quote from one of his histories. MJ's influence?"

This was a good opportunity to question Amber about her growing suspicions of Michael. "You and Michael seem to be getting close these days."

Katherine noticed Amber's eyes sparkle and how she inhaled quickly. "We're just like soul mates. He's not like anyone I've ever met. We just sync."

Katherine nibbled on her thumb nail then stopped herself, her worries contrasted with Amber's dreamy demeanor. "Just, be careful Amber. You haven't known him that long. The details of his past aren't clear, and I don't want to see you hurt."

"What I need to know is clear enough to me. I appreciate your concern Katherine, but haven't you ever known it? That magical instant where you know this person is the one? It's his eyes, his touch, voice, and those kisses that bathe your soul in love, and fun, and understanding like no one else can."

The young woman's confidence lit up her face and prompted Katherine to think back to when she too believed in true love. Seeing Amber, Katherine almost thought she could believe in that magic again. Almost.

"That's beautiful, Amber, and I'm glad you're happy. Just, please be careful, take some time. Don't rush in head over heels. Okay? I care about you."

Amber grabbed the last of the new purses left on the counter and turned her back on Katherine, walking over to the cupboards and putting the purses inside. "There's no looking back, no fear or hesitation. I want happiness and as MJ said for today's meditation - If you want something you've never had you have to do something you've never done."

Katherine frowned with concern as Amber stared out the little window over the front porch. Her frown deepened with the loud roar followed by the thunderous rumbling of a motor. Startled at the sound, Purrada jumped and skittered away from the gift shop alcove, running next to Katherine's leg, quivering. Katherine crouched down and petted her cat. "It's okay Purr, it's just some motorcyclist revving his engine and showing off his silliness at speeding as he takes the hill out of Bayside. He can't get to you. You're safe. See, the roar has stopped. All's good." Purrada nestled against Katherine's leg, enjoying the attention and the massage.

Amber turned away from the window with a big smile on her face. "I'm going to pick up Michael. We're chaperones at the homecoming but I'm hoping for one romantic dance with him. I'll tell you all about it and the purses tomorrow. I'm just going to go out through the back door. I parked in the alley. Enjoy your night."

Katherine got out a quick goodbye as Amber made a speedy exit. And then the doorbell rang.

Katherine answered the door. Jason smiled and held a trio of purple flowers. He was in tight jeans and a plain, buttoned shirt under his leather jacket. He held out the small bouquet to her. "Hey there. Katherine. What a crazy day. Still managed to drop off Hobbs, leave him dinner, and get here right at 18:30. Ready for some fun?"

"Let me get my purse. Do you want to come in for a minute?"

Jason stepped in and looked around. Katherine thought he can't help himself. It must be automatic for him to look for evidence wherever he is—a hazard of the job. She was starting to do that herself. "There's no crime tape left if that's what you're looking for."

Jason shifted his gaze to her eyes. "No. I was looking for that vase you had here. I brought these for you and thought they'd look good by your guest book, or something."

Katherine brightened at the flowers in his extended hand. "I don't know why I said that about the tape." She shook her head slightly and gave him a smile. "Thank you, Jason. They're very pretty." Katherine took the flowers and put them just up to her nose catching the scent. They both leaned toward each other, and then in an instant they were looking away again. He dropped his keys and bent down to pick them up. She sniffed at the bouquet and took that time to pull herself together. Oh no, she thought, am I getting pulled into some imaginary connection so he can turn around and belittle me again?

Jason straightened up and put his keys in his pocket. "You may not know, but these are hyacinth flowers. In the gardening world they mean 'I'm sorry'. And I want to add to that the meaning of a new start. I meant what I said on Sunday. I want us to be friends."

It struck Katherine that this sounded a little like making a beautiful purse out of a sow's ear, but she didn't want to be rude again, and certainly didn't want to antagonize him. "That's very nice of you. We just got off to a rough start at a bad time. I'm going to put these flowers in some water and then we can go." Katherine glanced toward the street but didn't see anything parked. Had he walked over? She should have just met him there. "Did you want me to drive?"

"Oh no, I'm happy to drive. Have you been on a bike?"

"A bike?"

Jason opened the front door again, stepped aside and revealed his motorcycle. "It's a fun ride. There's nothing like the sound of the engine and the feel of flying through the outdoors. This week if I've learned anything about you, adventure is what interests you. So, I'm betting you'll love a ride on my bike. It's really an experience. It's a fast Moto Guzzi California 1400. Custom."

Katherine couldn't tell if his enthusiasm for her to ride was a sincere misunderstanding about her character, or a cunning dare. Betting on the latter, Katherine wasn't about to give him the satisfaction of unnerving her. "I wouldn't want to miss that. How did you ever get these flowers here in one piece?"

"Oh, the bike has some hidden compartments, including a big one under the seat where I carried your bouquet."

Katherine walked back to the kitchen with the flowers, surprised when Jason walked with her instead of waiting at the door. She noticed that he continued to look everywhere as he walked. Was he working here tonight? Was he suspicious of her with this case?

Purrada perked up with interest from her favorite spot on the kitchen's bay window bench where she had settled for a nap. She glanced at Jason but was captivated by the colorful flowers and every move of those petals. Katherine filled the vase with water and flowers and on the way to the door grabbed her Capezio purse. She left the flowers next to the guest book and followed Jason out the door.

As Katherine approached the bike, Jason handed an extra helmet to her that had been hooked on the handlebars. "Let me know if you need any help fitting it on."

Katherine managed the helmet over her mane of long, wavy curls, realizing that when it came off her hair would be the worse for wear. This was some new friend. Why was she getting herself into this silliness? She wished she didn't feel a steady pull to this mischievous and yes, outrageous personality. Jason jumped on the bike and held out his hand to help her on behind him. She put her Capezio in an old western style saddlebag on the bike for safe keeping then held his hand as she pulled her long leg up and over and sat down. She did the best she could to sit on the fluffy folds of her full skirt and stuff the plentiful excess under her legs but away from the engine and wheel. She made a couple of attempts at holding onto him as she balanced herself, then placed an arm tentatively around his waist. She held onto some more skirt with her other hand. She leaned forward and spoke in his ear, "Where are we going?"

Jason turned his head to glance at her sideways. "It's a bar close by. You probably don't know it but it's somewhere I like to go. They have live music and a fun crowd. Is this your first time on a bike? I mean uh, you're going to want to hang on tighter than that when we get going. You'll want to squeeze me as tight as you can, like you don't ever want to let go, until we get there. It's for your own safety."

He laughed out loud, and she rolled her eyes and held on with her other hand, accidentally pulling her dress up a little higher. "Don't worry about me."

Jason strapped on his own helmet, patted her hands, and shouted, "Hang on tight."

He stood up and jumped down hard to start the engine. The engine below her roared to life, and then pulsed loudly as Jason revved it several times with the turn of his wrist. Her instincts kicked in and she tightened her hold on Jason with both arms now in a desperate hug. He kicked up the stand and started off. He made a U-turn and accelerated up the hill away from Bayside's little downtown. Gasoline was in the air as she hung on with her full body grip ever tightening. She was glued to Jason's every move and sway, as she mimicked it with her own, she leaned into every turn and motion. Her skirt billowed. Her sense of adventure grew. So did her temper.

The cycle slowed a bit now, into a turn entering an alleyway. Katherine bounced high at the bump in the road and clung to Jason to keep from bouncing right off the bike. Jason turned his head in the alley and

Katherine thought he might have said something to her, but she couldn't hear a thing over the thundering engine. He continued in the maze of alleys until he had left Bayside. That's when he sped up again onto the main highway headed north. It seemed like an hour, but it was just a few miles up the road when they pulled into a lot and stopped at the Endless Highway Biker Bar.

Countless bikes of various sizes and makes were parked at the side door when Jason pulled up amongst them and turned his engine off. They got a few casual looks from some of the people in the crowd standing around talking, drinking, and smoking on the patio outside the door to the bar. Katherine jumped off the bike as soon as she could get on the ground. She tugged down on the skirt of her dress and struggled to get the helmet off by jerking at the strap and shaking her head. She pulled it off with both hands. Jason sat on the bike, looking at her with his hands out as if he was going to help with her helmet. They stared at each other. Jason smiled. "How do you like the bike?"

Katherine punched the helmet into his hands. "Oh, it's a thrill. Next time I'll skip the dress and purse and go with jeans and fanny pack instead."

"The thrill is always worth the pain." Jason winked at her and his smile broadened as he got off the bike. He took a little care to be sure it was balanced with the kickstand. Katherine grabbed her purse. As he locked the bike and hooked the helmets on the bars, she walked toward the groups of bikers on the patio. She thought Jason's look was following her dress. She glanced back. He was walking along to catch up with her. She noticed the obvious looks from some of the people standing on the patio, as she approached it. By the time she stepped up onto the patio Jason was next to her.

Katherine could hear country music from inside the bar. The heavy smell of cigarette and other smoke hung over the patio. Conversations were loud and there was lots of laughter and leather. Some couples along the perimeter were holding hands and kissing. Jason opened the door and followed Katherine inside.

Chapter Twenty-Five

Amber knocked on the cottage door and smiled as it was opened by Katherine's grandfather. "Amber, you made it. Come on in. We're just getting started."

"Hi everyone." Her hello was returned including ahhs and compliments about the beautiful dress as she took her coat off and modeled it. Amber gave hugs all around. "What did you decide on your surprise, Pam? Were you able to find the old plane spotter bag?"

Amber noticed that MJ's expression lit up, and Katherine's gran's face wrinkled up more than usual and her lips briefly formed a small pout. "Are we all sure this is such a good idea? Katherine doesn't like surprises."

Her husband sat down on the couch next to her, with his arm around her and a grin on his face. "Go on now. It's a great idea."

MJ theatrically stood, stretched out her arms and looked with intensity into each person's eyes. She closed her own and spoke with great deliberation. "This fits perfectly into my meditation for today. If you want something you've never had, you have to do something you've never done."

A shade of enlightenment passed across Pam's face. There was no longer that trace of pout and her voice grew stronger now. "Yes. That's quite right. Yes, it is. Well, in that spirit then I will tell you I found my mother's old bag. It was packed well away but with some digging . . ."

"And help from a loved one." Her husband interrupted with a laugh.

"Oh yes of course my dear." She patted his knee. "Well, we found it. It is a treasure, but I'm afraid it's grown tattered and worn over the years in storage."

Her husband stood up again. "Let me get it, just a minute."

When he came back, he handed the relic to MJ. "I see what you mean, but it's so authentic."

Pam nodded. "It brings back memories of her stories."

Amber smiled. "It's a real treasure for the museum."

MJ put the bag on the coffee table. Still looking at the bag she crossed her arms in front of her. "I wonder if our team in L.A. could refurbish it. Just a few repairs so you don't lose the aging but just make sure it's preserved well enough for display. Of course, we'll have it in a glass case too. We want to be sure no one handles it. Is it all right if I take it and consult with someone on the team? I think Rosa can keep our secret."

Pam leaned forward on the couch now, animated and smiling. "You think Katherine will be delighted with this 1940's surprise display in the exhibit? I hope so. Oh, you girls are wonderful to conspire with me like this. I think it is going to be of interest to people. Remember how Rob wrote that article in the paper? And that's just the tip of the iceberg."

Amber reached into her backpack and pulled out papers. "I'll leave this with you then. If you don't mind reading over the stories you told me and marking the changes you'd like. Then the narrative will be ready to mount next to the display case."

"Thank you, Amber."

"Well, I've got to go. I'm picking Michael up and we're headed over to volunteer and chaperone at the High School Homecoming tonight."

MJ shifted her feet and said to Amber, "You're going with Michael? Be careful Amber. You know he's still on Katherine's suspect list."

Flames ignited in Amber's heart. "You're wrong MJ. He'd never do anything like that. You're on the wrong track." Amber thrust her arms into her coat and shrugged it on.

"Just be careful. Do you have any of that pepper spray in your purse?"

Pam cleared her throat then and chimed in, "MJ, you're on the wrong track with this accusation. I saw Michael leave the gala. I even spoke to him. I like that young man. He said the party was nice and he liked the food. He grabbed some more of the hors d'oeuvres on his way through the kitchen and out the back door. He said he just wasn't interested in the show. I asked him if he'd seen Amber." Amber was watching Pam intently and Pam said to her, "Oh my dear, his eyes lit up and his features softened in a grin just at the mention of your name." Pam smiled. Amber's pulse rate jumped. Pam continued, "He told me he'd seen you, Amber, but that you were too busy now, so he was going to catch up with you another time. That's part of the information that I gave to the police."

MJ stared at Amber while she spoke to Pam. "What did the police say to that?"

The question hung heavy in the room, and a growing chill traveled up Amber's spine. Pam answered, "Detective Grace wrote it all down in her notes and she said it could mean that Michael wasn't at Purse-onality when Brenda was killed." Amber's eyes met Pam's again. "So, Michael isn't a suspect then?" MJ pressed the point.

"Well, that detective also said that Michael could have said that he was leaving but instead had circled back. But she did write down what I said and I'm sure that Michael did leave when he said he did."

Amber picked up her purse. "I don't believe the police would suspect Michael anyway, but I'm glad you told them. I'll see you tomorrow."

Pam nodded. She patted her husband on the knee. "We must get down to the station and let them know what I think about that writer, that Anthony Marconi."

He answered, "Yes, we'll make an effort to get there in the morning."

She nodded with emphasis and looked at Amber. "Oh yes. Have a lovely evening dear." She patted her husband's knee again and beamed at him. "I have such lovely memories of so many times we used to go out dancing. So romantic."

Amber blew a kiss to the group and walked out the door. She warmed thinking of the happy couple and that she was on her way to be with Michael. Then felt a chill as she remembered MJ's last look, of concern.

Chapter Twenty-Six

Amber got her car keys out of her coat pocket and walked along the alley to her car. She thought of Katherine on her evening with Jason. Amber knew just enough about him to know that the two of them had very different outlooks on life. Or, she didn't know Katherine as well as she thought. Amber pulled off her coat, on this unseasonably warm fall night. Unlocking her Saturn Ion and getting in, her excitement to see Michael recharged.

On the short drive to Ida's house, Amber wished Michael could save enough money to rent his own place. The old woman seemed weird to Amber. She couldn't help but feel something didn't add up. She was nice to you when she wanted something and otherwise ignored you. It was odd she was willing to offer her new museum assistant a free place to live. Amber thought that seemed very unlike the Ida she knew. Ida's renovated attic was a big step up from Michael's run-down motel room when he first came to Seattle.

As Amber drove up to the house, she noticed again how it was surrounded by overbearing fir trees. Darkness gathered in this place. There was one light on inside. She parked the car at the curb, hoping for a quick getaway. She stepped up the front walk and took a deep breath before knocking on the door.

Some of the things Ida said, especially the tone of

voice she used, rubbed Amber the wrong way. She interpreted these conversations as if Ida felt a special claim on the town and its history that no one else had. Amber thought back on cold confrontations that she'd witnessed months ago between Ida and Katherine over the opening of Purse-onality. Amber had been uncomfortable with Ida's open hostility and Katherine had at times lost her temper. Now Ida seemed reconciled to a different kind of historical museum in her town.

At the door, bright floodlights flashed on, startling and a bit blinding as they lit the entire landing. She heard heavy footsteps inside, as if on a staircase. The door snapped open. Hoping to look up into Michael's grinning face, instead Amber was eye to eye with Ida.

Ida spoke first. "I wasn't expecting you. Do you want more of my books to sell at your gift shop? Come in and I'll get some for you."

Amber managed a slow smile and buried her discomfort long enough to attempt a diplomatic answer. "That would be great, but I need to write up an inventory accounting first. I'm actually here tonight to pick up Michael. He's been nice enough to volunteer at the High School tonight."

Then from behind Ida came that deep voice Amber thrilled at. "Hi Amber. I'm here, ready to go. Thanks for getting the door, Ida. Sorry to trouble you."

"No trouble. No trouble at all. Amber, whenever you need those books let me know."

"Will do."

"Come on Amber." Michael walked past Ida, in one swift movement and took Amber's hand, interlaced their fingers and led her down the front path.

Once they were in the car, Amber wasted no time starting the engine and driving away. She glanced at Michael. "You know, that lady always gives me the creeps, especially since we were almost caught in the basement. What is she hiding?"

Out of the corner of her eye, she could see Michael looking at her. He patted her leg. "She's just a very lonely busybody. She's harmless but sometimes annoying. And how are you, darlin'? You look so fine I could just scoop you up in such a long kiss until we're both forced to come up for air."

Amber blushed. "I'm glad you like the dress."

"No baby, I like you in the dress."

"And you look so good in those slacks and that jacket across your hot shoulders. You take my breath away."

"Even though we're volunteering, are you saving a dance for me tonight, darlin'?"

"I think we'll be able to steal away for one."

"So, in the meantime, what did you sign us up for?"

"It's just making sure everyone has a good time, no problems, no drugs, and no alcohol. It'll be very easy— a memorable evening for everyone."

They drove past the High School parking lot. As volunteers, they were early and there were still plenty of spots left, but Amber wanted the excited students, dressed in formals to have every opportunity to park close, so she parked across the street. They walked over to the gym hand-in-hand. Just outside the entrance Michael pulled Amber aside, in the little courtyard that was used for lunches in good weather. There were scattered picnic tables, stairs, and grass to sit on.

"I'm in a moonlit mood, baby." His strong arms surrounded her, and she reached up for his broad shoulders. As their lips met Amber couldn't imagine anywhere else she'd want to be.

When they paused, Amber giggled as he lifted her up and gently placed her on top of one of the tables. "I have something for you, babe."

"Really?" Amber's curiosity surfaced in her breathless voice.

Michael grinned. "Close those eyes for a second." He took a small, plastic box out of his jacket pocket and showed it to her under the sparkling light decorations hanging everywhere around the courtyard. It was a very small wrist corsage with a gardenia. As he opened the lid the sweetest, pure floral fragrance was freed and surrounded Amber. He took it out of the box and reaching for her hand he slid it onto her wrist.

"Oh Michael."

"Amber, I've never met anyone like you. I'm falling for you."

She reached for his shoulder and brushed his cheek with the gardenia, releasing another burst of the deep perfume. They gently kissed.

Michael held her around her waist. "Actually, I have fallen for you. Completely. I'm in love with you, Amber."

"Oh, Michael. I'm in love with you too. I've never felt like this. You're sunny kisses on the bleakest of days, you're a sweet dream on a bitter night, a familiar hug in the midst of strangers. You're my kindred spirit."

"I feel that too, baby. I want to spend forever with you. Honey, we're gonna have such a life together. I've got big plans for us and we've got our whole future to enjoy each other."

"I'm forever yours, Michael. Nothing will ever change that."

Michael kissed her. "You're forever in my heart too."

Amber kissed him back amid echoes of conversation and laughing. She nuzzled against him and fluffed her corsage. "People are arriving. We should go in. Shouldn't we?"

Michael laughed, and Amber enjoyed that familiar grin. He raised his hand to gently lift her chin and then joked. "Well, we did get all dressed up."

They both laughed as he lifted her off the table and onto the path. Their hands slid naturally into place, fingers laced together, and the couple walked into the gym. The lights were dimmed, and the huge room was transformed for the Homecoming with decorations. The High School's band was on a raised, makeshift stage and people were streaming in. Girls dashed from clique to clique, talking, showing off their dresses and accessories, instagramming their antics. The boys were scattered, talking to each other, checking their phones, and watching the girls. Volunteers and faculty bustled back and forth with last minute assignments and duties.

Amber recognized Sharon from the Bayside Boutique at the area set up for the coat check. She wasn't very busy because the odd, warm weather continued. As she and Michael walked toward Sharon, Amber noticed a smudge on his lip. She wiped it away for him whispering, "Lipstick."

"Thanks baby."

They got to the coat check and Sharon greeted

them. "Thank you both for volunteering. Amber, I've seen a lot of your donated purses. The girls are enjoying them, and the dresses."

Amber squeezed Michael's hand. "Where do you need us most right now?"

Sharon brushed a stray lock of hair out of her eyes. "Amber, if you could check the refreshment table over there, I just need you to make sure everything's been put out, and that there's plenty of cups for the punch. Michael could you run over to the stage? Please ask the band to get started with their first set."

Amber nodded and Michael answered, "Sure. No problem."

The couple walked toward the center of the large room and stood for a moment in the spot where tip offs happened in the school basketball games. Michael gave Amber a brief kiss on the lips. "I'll catch up with you in a minute."

Amber smiled as he walked toward the stage in the front of the room. She walked to the food tables set up on the back wall, at the opposite end from the band. There was Judith Sanders fussing with the desserts. After hearing about the harsh words and nasty scene at the city council meeting between Judith and team Katherine and MJ, Amber moved straight for the other end of the tables to avoid any possible unpleasantness. Her brief wave and smile in Judith's direction was seen and answered with a frown and shake of her head. Amber was more determined to keep out of Judith's way. Let Katherine fight that battle.

Amber took time to chat with a few of the girls. One of them was her friend Patty, Amber's inspiration behind the donated purse drive. Amber admired how hard Patty worked at her job to help her family, while trying to graduate from high school this year. Amber remembered how thrilled Patty had been to pick out a donated dress, purse, and she found shoes in her size too. How wonderful to see her looking so pretty and so happy now. Patty rushed over and gave Amber a hug and said hello.

When the music began, Amber recognized *Uptown Funk*. There was Michael, standing on the stage next to one of the students, helping him with his music stand. Amber touched her corsage to her cheek and inhaled the mystical scent. The room had filled up with students, and many were dancing next to the stage.

Loud voices in the doorway could be heard above the rest. A wave of people surged from the side of the dance floor, in response. Amber craned her neck and stood on tiptoes to see the situation better. A blue jacketed arm shot straight up into the air waving a silver badge as the crowd of students parted before it to the stage. Police? During Homecoming? Amber wondered what in the world was going on.

The uniformed entourage climbed on stage. The band stopped playing. With groans and complaints, everyone in the gym focused on the drama before them. It had taken the Band Director extra seconds to realize why his students had stopped playing. When he did, the officers had already brushed past him.

A huge lump formed in Amber's throat when the police approached Michael. She stiffened and forced her feet to move. When Amber walked by the desserts, she saw Judith nod at the police with a smile on her face. A smile! Amber lurched forward to run to Michael's side. He had just fixed the music stand when his arms were grabbed and pulled behind his back and cuffed. Amber could see that the cops were saying something to him. With tears forming, Amber fought to get past the crowds of students. It seemed they kept moving right into her way, and her chiffon dress was catching on bracelets and arms as she kept trying to push through. Everyone was glued to the scene front and center. A murmur flowed through the crowd and through Amber. "They say he's Brenda's murderer" . . . "they say he killed Brenda".

Amber made a final bold push to get to the stage. She slammed her hands down on it, the sound loud enough to startle those around her. She could hardly see Michael through her tears as he was walked across. Amber screamed louder than ever, "Michael I love you."

He turned to look at her as she was pushed up onto the stage by the people around her. She ran toward him. "Michael, I love . . ."

One of the cops held out his stiff arm before her. "Stand back, Miss. This is official business. You need to stay back." He motioned to the Band Director who came over and gently put his hand on Amber's shoulder.

She stopped there and pleaded to the cop, "Why?"

Michael tried to jerk back in her direction, but the other two officers held him tight and marched him down the stairs away from her. Just before they shoved him out the side door, Michael found a way to turn back in her direction with the saddest of expressions as he shouted back, "Amber, I didn't do it."

Amber shouted through her sobs, "I know."

She jumped off the stage and ran outside, only to

see him stuffed into the back of a squad car and driven off. Amber folded her arms around herself. She was cold and so very alone.

Chapter Twenty-Seven

Katherine's first glance in the biker bar revealed joyous chaos. The live band was in a corner on the left filling the bar with Country music. They were dressed in the full regalia of jeans, plaid shirts, and cowboy hats. The lady sang Tim McGraw's, *Live Like You Were Dying* into the microphone. Her loose, blonde curls dangled halfway down her back from under her black cowboy hat. She wore a plain white button-down shirt with sparkles that shimmered in the spotlight. Her blue jeans clung tight all the way down her legs. Next to the singer was a short blonde woman who tapped her foot to the beat as she slid her bow deftly across an electric fiddle, producing a smooth tone. The tall men who played guitars bookended the group, each of them was sporting a white cowboy hat with dark leather bands. They were strumming with enthusiasm and singing as back up. The drummer was hidden behind them, hardly visible from the front door, but his musical contribution was undeniable.

A handful of couples danced in front of the band. Most were just moving to the music, a few were still holding their beer bottles, and one expert couple moving on light feet executing swing dance moves. Scanning the room, there were few empty bar stools and no empty chairs at tables. Jason stepped forward with his hand against the middle of Katherine's back.

He nodded to a table against the far wall that a waitress was wiping down. They stepped over there and sat down on the high stools around the tall table. The waitress greeted Jason effusively with a hug and an excited shout, "Jason." She gave Katherine a smile over Jason's shoulder. She left them with menus.

Katherine raised her voice over the band, "Friendly place. I've never heard of it."

Jason leaned forward with a broad smile. "Everyone here is great. I think you're going to like it." With the band blaring and the conversations all around them, Jason raised his voice too and leaned further in toward Katherine. "That's Janet. She's a waitress by night and an artistic painter by day. She's working to get a gallery showing in Seattle. So, are you hungry? How about starting with some loaded potato wedges? They're great. What else should we get?"

Katherine glanced at the menu. "How about having the spinach dip and chips?"

"You got it." Jason waved at Janet and she came back over when she had a chance. He gave her the order, and added, "I'd like a coke. What would you like to drink Katherine?"

"I'll have a Diet Coke, please."

Jason nodded and winked at Janet. She winked back at him as she walked away.

"So, you're okay with the place? Just wait 'til you taste the great food. I feel like I can relax with this crowd."

"Oh yeah, this is great." Katherine raised her voice again as the band went into a fiddling frenzy.

The song ended, to scattered applause and cheers. The glittering singer announced they were taking a break and would be back in a bit.

Jason stopped clapping. "You're a good sport about the bike. I'm glad we've been able to get to know each other better. How's the museum business going?"

"We've had pretty good crowds this week. The café has been busy, which is a great bonus and we're having an event we're catering tomorrow. Some of the people are stopping in to see the place where Brenda was murdered. I don't like that, but I pay attention in case their interest surfaces clues." The waitress came over with their drinks.

Jason nodded to her. "Thanks. You've got a good crowd tonight keeping you busy."

Janet shifted closer to his shoulder. "I'm never too busy for you. I'll be right back with your order."

Jason slurped his drink. Katherine fidgeted on the tall stool. "So, what are you and Hobbs working on now?"

"Our patrols have been routine the last couple of days. I told you, we don't work cases. That's the detectives."

"Why is that? You know just as much about the clues as they do, and you were there that night, so you have a better understanding of the logistics."

Jason leaned forward in his chair. "It's the downside of working with the dog. We're assigned for tracking clues and pursuit of the perp. We don't get the luxury of a case load. Our work is the immediate incident. I admit, that's a frustration I have with the job. The adrenalin of the immediate chase is addicting, and I love that part, especially when we're successful. But I know I have the skills to take on a full case and solve it. I wish I could get the assignment to follow it through."

The food arrived and they both started sampling. "I like working with the dog. It's an incredible set of skills working the field. Hobbs is intelligent. I'm not complaining. I'm just wishing, I guess. It's aggravating to turn a case over. I get to know the people who've been hurt, like you." Jason put his hand over hers resting on the table. "I see their pain up close and in the moment. I know I can't take that away, but I want to help see them through it. And I want to stop it from happening to someone else. I'm dedicated to serve and protect, and I feel like I can do more. That's just not how it works. The mayor's case is one I really wanted to be on. I wish Hobbs and I had got the killer that night."

Katherine perked up. "What if you worked on the case outside of your job? Can't you do that?"

Jason leaned back again in his chair with his drink. "The detectives are on it now. And they're good at it, Katherine. I know you don't think so from what you've seen, but I know these officers are dedicated to it. Someday I'll get to continue on a case. One day I'll make Detective grade."

"Jason, what if you share information with me? And I can do the same. We can collaborate and get this killer. Let's do it."

"I don't know. I can't jeopardize my job by revealing confidential information on an ongoing case."

"Absolutely." Katherine nodded slightly. "But when you solve the case with me then you won't jeopardize your job. They know you're good at your job. This is an opportunity to show them you'd be good at this detective job too. I have some information I can share with you. If nothing comes of any of this and your detectives solve the case, that's great. What we all want is for this case to be solved and the killer locked up. Was an autopsy done? Do you know if they found anything unexpected? I mean, it seemed pretty obvious how she died. I don't understand why an autopsy was asked for. I don't think that's automatically done."

Jason cocked his head and gave her a puzzled expression. "You really are trying to dig up clues about this, aren't you? I don't think anything is going to stop you."

Katherine gave her head a definitive shake.

Jason leaned forward. "Okay partner, I probably shouldn't encourage this, but I can tell you a little, if you tell me yours too."

Katherine leaned in with her little finger extended in his direction. "Pinky-swear I will."

She watched with a grin as Jason turned his hand a couple of ways then with his elbow stuck out was able to wrap his finger around hers. "I know how to swear but this is my first pinky-swear, whatever that means." He laughed. "There was an autopsy done. I took a look at the report out of curiosity and I was surprised that they found a drug in Brenda's system."

"What? Brenda never took any drugs. That's ridiculous. Unless she was drugged and didn't know it."

"Could be. Or more likely she was attacked with it in a syringe or some other method. This drug is used as an anesthesia. The drug is…wait let me make sure I say it right. I wrote it in my notebook, but I don't have that with me." Jason stopped, deep in thought. "Okay, the drug is called suck-in-chlorine or something like that. It said that the affect it has is paralyzing, and with the right dose it takes you down in less than 30 seconds.

And it leaves the body quick so it's hard to detect. They performed the autopsy in time to register traces of it."

"Whoever insisted on that autopsy had good instincts."

"Actually, I recommended it to my chief. He passed that along, and the powers of Bayside acted on it since Brenda was the mayor. That's why I followed up to see what they found. It just didn't seem to me that a killer could hoist her onto that wheel. She would fight them off if she had all her faculties."

"And it may also give credence to the killer being either a woman or a man."

Katherine's cell rang. She grabbed it from her Capezio bag. Amber was calling. She sent it to message. Jason munched on a potato wedge and watched the band head back to their corner.

"Jason, why are we here?"

"It's a great little place, fun music, thought you'd like a night out."

Katherine repeated herself and made sure the emphasis was on the word we.

Jason fidgeted in his seat and wiped his hands on a napkin. He lost his smile and cleared his throat. Leaning forward, he took her hand and said, "You captivate me."

That was the last thing Katherine expected to hear. Katherine's cell rang again. She pulled back her hand and looked at her phone. It was another call from Amber. She frowned and sent it to message. When she reached for Jason's hand again, she saw the band's singer had stopped to chat with him. When he noticed her off her phone, Jason introduced her. They continued talking until the singer promised to come back for a chat after their next set.

Katherine's cell rang from Amber a third time. This one she answered. "Sorry Jason, it's Amber. Something's wrong. Hello, Amber?"

As Amber spoke, Katherine heard desperation. "Amber, where are you? I'm coming there." Katherine's features shuttered as Amber talked. She told Amber she was on her way. As she hung up her brain was running like a racehorse on the track—full out.

"Jason, they've made an arrest. I have to go. I have to be with Amber."

"They've arrested Amber? Wait, I'll drive you. Hang on a sec." Jason got Janet's attention and the band started up again. She walked over with the bill. Jason took out his wallet as Katherine headed toward the door.

Rushing outside, Katherine bumped into a couple of men. All Katherine could see in the moment was a lot of black leather. One of them held her briefly by her arms and said, "Watch it there, sweetheart. You okay? Am I in your way?"

Katherine muttered her, "excuse me" and wiggled her way out of his hands. She squirmed around him and his friend, and out onto the patio making a beeline for Jason's motorcycle. When she got there, she grabbed one of the helmets expecting to see Jason hurry toward her. No such luck. Katherine sighed and scanned the patio. She slapped the top of the helmet with her palm and frustration built fast, along with a stinging on her hand. She paced along the motorcycle. Every laugh in the conversations around her particularly deepened her frustration.

Jason walked through the door carrying a large to-go bag. Katherine couldn't believe it. Amber was in an emergency state. Michael was in jail. Jason waited for leftovers. Katherine pulled her helmet on. As he approached, she scowled from under her helmet and pointed to the takeout bag. "Really?"

Jason unlocked and opened one of the bins on his bike. "What are you talking about?"

"We're in a hurry. We have to get to Amber, and Michael." Katherine touched his shoulder. "They've arrested Michael. Jason, you should have told me this was going to happen." As she stuffed her oversize skirt around her, she did feel one thought of relief - now Russ was cleared, but how did he react to hearing Michael killed his wife?

Chapter Twenty-Eight

MJ joined Katherine on the porch as the sun came up. "So, you were able to talk Reggie into working on the pond for the Memorial. He's cutting it tight starting Friday morning. On Sunday your Brenda Dirling Memorial might be a pit on the edge of your yard. That's okay. People will understand. Maybe it's more meaningful that it's all under construction."

Katherine leaned forward on the porch railing, holding her chai tea latte. It had been another short night, but worth it to have this construction started. "Reggie's being very nice to fit this in. He's going to work with the landscaping this afternoon too. By the end of the day I intend a Memorial Garden to exist."

"You're pushing yourself and others pretty hard."

"The garden is the least of it. I wanted the murderer in jail by now and we all know, except the police apparently, that Michael is no killer."

"Well, I'm meditating on today's mantra—When Plan A doesn't work, there are 25 other letters in the alphabet. We'll need to figure out Plan B next. And if Plan B doesn't work then we'll go on to a Plan C. How's Amber doing?"

Katherine yawned. "She's so emotional, as you can imagine. Michael's arrest was a total shock. We took her to the jail, hoping we could all see Michael, although Jason warned us, we probably wouldn't be able to last night. He was right, but at least Jason was able to get a message to Michael from Amber. I know she appreciated that. I wanted Amber to spend the night here, when we finally dragged her away from the jail, but she insisted on going home."

MJ took a long sip from her blended fruit drink. "Maybe she can see him today."

"She already texted me this morning. I bet she didn't get any sleep last night. She's going to visit Michael. She wants to come by this afternoon and talk about clues and suspects. She's sure that the evidence we've got has to free Michael."

"She's sure, or she's wishing? I wonder if she's found out something on her own. Did you know she was investigating?"

"No, not really. She mentioned something about tracking down a mysterious love letter she'd found, but I think that's for an exhibit, not Brenda's murder. I want to try and see Michael myself, to hear his story. Maybe the detective will tell me what evidence they think they have."

MJ shook her head. "I doubt that detective is going to talk with you about anything. Did they drop the charges against Russ? Does he know Michael was arrested?"

"Christine was there. She was playing in the band at the Homecoming. When I got there Christine was just heading home, in shock. I was torn whether to help her or Amber."

"Poor girl."

"She was shaken up. Her boyfriend, Sam Corey came over. He took her home."

"Christine is going out with Tom Corey's son?

That's interesting. I've seen them together in groups of kids in town but didn't realize they were dating. That feels odd with the tension that was between Tom and Brenda. At least Christine had someone to help her. And Amber had you, and did you say that Jason was at the station? Was he a part of Michael's arrest?"

"Yes. Actually, he didn't know about the arrest. He and I were together when I got the call from Amber. Oh no, don't look at me like that, all shocked and shaking your head about fraternizing with cops or something. He gave me some interesting information about a sedative discovered with Brenda's autopsy. I researched it this morning. It's succinylcholine, a chemical for temporary paralysis, and can be given in a shot. Can you imagine poor Brenda's terror, conscious of what was happening to her and paralyzed unable to do anything to fight back?

MJ visibly shuddered. "What a terrible destiny. Was it the same drug used in the attack on you at the library? Someone is getting that drug somehow or making it themselves."

Katherine sipped her tea and tried to shake off her own fears. "I don't know any more about the drug yet. Actually, Jason was such a big help for Amber at the jail last night. And then thank goodness he was there when Russ ended up at the jail last night after Christine told him what happened. Russ ranted and raved and demanded to see Michael. Of course, he was refused which made him madder. Jason was able to get him out of there. He drove away in a rage. I wish I could check on Russ and the kids today, but it was obvious he was still furious with me too."

"You're working with all this construction, friends,

investigation, business, and something about service dogs? You've taken on a lot."

"How did you find out about the dog?"

"I wasn't snooping. The screen was on in your office when I was looking for your design on the new exhibit. I have good news. I started work on that preliminary set up."

"That is good news. The dogs are just something Cynthia told me about. Jason is looking for his Army dog now that the dog's service is over. I thought I might be able to help, that's all. His dog's name is Robby and he was trained to sniff out roadside bombs and save lives. I haven't found him yet, but I have narrowed down the search to Texas. That's a big state to look in though. So, I don't know if I'll be able to help or not. I'm learning a lot about these amazing animals though. Did you know these bomb sniffing dogs are over 98% accurate in their detection skills? And, they're not all German Shepherds. Jason's dog was a Lab."

"Well I wish you the best with that. The dog deserves some peaceful days. Sounds like you've got a heavy day ahead with this and all. I'm going to work on a few of the details for the Memorial reception Sunday and let me know anything else I can help with."

"I think Amber and I could use your help late this afternoon going over clues and suspects."

"I'll make sure I'm available."

Chapter Twenty-Nine

"Miss, we're going to have to search your backpack, or you'll have to leave it out here. And we'll have to search you as well." Amber had never been to the police station before and had no idea what to expect as she listened to the desk officer in front of her.

"Okay. I can leave my backpack here. There's something in it that I'd like to give him though."

"We'll have to check it and let you know about that. I can hold your backpack here. I'll give you a receipt for it. You can sit over there until the officer calls you."

Amber took off her backpack and unzipped it to take out the gardenia wristlet. "Is this all right for me to give to Michael?"

"You can ask the officer. Here's the receipt for your backpack." The Administrator handed Amber the receipt, put the backpack in a locked cabinet next to her desk, and resumed typing into her computer.

Amber sighed and went to sit on a rigid, metal chair, one in a row of about a dozen chairs lined up along the beige, windowless wall. She stared into space, waiting. It seemed like a cold, long isolation until he called her name. Focusing her eyes, she was surprised to see it was Jason walking toward her.

"Amber, they said you were here. They're getting ready for you to see Michael. What can I do to help you? Do you have any questions?" He sat down in the chair next to her.

Amber took in a deep breath. "Do I have questions? You mean like how could anyone think Michael did such a monstrous thing? Like how could they surround him, and attack him, and arrest him like this? Like…" Amber ended in a sob.

"I'm sorry. Are you sure you want to see him now? It can be a tough time for both of you."

"Of course, yes. I wanted to see him last night. I want him to know I stand by him, that I know he didn't do this. I want him to know I believe in him and he'll be proven innocent."

"Okay. Take it easy. You'll see him soon. Try to breath. Prepare yourself Amber. He's going to be depressed, scared. Don't be disappointed if, well with how things go on your visit. I mean, if it doesn't go how you want. He's in shock too."

"Of course, he's in shock." Amber shifted in her chair. She sobbed again and pulled tissues from her pocket. "I think, I'm going to splash some water on my face. Excuse me." She stood up and walked into the women's bathroom.

The mirror reflected Amber's concerns and fears in puffed, red eyes and frowning lips, framed by disheveled hair. She ran the cold water and could feel stinging in her left eye. She pressed wet paper towels against her eyes for as long as she could summon the patience. She wanted to fix her hair but didn't have the energy to go and get her brush from her backpack. She tried to pat it in place, to little effect, but it gave her time to take a few more deep breaths and gather her thoughts. She wouldn't have much time with Michael.

She wanted to be sure to say what was most important, hear anything he needed, and give him the gardenia to keep.

Amber walked out of the bathroom with more confidence. She saw Jason talking to another officer who had his hands on his hips and an impatient expression. Jason nodded to her with a faint smile that she took as encouragement. The other officer took his hands off his hips. "Are you Amber?"

She nodded. "Yes."

"I can take you into the visitors' area now. We're a small facility, so a female officer will pat you down there. Once you're cleared, we'll bring the prisoner in. You'll have ten minutes to meet, and then this visit will be over. We'll take the prisoner back out of the room first, and then you can leave."

Amber cringed when he used the word prisoner. She held her hand out in front of her and uncurled her fist palm up to reveal her small gardenia. "Can I bring this in and give it to Michael to keep?"

When the officer gestured with his hand she said, "Please be careful with it." She handed it to him. She thought his eyes lingered on her a moment, and that his gaze appeared to soften.

He looked at it and handed it back to her. "This flower can be given to him if you take off the attached wristband."

"Okay. Thanks." With care, Amber twisted the flower until it loosened, and she could pull it off the band. She carried the flower petals in her hand. She followed the officer into a smaller room which had a table in the center and a chair positioned on each side. Amber felt numb as she was searched. She sat stiffly in the chair that the officer indicated.

She waited until the door in the opposite wall opened and framed Michael. Steered by the guard next to him, he stumbled toward her. His head was hanging down, not looking at her at all. So characteristic of Michael, his hands were positioned where pockets would be if orange jumpsuits had pockets. When he sat down the guard stepped back a few steps and remained.

Amber leaned forward on the table but was still about 3 feet away from Michael. He sat still and although she waited, he didn't lift his head to look at her. "Michael, are you okay? This is the first chance they let me see you."

There was silence and no movement on the other side of the table. Amber started to get up and reach to him. In a fast move the guard stepped forward and shook his head at her. He ordered, "No."

Amber sat back down. Michael glared at the guard and looked like he would yell but Amber interrupted him. "Michael, I love you. Please talk to me."

He dove right in her eyes and her heart warmed. He continued to face her, but his eyes drifted just off to the right as if there was something interesting sitting next to her on the table. Her forehead wrinkled and her mouth pouted as she tried to calm herself. Then, his voice. It was grave as he started with her name, which made her smile, until he continued.

"I want you to forget about me. Don't come here again. We were together for a fun time, and it was great. You're great. But now that's over. You get it? I've got my own problems now and these are real problems and I don't want you involved."

Amber wasn't expecting to hear anything like this.

She started to say something, and then the meaning of his words sunk in. "What are you talking about? I'm here to help you. I love you. I'm with you. Don't give up. I know you didn't do this. Other people know you didn't do this. We're going to prove it."

"Amber, you don't understand what's going on here. It doesn't matter that I didn't do it, and I don't want you with me. I wasn't even going to come out and see you. I did to make sure you won't come back. We're through. Do you get that? We're done. Go enjoy your life and don't look back."

"You don't mean that. Do you? Look me in the eyes. Don't talk to the other end of the room. Talk to me. If you don't love me anymore, then you tell me straight. You're looking away from me because it's not true. I don't know why you're saying this, but you don't believe it."

Michael shifted his eyes to meet hers. He blinked several times, then paused. Were his eyes watering? He twisted away, leaned forward, then he chilled her to the center of her being with the coldest look. "I mean it. Don't come back here to see me."

Amber's throat filled with regret and such sadness she thought she'd be unable to breathe, let alone speak. Her last look at him was blurred as she stumbled to her feet. She held out her hand and let the gardenia flower fall on the table. Two of the petals had fallen off and they floated down to land next to the crumpled flower. She ignored the guard who walked forward. She pushed back the chair, which fell over backwards. By the time it clattered onto the floor she was halfway to the exit. Michael never spoke a word as she opened the door and walked out.

Chapter Thirty

Amber surveyed the shining water from the bow of the Kingston ferry boat. She'd walked on board at Bayside and was heading across on the twenty-minute ride to the Peninsula. She was in search of answers to their mystery. It was the last part of him she could cling to. This would also give her time away from the misery of Bayside. Her world had crashed, and she didn't know how to pick up the pieces. She was going to meet today with Francine Blakely and Felisa Ocampo, just as Michael and she had arranged to do, before he was arrested.

The ferry rode smooth waters today. As it crossed, in the southern distance she had a clear view of grand Mt. Rainier. There were no fun selfies posted, or joyful videos from Amber today. Near where she stood was a family, parents with their two elementary age sons. The adults were commenting on their appreciation for such a warm, sunny day in fall. They were smiling and chatting, and the children were pointing at the sights and the attentive seagulls. Amber couldn't stand it. She turned around and walked over to the heavy doors. She tugged hard to open one and went inside to sit down and wait out the trip in solitude, without even a single glance at her phone to look for messages.

With the dock in sight, an announcement came over the loudspeaker urging walkers to move to the front of the boat to disembark, and for drivers to return to their cars. Amber let the other passengers disappear down the stairwells in front of her. When the boat pulled into the dock, the staff tied up at the pilings. Then Amber got up and began her lonely walk off the ferry. One of the crew members standing on the dock smiled and waved at her as she walked onto the dock. She put her head down and sped up. She just wanted to get all this behind her. She was running out of aspirations.

Amber dragged herself up the long hill, head down. She passed the small cluster of businesses including fish and chip shops, boutiques, lots of souvenirs, and then a couple of gas stations. The stores faded away, and she was in a neighborhood of small homes. Checking the street signs, she walked a couple more blocks and turned down the road Francine had said she lived on. Amber thought how grateful she was that Francine was still alive and was willing to talk with her and Michael—then she mentally corrected herself, to talk with her.

She walked up to a modest, split level home with wooden sideboards that looked like they'd recently been painted a creamy ivory. It was well kept with a mowed, green lawn, tidy flower beds, and a short rhododendron hedge that was so common in the Seattle region. She knocked on the wooden door that was painted a bright red.

Amber was surprised when a man who looked to be about thirty years old appeared in the doorway and greeted her. She paused and looked up at the street number that was on the front of the garage. "I'm sorry. I may have the wrong house. I'm looking for Francine

Blakely? Do you know her?"

"Oh yes. I'm her grandson, Steve Colman. You're Amber?" He extended his hand to her.

Amber shook his hand. "I'm Amber."

"Come on in, she's waiting for you. She's been very excited that your friend Michael contacted her. She's finally ready to tell her story." Steve motioned to Amber to follow him up the stairs to the living room where two women sat and knitted. Steve did the introductions. "Amber, I'd like you to meet my mother, Harriet Colman, and my grandmother Francine Blakely. Ladies, this is Amber."

Francine leaned forward with her arms outstretched. "I'm delighted to meet you."

Amber gave her a hug. "It's so nice to meet you as well."

Harriet spoke next. "Thank you for traveling over here to see us. We don't go to Bayside. Please have a seat." She gestured to the sofa that was across from their armchairs.

As Amber took off her backpack and sat down, Steve asked if she'd like some tea. Amber nodded and smiled.

Francine asked, "Harriet started to explain to me, but you tell me dear what got you so interested in our family?"

Amber locked onto the woman's deep, green eyes, and then unzipped the backpack and pulled out a sturdy cardboard box. She took off the rubber bands that secured the lid and opened it. She gently lifted the Whiting and Davis flapper bag and held it out for Francine to see. Francine's hands went to her cheeks and her mouth popped open. Amber got up and handed the purse to Francine who took it and caressed it ever so lovingly. Tears welled in her eyes. "Do you know what this is?"

Amber sat down again. "Tell me."

Francine gathered herself for a moment. "This was my mother's bag. She told me my father saved his money for a long time to buy her this very special purse she'd admired in a store window. You see, my mother came from the rich Hansen family, and she was used to a rich lifestyle in those days. When she met my father, when he moved to Bayside, he was not moneyed at all, but he adored her, and she fell deeply in love with him. Her family was angry and forbid her to marry this accountant who worked for them. Just a lowly number cruncher they called him. But she did it anyway. They loved each other, and their lives were joyful."

Amber nodded.

"It all seemed to work out with the family. My dad even kept his job working for them. But this purse! My father was so proud to give it to her, and my mother carried it always. I was young, but even I remember this purse. As a child I played with the dangling metal, and the colors of the pattern were bright then and cheery. When my father was hanged, my mother was broken hearted. She never recovered from it, and we moved out of Bayside to here. She always blamed her family's meddling for what happened to my father, along with a corrupt court and police force. To add insult to injury, she somehow lost this treasured gift from him."

Amber was silent as Steve came back in the room with her tea and with a plate of shortbread cookies and put it all on the coffee table. Amber thanked him and then spoke again to Francine. "In Bayside I work at a women's history museum where we have a lot of purses for exhibits. This purse ended up as a donation. Inside there was a letter that your father wrote. We did some research and found you." Amber reached back into her backpack to retrieve the letter folded in her textbook.

Harriet asked, "You and Michael, is it? Is Michael coming today too?"

Amber froze in her movements. She continued to stare into her backpack as she answered in a trembling voice, "No, it turned out he wasn't available today." Amber pulled the paper out of the textbook from the backpack. Harriet and Francine glanced at each other as if they had a follow up question poised to leap out, but they remained silent. Francine stared back at the purse.

Amber handed the letter to Harriet, since Francine's hands were full. She showed the paper to Francine who sighed, and her eyes teared up. "Yes, that my father's handwriting. Harriet, my eyes are too old to make out the words, would you read it for me?"

Harriet smiled. "Of course. I may struggle because the ink is very faded. Here goes." Harriet read the letter her grandfather had written from jail to his beloved wife. She was choking on the words toward the end as she read, "I'll think of my two beautiful girls there. That will be my dying vision through eternity. Will you do that for me? And know I'm there, with you both. All my love, Harry."

Now everyone had tears in their eyes.

Francine sat back with the purse on her lap now. She took a tissue out of her pocket and wiped her eyes. "You know, my father was completely innocent. We couldn't prove it, but he was framed. He didn't have a mean bone in his body and certainly not a murderous one. I can't prove it, but my mother told me what happened. He was the accountant for the Hansen family. He kept their books for their many businesses around town and in the larger city of Seattle. My mother said Seattle was a terrible city full of crime and very scary to visit. She made only rare visits outside Bayside, unless with my dad. She told me what my father had told her when she visited him in jail. The same as what he told his court appointed lawyer." Amber sat in rapt attention, her own troubles replaced for now by the heartache of decades.

Francine appeared to get a surge of strength, like she was determined to convince this audience of her father's innocence. "My father was very good with numbers. He was also as honest as the day is long, and more so. He suspected mis-dealings, even illegal dealings with the Hansen businesses for some time. Then he found the proof in the numbers. He confronted Theodore Hansen with what he'd found. Of course, Theodore, my mother's brother, was defensive. He denied everything, but as my father used to say, figures don't lie, but liars sure figure. Finally, Theodore seemed to realize that my father wasn't going to back down, so Theodore told him that he would make everything right again. He said he would come up with a plan to fix it all, return money and stop illegal activities. He told my dad to meet him at the dance hall in Seattle later. Theodore said he was on his way there and to meet him there at 2:00 a.m. when the place closed. Then he would show my father his plan."

Francine paused to drink her tea. "My father got there late. When he walked into the office Theodore was holding a revolver and standing over a dead cop on

255

the carpet. My dad went into shock. He couldn't talk, he couldn't move. He stood frozen. Theodore charged him, wielding the gun high in the air. When he woke up, he found himself on the floor, now near the dead cop and surrounded by living cops demanding he come to and accusing him of murder."

As Francine finished speaking, Amber took up the story. "In my research of the courtroom testimony Theodore denied all knowledge of the murder and the illegal activities at the dance hall. He accused Harry, your father, of manipulating all that without Theodore's knowledge. Theodore said your father had control of all the money. He also said that he'd been at the hall that night but had left before Harry got there, and there were no witnesses."

Harriet spoke up now. "But that's not true. Felisa was there. She was one of the girls working at the dance hall. She was late leaving for home. There was an argument between Theodore and the cop. They never saw her hide in the hallway."

Amber asked, "How do you know that?"

Harriet sat forward. "Felisa became a friend of my mother's. She ended up moving from Bayside too. She was afraid of the Hansen family and what they could do to her. She was there when Theodore killed the cop. She was afraid for her life. My mother forgave her for running away, didn't you?" She turned to Francine who nodded.

Francine said, "My mother had passed away by then. A person has to forgive. Life must go on. Felisa ended up living a long life, just passing away a few years ago."

Harriet continued, "Before Felisa passed away she

gave me something she'd hidden all these years." Harriet dug into her sweater pocket and showed Amber a well-worn men's wallet. "She said that she hid when she heard the gun shots, during their struggle, and she stayed put when my grandfather, Harry arrived. She came out of hiding later when Theodore left the building and went into the office to help anyone she could. She said the cop was dead; she tried his pulse just in case. She was helping my grandfather when there was a commotion in the street and police coming. She didn't want to be discovered so she ran, pocketing the cop's wallet that was clutched in his hand. This is it. See the sheets inside. They prove it was Theodore who ran illegal activities, and he was the one bribing cops. There's also a letter signed by Felisa on her death bed saying she witnessed all but was too afraid in life to tell. I've kept this because she gave it to me. Take a look."

Amber unfolded the wallet.

Chapter Thirty-One

Katherine worked in her office. Outside her window Reggie checked equipment and talked to his assistants. Poised at the edge of the pond, he raised his arm. That pond would be drained today. The noise from the machinery echoed off the walls of the museum. When the pond was drained, the wheel and shed would be demolished and removed. The machinery sounded powerful as it sucked the water up and into a huge tank Reggie had trucked in. The surface of the pond became wavy.

Katherine checked emails and texts on her phone and after a while there was a noticeable difference in the level of the water. The pond was shrinking. Katherine gave a sigh as an imagined burden on her shoulders lightened. This pond and wheel that had once seemed so quaint was now a deadly nightmare that she wanted destroyed. She stared at the shrinking pond and raged inside. She'd never see Brenda again, and she wanted the killer to pay with their life. She wanted to be the one there when the killer's life was over. Katherine gasped at what she was thinking. "What has this turned me into?"

Her cell rang. It was Rodeo Drive. She needed to calm down, and business always calmed her. Switching to a live conference call on her computer, Katherine was able to connect with her staff and finish an effective review of the California inventory, discuss details about the line for the Los Angeles Spring Review, and plan a new runway show that Watson Designs had been invited to as a featured designer. At the end, Katherine clicked off, stretched and got up from her desk. She noticed the machinery noises had stopped. The pump was disassembled. The bulldozer was ready to start destruction.

Katherine walked over to chat with Reggie. He reassured her everything was on schedule. Katherine was amused to see some objects shining in the sunlight on the muddy pond bottom. She had no idea people had thrown coins into her pond, perhaps for wishes or for good luck. There were a couple of broken children's toy boats too, and who knows how old those were. Plastic never seems to decompose. There were a lot of big rocks on the bottom, and some on the edges. Her eyes wandered to the wheel. How hideous it was. It was hanging over a big hole in the ground. She couldn't stop from staring into the pond below the wheel. She couldn't stop her mind from calculating where Brenda's body had fallen into the water as her mind's eye reminded her of the sights that terrible night.

Her eyes locked onto the glint of a smattering of coins lying below the wheel. Just off to the side from there was a metal gleam. She started walking around the hole now, not wanting to get stuck in the mud, but wanting a closer look at what this could be. She approached it. This was way too big to be a coin, or even a small pile of coins. She was next to the wheel now. The band was too far out in the mud for her to reach. She glanced around for a stick or something. They'd already emptied the shed for demolition, so there were no tools to be had from there, but a pole leaned against the pump. She grabbed it and tried to pull that band closer to her. She launched the pole out, hanging onto the end. It crashed down near the metal and splashed mud all around. She tried to maneuver it over, but it buried whatever the object was deeper.

"What are you doing?"

Katherine jumped at the unexpected voice, although she recognized it as Reggie's. "I want to find out what this is without sinking up to my knees in mud."

Reggie laughed. "Maybe it's buried treasure? If I help you, do I get a share?"

Katherine put her hands on her hips. "Well if it's worth anything you'll get your share."

He shook his head and pushed the cuffs of his jeans into his boots. Then he stepped into the mud, sinking up to his ankles, and squished his way out to where Katherine was now pointing. When he reached it, he pulled a trowel out of his pocket and pried around the item, loosening it from the mud. He walked back to Katherine with it, and she grabbed his hand to help him out of the hole.

Despite the remaining mud, Katherine recognized it at once. It was the waterproof wallet she'd made Brenda decades ago for her scuba diving. And she felt something inside. She couldn't wait to wash it off and open it up. "Thank you so much Reggie. This is not a treasure, but it's definitely a keeper. You may have just found something that could help find Brenda's killer."

Reggie tilted his head and put one hand on his hip. He held out the trowel and pointed it to emphasize his words. "Does this mean we need to stop for the day?

Do the police need to come back?"

Katherine stopped in her tracks to answer him. "Oh no. No need to stop. I'll give it to the police if it's what I think it is. The police already searched everything out here and declared it no longer a crime scene. To make that true, we still need to level that wheel and shed and then make something beautiful for Brenda."

"You're sure?"

"I'm sure and the longer we talk, the less daylight you're going to have to finish." Katherine ran to the back door of her house. There was a hose there, and she wanted to wash the mud off this wallet and see what was inside.

Chapter Thirty-Two

Having washed off the precious scuba wallet, Katherine ran in the back door and grabbed a rag off the mud room shelf to wipe off the excess water. She held it between her hands, gleeful and certain that there was something inside. Katherine's hope soared that Brenda's personal cell phone had been found. Thank goodness for draining that oppressive pond.

She was about to dash into her office to discover the contents when there was a loud knock on the door behind her. It opened, slamming into her back. Katherine moved out of the way and turned to see Rob push into the room. "Oh, I didn't hit you with the door, did I? Man, I didn't think you'd hear me knock with all this construction noise going on."

"Hi Rob. Anything in particular you need?" Katherine sneaked the wallet into her jeans pocket as she cursed the designer jeans she'd chosen this morning with the tight, shallow, useless pockets. She moved toward the kitchen to mask her casual shimmy to get her sweater to fall over the top of her jeans and the piece of the wallet that was peeking out. Rob slammed the door shut and followed her. When she stopped, he bumped into her.

Katherine caught her breath as his arm went around her waist and his green eyes met hers. She pushed back against him with the palm of her hand. "I'm busy this morning. I'm getting ready for the memorial, and we've got a lot to get ready."

"Sure." His grip tightened for just a moment, and his warm breath was against her lips. "I have something for you. I think you'll like it." He chuckled and stepped back. "It's a clue I found about the case when I was researching background material for the article on your memorial. It's something unusual. Can we talk in your office? Or are you too busy for that?"

Katherine wasn't ready to share all her information on the whiteboard with Rob, so her office was out of the question. The construction noise made the porch awkward. "I can always make time for information that could solve the case. My office is a mess right now, due to planning for the new spring line. Let's just sit here in the kitchen. Do you want a cup of coffee or anything?"

Rob took off his backpack and sat down. "Coffee sounds great. I got in late last night, and I'm still waking up." He glanced at the vase with the hyacinths in the middle of the table. "Nice flowers. Mind if I move them out of the way?"

"I'll put them on the counter." Katherine could still hear the construction noise, but it was dulled now. As she waited for the coffee maker, Rob got a laptop out of his backpack. He turned it on and started working the keyboard. "You're going to find this interesting."

Katherine brought over a mug of coffee, and Rob took it from her. He tried to drink some despite the steam rising off it. "Thanks. This is just what I need."

She sat down opposite him, conscious of the lump in her pocket underneath the table. He pecked at the laptop keys and then smiled, turning the screen so she could see it. The screen was filled with some kind of legal agreement about building space. Katherine skimmed it. "This looks like some kind of purchase of a building downtown. The address is in Bayside's main core. Hmmm, a record of some purchase."

Rob leaned back with his mug of coffee. "Skip down to page five. That'll tell you what the purchase is dependent on, and what's being requested in this agreement."

Katherine scrolled. "It's a request to proclaim the building a historic site. It mentions endorsement and certification from the Bayside Historical Society. That's Ida."

"Check out the appendix where the purchasers are named."

Katherine skipped through the document again. "It's Judith Sanders and Tom Corey in a partnership. I didn't know they did business together. How does Corey fit into it? He wants to bulldoze history and Ida wants to preserve it, or at least preserve her founding family's legacy. I'd be surprised if Ida would endorse a fake historical status knowing Tom Corey is involved."

"It may not make sense on the surface, but there's the request in black and white. And guess what. This isn't the only one. There's a series of similar requests and purchases that were each filed separately. And here's the interesting part. Take a look at the link at the bottom."

Katherine clicked on it and waited. The page came up in a window next to the one she already had open. She scrolled back to the beginning of the original document. When she compared them, she could see that this new window was a review of the agreement regarding the historic declaration request. "Upon review, blah, blah, blah . . . Okay, the request was denied. It's citing some criteria that haven't been met." She shrugged her shoulders. "So, I'm guessing the purchase never went through then."

"Check out who denied it."

"Was it Ida?" Katherine looked at the last page. "No, it's Brenda as mayor. It doesn't look like Ida ever even saw it, although we don't know that."

Rob leaned forward, put his mug down and rested onto his elbows on the table. "That's right. All the requests were denied by Brenda. There was a lot of money on the table, because if a building's declared historic a developer can ignore the building height restrictions and lease space to even more businesses. There was just one person in the way."

"Brenda." Katherine slid the laptop back toward him. "So maybe Judith and Tom were business partners and murder conspirators. But historic buildings have particular requirements that the owners have to comply with."

"I looked at that, but those requirements by Bayside are minimal maintenance specifications, nothing that would get in the way of adding on. You know that with your building here. You have the extra floor, although this old farmhouse does meet the definitions of historic. There's no fraud about this."

Katherine frowned. "Did you check on that during your research too? So, with Brenda out of the way they'd have Judith stepping in as temporary mayor. Tom could resubmit the paperwork to Judith and bury the conflict of interest. If it worked, they'd have it approved and could get busy building and counting their money. This could be motive. Brenda's life brutally traded for money."

"We need more proof. It could be both of them, or just one. Or this could be just a dirty business deal that failed, and that was the end of it. Did you hear that they arrested Michael? Maybe that solves the case. Did you see my story on the front page? I was listening on the police scanner and hustled over there just in time to get a photo of them putting him in the cop car at the school."

"I saw your story, and Michael didn't do it."

"What makes you so sure?"

"Amber. Well, to tell you the truth I'm not sure he's innocent, but she is. I have to admit, I'm not sure of the timing of where he was that night when the murder happened. I think he was in the wrong place at that time to be in the shed. My gran says she saw him leave. He didn't stay for the runway show. On the other hand, Tom Corey's unsubstantiated alibi is that he was out on the front porch smoking. It's unsubstantiated because my darn security camera was broken. Ida was in the gift shop looking for Michael, and I have no idea where Judith was. I'm going to the jail to talk with Michael today."

"You're going to see Michael at the jail? Want some company? I could use a scoop."

Katherine had a fleeting thought that if Michael was innocent, a feature story by Rob might be helpful for him. "I'll let you know if I find out anything."

"Is there anything else you've uncovered since we talked?"

"There is something I'm working on. It's the notes, all those threatening notes that went out so far. I'm trying to isolate their similarities to see if either someone, or some type of person surfaces. They are newspaper letters. It's kind of strange. If I text you the pictures that I have of the notes, could you see what you think?"

"Sure. What you showed me before, right? Yeah, text it to me this time. Words are my business, so I have a head start on it. The police didn't let me see any of the notes. This would be great."

"Don't use them in a story though. We don't want to tip off anyone in case there is something to this. Maybe I better just send you a partial picture of one of the notes and see where it goes from there."

"If it makes you feel better. Knock yourself out." Rob turned his laptop off and started to shove it back in his backpack. "I need to get going. Let me take a quick look at this stingy little piece of note that you just texted." He checked his phone. "Oh yeah. This font is unique to the paper. It's the daily jumble puzzle, I'm sure. We ran a contest of fastest solvers a couple of months ago. I'll email you the top ten winner names. Let me know what Michael says to you. If he's innocent we may not just have a news article, we may have a book."

Katherine stood up, but something caught on the edge of the table and tugged at her pocket. Her secret contents fell onto the floor right in front of Rob.

"Wait, you dropped something." He bent down and reached for it.

Katherine jumped to grab it first and then steadied herself. She needed to act nonchalant so Rob wouldn't guess this was something important and connected to Brenda. She paused and waited for him to hand it to her.

"Is this something for your spring line? It doesn't look new."

"No. Uh this is a donation I grabbed out of the box. I need to remember to clean it up and evaluate it. I just didn't have a chance to get to it yet. Busy morning you know."

Rob walked through and opened the backdoor. The construction noise boomed inside. "You're really going to be ready in time for a ceremony?"

Katherine nodded. "No problem. Reggie and his crew are hard at it. Be ready to write a great feature about it and bring your photographer. Maybe we'll catch the killer in time for the ceremony with that information you found."

Rob took a step toward Katherine, touched her cheek with his hand, and whispered, "If you find out anything that leads you to the killer, I don't want you taking any chances on your own, okay? Before you go chasing anybody down and dragging them off to jail, don't call the police. Text me right away." His voice grew louder. "I want to be in on it."

As he stepped back, Katherine couldn't help but wonder if their reconciliation had meant more than friendship to him, or did he just want to break another story? "I'll text you, but at some point, we'll get the police involved so we can free Michael. Then write your book and accept your Pulitzer?" She grinned.

Rob laughed. "Sounds like a plan. See you later."

Katherine closed the door and rushed into her office. She sat down at her desk and zipped open what she'd once christened as the 'submersible purseable'. The zipper caught but she adjusted her hold on it and then gently tugged again, and again. It opened, and

Katherine gathered her breath in. It was Brenda's personal cell phone.

The inside of the wallet, and the phone was dry. Katherine smiled. "Excellent." She tried pushing the side button, but nothing happened. Katherine hoped that it was just the battery that was dead and not the phone ruined. She and Brenda had the same model, so she put the phone in her charging station and waited, foot and fingers tapping with impatience, hoping it would come to life.

A low buzz, then light flickered on the screen. Katherine played a rapid drum roll with her fingers on the desk in delight. She leaned back to let the charge build as she contemplated the password. She could ask Russ, or Brenda's assistant, but that would raise questions. Russ would refuse to tell her anything right now, and she didn't want word to get back to the police about withholding evidence or anything like that. She wasn't withholding evidence. She was checking first to see if the potential evidence was pertinent information. Then she'd take it to the police. She'd have to try and figure out the password without bothering anyone else.

Katherine leaned back in deep thought. There had been occasions when Brenda was driving her to events they were both attending, and she'd asked Katherine to text messages for her on the business phone when issues were heated. What was that password Brenda had given her to enter? Livfreeordi. Did her personal cell phone have the same password?

Staring at the phone in the charger, willing it to give up its secrets, she grabbed it and tried the password. No luck. The screen alerted that it was a bad password and asked if she'd forgotten the password or wanted to reset it. On impulse she wanted to click that but stopped herself thinking that the reset would go through Brenda's email and she had no access to that. Someone else might have that access though, and then they'd get suspicious.

She groaned and put the phone back in the charger. "Oh, wait a minute." She focused on a memory that popped in her head. She was sitting with Brenda in her Tesla, staring at the ferry as it left the dock. The car windows were down, and the sounds of the small waves lapped up against their harmony. Brenda had enticed her to enjoy a day together at the Seattle Women's Conference. The conversation was easy in the car. Katherine remembered savoring the relaxed company, and she'd thought then that she wasn't the only one reluctant to rush back to her busy life. They watched the ferry on its return trip. Brenda started the car and pulled out to the road. Katherine had just rolled up her window when Brenda's phone beeped with a text.

"Oh, can you grab that out of my purse and check it for me? That's my personal phone and with Christine driving now I get especially anxious she might be texting me if she needs help. And there's always the worry Danny could be injured with all his sports."

Katherine rummaged in the purse looking for the cell. "Unfortunately, that maternal feeling is subdued but never goes away as they get older. I still open texts from the twins quick, just in case of trouble."

Brenda nodded. "Having them living away from home must add a new dimension."

"Where's your cell?"

"I keep it in the old waterproof wallet you gave me forever ago."

"You're sentimental. Here it is. The skin feels a little thin from years of wear."

Brenda smiled. "I like that. I can just reach down and operate some of the functions right through the bag. You don't need to unlock the password to record if I want to make a note to myself or record my thoughts on the go about something. Also, I can automatically call someone on speaker, I can start the GPS. I can even take pictures through the clear plastic on the back."

Katherine had the cell phone out now. "It's asking for your password."

"Oh, it's narcosis." Brenda spelled it as Katherine typed it in.

"No worries, this text isn't from either kid. Something from Judith it looks like."

"Judith on my personal cell? That's funny. She usually sends everything on the government cell, whether it's council business or not. Her text can wait. Thanks for checking for me."

Katherine put the phone away. "Narcosis? That's an odd password. Sounds like a medical diagnosis or something."

Brenda giggled. "Sort of. In scuba its nitrogen narcosis and it's dangerous. It has to do with the effects of breathing nitrogen under water at high pressure. But the condition is also known as rapture of the deep. I haven't breathed in the dangerous levels of nitrogen, but you know I suffer from a rapture of the deep. That's too long to type for a password. So, it's narcosis."

Now Katherine hoped the password hadn't been changed in the meantime. She picked up the phone. As she typed it in, she noticed she was holding her breath. "Silly. It either works or it doesn't." She took a breath and typed the last s on narcosis. The screen opened to a dashboard of apps and functions. "That's it. Okay, now, where do I begin?"

She started with anything near the time of the murder. Katherine took a quick look at the emails for anything sent or read by Brenda that night. She didn't see much of interest. There were only two from Friday that even showed as having been opened.

One email from Friday morning turned out to be from Anthony Marconi about her book group. He was asking to confirm the time of their next meeting on Tuesday at the library. He said he was happy they'd chosen to read and discuss one of his books. He added that he'd like to chat with Brenda before the meeting. He wrote that he'd try to catch her alone for a few minutes at the museum opening. The email indicated a reply sent.

Katherine checked the 'sent' folder and saw that Brenda confirmed both the date and time, thanked him for planning to attend, and agreed that she'd make time to chat with him that night. She ended her response saying, "You're right, we do need to talk." Katherine cocked her head to the left and frowned. She didn't remember Anthony saying anything about talking with Brenda at the gala. Was it just about the book club? Why was he hiding his intention, and did he get any private time with her that night? Did he talk with her in the shed and did things get out of control?

The other Friday email was from Judith. Did Judith send government topic emails to the personal address so there wouldn't be a public record of what she wrote? Skimming down, Katherine widened her eyes as she absorbed the diatribe of threats and criticism of Brenda.

There were many screens of text sent from Judith, complaining that Brenda had not responded and then diving into bitter content again. The central theme was the imminent building heights vote. There were complaints about Brenda insisting on an open forum for citizen comment. After the council meeting there were complaints about the delay of the vote. And above all there was the continual argument that building height restrictions would stunt the future growth of Bayside and instead of thriving, the community would shrivel up as progress passed them by.

"That's very dramatic, Judith," Katherine muttered as she leaned back to contemplate this discovery. "I had no idea you were so invested." Katherine thought about what Rob had found. Was Judith's Plan A to turn Brenda so she would sign that historic designation paperwork, and when that didn't work, Plan B was to murder Brenda so Judith could bury the height restrictions proposal as temporary mayor? Did she corner Brenda in the shed that night for a talk and then her fury grew out of control, and she ended up violent, killing Brenda? Was Tom there too?

Katherine switched from the emails to Brenda's calls. During the day, Russ called her once in the morning and left a loving voicemail suggesting he take her out for dinner after the gala for a romantic date night. The cell phone recorded that she called him back later in the afternoon, for a ten-minute call. There were a couple of calls from phone numbers that didn't have contact information and no message left. There was a voice message from some friend calling about their college alumni group and asking if Brenda could volunteer some time for their next event. There was the call she had made to Brenda thanking her again for coming to the gala.

None of these calls were intriguing. Katherine glanced at the previous day. One call that morning got her curious. It was from Cynthia at the library. She left a message that she'd found the historical records Brenda had asked for, and they were available for pick up anytime.

Katherine checked the texts. Of course, there were the texts from Katherine trying to find Brenda before, during, and after the runway show. She could also see some from Russ during that same timeframe. And earlier, there was the text from Christine that she was on the way to the museum from school practice. There was a previous text from Tom Corey. He wanted to talk with her about her daughter seeing his son. He said this was a discussion he didn't think she'd want to have in front of a lot of people, and he suggested meeting her out on the back porch after the ribbon cutting. Brenda responded that she would meet him. Katherine's grip on the phone tightened, and she stared at the screen. If he went ahead to meet her when getting this text, that would have been about the time of the murder. Once on the porch, had Tom led her over to the shed so they'd be farther from the crowd in the house? Had he murdered her?

Last, Katherine checked the photos on Brenda's phone. There was a lovely selfie of Brenda and Christine in the alcove during the gala. There were a couple of pictures she'd taken of Katherine during her talk with the press from the front porch, and a shot of the new, prize purse as well, and one of Purrada in the den that night. Katherine was touched by the picture

Brenda had taken of her, MJ, Gran and Grandpa. She texted it to herself. The final one saved that night was a video. She clicked on it, and the screen went dark. She touched it. A video was on and tracking. She turned the volume up.

"I know more about this than you realize." That sounded like Brenda's voice. Was she recording with her phone in her pocket or purse? Who was she talking to, and where were they?

Someone was talking again, but she couldn't make out what they were saying or whose voice it was. Then there was Brenda. "No more secrets. It's all wrong. It's all tarnished in blood."

There was more muttering. The tone became urgent.

Then Brenda again. "The price is too high. Wait. Stop!"

Chapter Thirty-Three

Katherine had to give Brenda's cell phone to the police. She didn't want any question that she was withholding evidence. She guessed that could have serious consequences if they wanted to enforce it. She wanted copies of some of the emails, texts, pictures, and definitely that video so she could analyze further. She got busy saving copies. Maybe she'd be able to enhance the audio on that video and recognize the killer. She was deep in thought and action when she was startled by a loud knock on the French doors to the porch.

Jason stared at her through the glass. She swallowed hard and stared back at him. He smiled and opened the door and walked over to her desk.

"Sorry for the loud knock on your glass, but with all the construction noise no one heard me at the front door. How are you doing?" He put his hands on his hips and told her about how Michael was doing at the jail, the time he'd spent with Amber, and how she'd left looking very upset after talking with Michael.

Katherine said, "Thanks for letting me know. Poor, dear Amber. She's coming over later. Jason, we're still partners on the case, right?"

Jason nodded. "We're both sharing our information, right?"

Katherine nodded. "Right. Well, do you have

anything new?"

"Nothing I haven't told you about."

She glanced at her screen, then stood up and walked a few steps forward, swinging her arms broadly, knowing that she had exciting news. She was debating though, was it too early to share what she'd found? She'd captured his full attention. There was no turning back. She didn't want to hold back. This was something where sharing could be helpful in solving the mystery. "I have big news. I've found new evidence. I was headed over to the police station but first I had to check it. But wait until you hear this. Just a few minutes ago, I was outside looking at the drained pond, and I found Brenda's submersible purse with her cell phone in it. And it's still working. I've retrieved some terrifying and intriguing information off it."

"Katherine, we've had this conversation. You can't tamper with objects related to the case. This is serious. There's forensics that could get disturbed or polluted. You should…"

Katherine groaned and sat down at her desk again as she tried to conceal a grin. "Yes, we've talked about it, and that's why I'm on the way to the police station. Maybe I should leave right now without wasting any time filling you in."

"Well, yes, but a few more minutes won't make a difference now that the pristine scene has been disrupted." Jason sat down on the edge of the desk next to Katherine. He pointed to her screen on the wall. "Why don't you go ahead?"

Katherine smiled. "Now you're talking. I think your insights could be helpful, along with my analysis." Katherine told him the highlights of what she'd discovered on the screen and explained what she'd found.

He was interested. "Katherine, this cell phone is going to register all your activity at the station. If they check it, they could trace it to your place here with the cell towers and GPS activated. I think you should get it to the station sooner rather than later. It's easier to explain when you're handing them the phone rather than after they've barged in here. Do you want me to go with you?"

They arrived at the police station within half an hour and let the assistant at the front desk know that Katherine had evidence in the Brenda Dirling case to turn over to a detective. She was asked to take a seat, and Jason went into the back. In just a few minutes the door to the inner sanctum opened, and Detective Grace Adams motioned at Katherine to follow her. They walked to her cubicle.

Grace didn't invite her to sit down as she sank into her own chair behind the desk. "This is a popular place for the Dirling case today. You have information?"

The detectives were each shielded by the walls of their cubicles, but loud echoes indicated that lots of officers were at their desks today and many were either on their phones or were talking with someone at their desk. In contrast, the other day when Katherine had been here it seemed they were the only ones in the building. Katherine sat down in the visitor chair, and Detective Grace typed on her computer, eyes fixed on the screen, not Katherine.

"This is a popular place today? I don't understand?"

"We've made an arrest. What can I do for you?"

"Oh that." Katherine reached into the outer zip compartment of her Swagger purse. As always when she carried this unassuming black bag with the swinging jewelry, she was pleased with its quick access and organization. "It's not information, well I guess it is that, but it's something that I found. It's Brenda's zip case with her cell phone inside, and the phone is still working."

The detective turned to Katherine now. It was impossible not to notice Grace's sudden interest. Katherine produced the case and started to unzip it. Grace gasped. "Wait. Stop. Put it on the desk, please. Let me get an evidence bag and some gloves out of the drawer."

"Oh no, don't worry. This was found at the bottom of my pond when I drained it. I bet it fell out when she dropped…" Katherine was suddenly cold all over as she thought of what it must have been like the last moments of her friend's life. She couldn't finish.

"We'll still follow procedure. We don't know the forensics they might be able to pick up." With great care, Grace put on gloves and examined the wallet, then unzipped it and pulled the cell phone out.

Katherine wiped away the sweat on her forehead with a tissue from her purse. "I touched it already. I charged the phone to see if it was still working. See, the bag it was in is one of mine and I had made it waterproof for Brenda because she's a scuba diver. Anyway, that's what happened. But I'll leave it to you. Okay? Do you need anything else from me?"

Grace watched her as Katherine stumbled through this brief explanation. "Yes, I will need a statement from you about how you found this, and I have questions. We'll use examination room one. Right this way."

Grace led Katherine to the room and as she sat down on a plain, metallic chair next to the table Grace told her, "Let me get this over to our lab, and I'll be right back to record your statement." The door closed, and Katherine sighed. She had too much to do in too little time.

Chapter Thirty-Four

After recording her statement, Katherine wanted to see Michael. The police did not keep her waiting long before bringing her into the inmate visiting room. She sat and gathered her thoughts. She wasn't sure what information Michael had about the night of the gala that might help her. Now that she was here, she wasn't sure what she even wanted to ask him, although questions tumbled in her mind. Who would want to frame Michael? What evidence did the police have against him? She'd seen him that night when he told her Ida was looking for her; what else did he do that night? Where was he at the time of the murder if he wasn't in the shed?

The door across from her opened, and Katherine lost her train of thought to sadness when seeing the once bright, funny, overconfident, lively young man walk into the room, head down, handcuffed, and in jail orange clothes. He'd never earned her complete trust, and she was concerned that Amber was so enamored with him, but guilty of murder? Looking at him now, it was hard to picture him as a cold-blooded killer. She'd never seen him lose his temper or be violent in any way.

She smiled at him as he sat down on the other side of the table. She had to wait until he looked up at her. "Ms. Watson, if you're here because of Amber's visit, if you're here to say I'm wrong to send her away, you're wasting your breath. I know that with these charges it's better for Amber to stay far away from me. It's better to break up."

That pronouncement took Katherine by surprise. He was looking her in the eye now, almost daring her to disagree with him, but she noticed a slight tremble in his bottom lip and a tightening along his jaw line. She shook her head. He cleared his throat. "I told her, we weren't serious, we just got caught up in it. She'll forget me soon. When I get out of here, I'm going to get as far away from Bayside as I can. Maybe I'll get lost down in L.A. like you do."

Katherine sat up straighter. "I didn't come here to talk about Amber or me, although I think you're underestimating her and probably yourself as well. I came here to talk about the serious trouble that you've stumbled into. Amber says she knows you didn't kill anyone. I don't think you did it either, but I want to hear from you. Did you kill Brenda?"

His gaze never left her eyes. "I did not kill Brenda. I wasn't anywhere near her or the shed that night. I could never kill anyone."

"There were only a couple of times I remember seeing you that night. When you came to the office to tell me that Ida was looking for me was one. Michael, were you listening to what Brenda and I were talking about?"

"Listening? No, I had other things on my mind. I just needed to get that message delivered. I was kind of in a hurry." Michael sat still, with a blank stare.

Katherine continued. "You were talking with Amber in the shop. You were enjoying each other's company very much. Was it Amber that your mind was preoccupied with?"

"Amber doesn't have anything to do with any of this." Michael leaned forward with his elbows on the table and held both hands out palms up.

"Tell me about what else you did that night. Do you have an alibi for the time of the murder? Were you still with Amber?"

"I don't know. The police went through this with me over and over. I was with Amber for a while in the shop, and then she was busy, so I made a date with her for the next day. I wanted to stay, but she was headed to work on that fashion show and that's not my thing. I went in the kitchen and grabbed some food off the trays. I was hungry. Sandy's food is great, and she's real nice, so we talked, then she headed into the café because people were going to the show. I went out the back door, walked down the alley, and headed back to my place. I didn't even know that anything had happened until Amber told me the next day."

"Ida didn't say anything when she got home?"

"No. I heard her get home, but I was up in my room doing stuff on my computer. The next morning she'd left to go somewhere while I was still asleep."

"So, no one saw you leave, and no one can say for sure you were in your room that night."

"Yeah. That's what the police said too."

"I've been told that the police have evidence against you including newspapers that are cut up, like they may have been used to make the threatening notes. They say you set up a chemical lab for drugs hidden in the basement at Ida's. She didn't know anything about it. Do you have a lawyer, Michael?"

"I haven't seen one yet. I told them I couldn't afford one. No way. The cops said the judge would assign one when I go to court on Monday. I don't know anything about newspapers or chemistry. None of that is mine. The police are framing me. They were trying to get me to say that I killed Brenda because she caught me hacking into the city's computer system and changing data, and she was going to throw me in jail for it. They said I must have got real mad when I saw her at the party. Yeah. And my temper got out of control when I had the chance to get her out to the shed and kill her. Crazy. Did I look mad at her when I came in your office? That was the only time I even saw her that night."

"Did you hack into the city's system and change things?"

Michael sat back and folded his arms across his chest and raised his face pointedly up at the camera filming them. "Did you ever notice they have cameras everywhere here, following every move? Probably recording somehow everything said, in case you admit to some crime or something."

"So, the police told you why they think you killed Brenda. Do they have any evidence? That's just a theory, and they can't prove you were in the shed, and they can't prove you weren't in your room. What evidence?"

"They say they found some drug in my room. They say it's a drug that Brenda took. First of all, I don't do drugs, and I don't deal drugs either, so she didn't buy any drug from me. I don't know how they found any drugs in my room. They probably planted it there." Michael faced up to the camera again then frowned at

Katherine.

"A drug?" Katherine rubbed her temples for a few seconds. She needed to take some more pain-reliever for the remnants of her concussion. "The drug was in your room somehow. Who else could get in your room?"

He shook his head. "The cops were probably so busy planting evidence they never found my hidden USB. There's some weird, secret stuff about Ida's family Amber and I found out. They should look at that for Bayside lies, but the cops only think guys like me lie."

"Michael, stop accusing other people of being dishonest. You're doing what you're accusing them of doing. How can I get in your room and look at that USB?

"The cops took my keys when they arrested me."

A plan began to form in Katherine's mind. "I'll ask Jason how you can give me permission to take your keys. I can go take a look at that drive if you tell me where to find it. Is there anything else I should look for, or anything I can bring or do for you?"

Michael leaned forward again, and Katherine thought his face brightened. At the very least the scowl he'd had for the camera disappeared. "I am innocent. I want to get out of here."

"I'm going now, Michael, but I'll see you again soon."

Katherine got up to leave. The officer stepped forward and pulled up on Michael's arm to get him to stand. Michael left, his shoulders hunched over. The two of them walked back through the door they'd come through earlier. When it slammed shut behind them, the sound reverberated across the small room.

Chapter Thirty-Five

"We've gone over this Brenda board a hundred times. The murderer's not on it." Amber seemed unaware she'd started tapping her fingers on the arm of the chair.

"Or, maybe we just have to go over it one hundred and one times to find the right answer," Katherine said, looking with a grimace from the board to the abyss of despair that used to be her enthusiastic, gift shop gal. Sitting cross legged on the floor next to Amber, MJ was doing arm stretches and what appeared to be breathing exercises. Relaxing in the easy chair behind them, Pam had dozed off with Purrada snoozing at her feet.

Katherine groaned and let her frustration out on the blinds as she carelessly lowered them, and they dropped with a bang on the sill. The startling noise had Amber looking up as if expecting an announcement. MJ stopped mid-stretch and sat at attention. Purrada startled awake and glared with indignation. When Katherine glared back the cat stood up, stretched, turned around and lay down again with her back to her owner. Pam was awake at the bang of the blind and blinking at the whiteboard.

Katherine focused in on her grandmother. "When I talked with Detective Grace today, she told me you'd talked with her too. Did you hear anything new when you were there?"

Pam cleared her throat. "Yes, I was there with your grandfather. I wanted to talk with the detective about that writer, Anthony."

Katherine was puzzled. "About what?"

"Well, don't get upset about this. I know you're friends with that writer, but I was always uncomfortable about him. I couldn't talk to you about it because I didn't think you wanted to hear it, but I needed the police to know in their investigation that the writer talked with Brenda. During the gala I walked back from the kitchen, had a chat with Michael, and headed down the hallway with my cane toward the café to settle in for the show. There were voices in that new 1940's room. and the door was ajar. I was surprised anyone would be in there, so I paused outside. I couldn't hear them well, but I recognized Brenda's voice right away. She had that calm tone of voice that she sometimes gets when she's trying to manage a situation, you know? And then a man spoke to her. He sounded very angry."

Katherine folded one arm across her waist and leaned her chin into her other hand. She'd had no idea this had occurred at the party. "Were they arguing about something?"

"He was saying she broke his heart. He'd never loved like this. Why did she put him on like this? Was she trying to hurt him all along? He went on about her not being the woman he'd thought she was. Brenda said something then, and her hand appeared on the doorknob. I thought I was going to be discovered eavesdropping, but then her hand disappeared, and it sounded like she was pushed against the wall right next to me. I got nervous then. The man said that he'd tell Russ. All I could think to do was make some noise and get someone else there so I shouted as loud as I could a hello to Rob and asked him to come over to help me. He walked over right away and, in the meantime, the two in the room became silent. Rob and I continued down the hall, but I turned around to make sure Brenda got out of the room, or else I would have asked Rob to go check on them. Brenda walked out and headed for the kitchen. The man never came out, but I recognized that voice at the Round Table this week, Anthony Marconi."

Amber brightened. "Did the detective say she was going to investigate him?"

"Well, she put it all in her computer."

Amber nodded. She pushed herself up and off the floor. "I'm going to check on the tea," she said over her shoulder as she walked into the kitchen.

Katherine scowled at the all too familiar white board. The excitement that had begun it was now well worn. When not flipped to the wall to hide its contents, the fluttering post-it notes and thickly penned sketches mocked her. Initially casting about and identifying suspects had been so easy. Then tracking had uncovered some valuable clues, but now it was like the murderer had gone to ground and eluded them. There were so many challenges narrowing the hunt to the one murderer. The clues, arrows, smudges, sketches, and theories blurred together, and Katherine rubbed her tired eyes.

MJ got up off the floor and rolled the Brenda board up against the wall. "Let's try something new." She went to the easy chair and raised her voice. "Pam, are you awake?" She gently rubbed the old woman's hand.

Pam yawned and replied, "I'm with you." And the

edges of her mouth turned up slightly as she drifted back to sleep.

MJ smiled and stepped over to the doorway. "Amber, we're headed outside."

"I'm right behind you with tea mugs and cookies."

"Maybe we should have something stronger," Katherine muttered.

MJ patted Katherine's shoulder and motioned her toward the porch door. She flipped on the outside lights as she walked out. Katherine moved over to the railing and leaned against it with her back to the yard, gazing at her museum and house. Through the window, she saw that Purrada had moved to curl up on the desk, and she could see Gran resting. She could just see the corner of the whiteboard sticking out, as if taunting and daring her to find the killer. The sun hovered low in the sky, but this time of year its farewell setting would be brief.

Katherine muttered, "Maybe our real fall is about to start."

Amber had walked out and put snacks on the low, rattan table that stood surrounded by a matching rattan couch and three chairs.

MJ said, "We can celebrate the end of all the construction noise draining that pond. I can't believe they were able to get it drained and landscaped. It will look nice for the memorial."

Everyone grabbed a seat, and Katherine ended up with the couch to herself. Amber's eyes teared up, and she fought to regain composure. "I was out there checking for any evidence too. Just anything that could clear Michael. But I didn't find anything."

Leaning forward with her chin on her hand,

Katherine shook her head. "Tell me it can't be done. Tell me that some mysteries can't be solved. In the end is there such a thing as a perfect crime? Can this person get away with murder?"

"You mean get away with framing dear Michael."

MJ reached out and rubbed Amber's back. "Come on you two. We'll get him out, Amber. Remember today's meditation, when Plan A doesn't work, there are twenty-five other letters in the alphabet."

MJ gave a hopeful smile and then took a cookie for herself and offered the plate to Amber who passed the plate over to Katherine. "I did solve one other mystery in the middle of all this. I learned some things about mean Ida's real family history back in the 1920's. It's not pretty. It all started last weekend when I found a letter in a donated purse that was in the box you gave me out of your office, Katherine. It was a Whiting and Davis. I have a picture of it on my phone, hang on." As she scanned her phone, Amber explained that today she had returned the purse to its real owner. Katherine looked at the photo and then texted it to herself. The ladies sipped tea and gave Amber their rapt attention. She told them about the mystery she'd solved with Michael. Katherine had the USB drive and wanted to finish looking at that information tonight.

Katherine remained thoughtful at the end of Amber's tale. She wondered how she hadn't noticed this historic, vintage purse when she'd gone through that donation box in her office. How did it get in the box? When did it get in the box?

MJ held her mug, blowing on the steaming tea. "Imagine that skeleton in pure Ida's family closet. We'll solve Brenda's case just as you solved that one.

There is peace and truth in the universe. Come on now. Put your hands around your mug and close your eyes."

Katherine reached for a mug and tried to avoid seeing the gap in the garden where the water wheel had once been. She leaned back and closed her eyes. They sat in a comfortable silence, and MJ spoke in a soft voice, "Smell the wafting scent of lavender, honey, and lemon. Hold that mug close to your face and breathe deep. Feel the warmth of the cup, the silken depth of the blend as you sip with your eyes closed. The liquid sustains us as it travels and spreads within us."

MJ paused, and silence wrapped around the trio. MJ whispered, "The answers exist. See that they are tangible and they're in a place in the universe, waiting for you to find. Clues on the board, people, motives, suspicions. Now these are in your head, and Brenda is in your heart. Love from your soul, and you'll find what you're looking for."

A bit more relaxed, but not convinced of success, Katherine opened her eyes. Jason stood on the lawn grinning. Next to him, Hobbs seemed torn between his partner and a tempting chase at a crow taunting him from the bird bath.

"Oh, for Heaven's sake, what are you doing standing there?" Katherine rubbed her forehead with the palm of her hand and blushed.

"Just seeing how the sleuthsayers work cases." Jason smiled.

"Well, we all have our methods," MJ said. "I'm going to help Gran home, or she'll spend the night sleeping in your office, then I've got things to do so I'll see everybody later." She grabbed a couple more cookies. "These are for Gran." She walked out through the French doors amid a chorus of good nights. The glass of the French doors framed MJ as she headed toward the big chair that wrapped around the snoozing grand lady herself.

Amber got up and walked onto the lawn. She kneeled down to give Hobbs a pet and a cuddle. She looked up at Jason. "Thanks for this morning. You know, helping me at the station." Jason nodded.

She lingered, scratching behind the big shepherd's ears. The dog gazed at her, gave an exaggerated yawn, and nestled closer to her. Jason's and Katherine's eyes met. With a final flurry of pets for the dog, Amber stood up again. "See you tomorrow, Katherine. I'll be here early to help get ready for the memorial."

Katherine shook her head. "You have a lot on your mind and in your heart. Don't feel you have to be here early tomorrow. Take time for yourself if you need to. But I'd love you to be here for the Sunday memorial if you can. And let me know if you need anything at all. You're sure you don't want to stay here tonight? You know you're welcome."

"Thanks, but no, I'm going home. Maybe tomorrow some clue or idea will surface that will free Michael." As she walked past Jason, she said, "Please find the killer, the real one." She continued out to her car parked at the curb on Main Street. She lifted her hand to brush back her hair and wipe away tears, then climbed in and drove off.

Jason and Hobbs had walked onto the porch and looked through the windows. Was he studying the whiteboard, or looking for clues on her big screen? Katherine cleared her throat. Jason didn't move so she stepped over to stand next to him. "It's a nice surprise to see you tonight."

Jason faced her. Hobbs wagged his tail. She scratched behind the dog's ear. "It's always nice to see you as well, Officer Hobbs. If you're here looking for a dog treat, you've come to the wrong house."

"All these purses and none of them are carrying dog treats? That seems wrong somehow, doesn't it, Hobbsie?"

The dog cocked his head to one side and then looked back and forth between the two of them. He lay down as Katherine spoke again. "You were quiet when Amber was wondering about Michael. You don't doubt his innocence, do you? Because with the evidence I've seen, the one thing I feel certain about is that Michael didn't kill anyone. He may have used some skills and talents in questionable ways on the websites and so on, but he's not violent."

Jason put his hands on his hips. "I'm not supposed to talk about an ongoing investigation."

Katherine shook her head. "They're saying the case is closed."

Jason smiled. "Well, we each know someone who is still investigating." He smiled at her with a glint in his eye. "I just don't see it in that kid. Detective Grace was talking about one of the interrogations. I think they're still fishing for facts to prove he did it. So, the killer may still be on the loose, and the public could let down their guard thinking they're safe. I don't like the idea of that any more than the idea that Michael may be sitting in jail and shouldn't be."

Strains of music surrounded them. Jason's expression turned puzzled.

"That's Gran in her cottage." Katherine laughed.

"She likes to turn up her music and sometimes we can hear it all the way across the lawn like this. We can't hear it much, just enough . . ."

Jason smiled. "Just enough so you can't quite recognize the song she's playing. At least, I'm struggling to figure it out." He put his finger across his lips and concentrated in the direction of the cottage. Hobbs sniffed the air. Katherine waited.

Jason's smile broadened. "Nice. I recognize it now." Jason stepped forward, tentative as he took Katherine in his arms, and they began a dance. His embrace was strong, sure, and yet loose and guiding. He was close to her, and there was an air of cloves when his cheek brushed against hers. His gaze turned toward her lips. She stumbled against his shoe. She missed a step and fell against his shoulder. He was holding her tighter now to stop her from falling, but she was off balance. With one more step backwards at the wrong angle, Katherine fell over Hobbs. Grabbing to help her, Jason fell forward, twisting somehow and ending up under her on the porch floor, cushioning her landing. Hobbs stood, looking down at them both. Katherine couldn't stop laughing, and Jason joined in with her as the music continued, and Katherine's mind filled in the next words, "dancing cheek to cheek."

Chapter Thirty-Six

Jason's radio erupted with static and a voice. He helped Katherine up and walked a few steps away to respond. Hobbs was sitting up, full attention on his partner. Jason said, "Looks like unexpected escort duty for a city official. I've got to run Hobbs home and get over to City Hall on the double. I'd like a rain check on that dance though."

Katherine blushed. "You can leave Hobbs here if you want to save time. I'll be home with him, and you can pick him up later."

Jason hesitated. "That would be great, but is it too much—"

Katherine interrupted. "It's no problem. We'll see you later."

Jason petted Hobbs on the head. "Great. Thanks. Hobbs, I'll be back." He reached in his pocket and gave his dog a biscuit, then handed the small bag to Katherine. "In case he wants a treat. I'll be back as fast as I can."

"Come on Hobbs." Katherine found the German language commands cumbersome and was glad that, when off duty, Hobbs followed commands in English. "Come on, let's go in the house now. I want another look at that whiteboard."

Hobbs' confusion was obvious as he stared at Jason who was walking away at a fast pace and opened only the driver's door to the car. He didn't call or signal the dog. Instead he got in and started the engine.

"Hobbs, come on. Come on." Katherine held open the door to her office and waved a biscuit at doggy nose height. Hobbs bounded over, grabbed the cookie on his way inside, and settled in on the braided rug by the bay window. Purrada jumped up from her nap and vehemently hissed at the dog. That was followed by an indignant look at Hobbs and then at Katherine. Purrada twitched and jerked her tail up, then turned her back on them both as she sat down.

Katherine attacked the whiteboard while Hobbs crunched his cookie. She stood in front of the board, leaning on one leg with the other foot curled around her ankle. She tapped her finger against her chin. "Hobbs, the killer is on this board, I just know it." Katherine walked past the dog as he put his head down on the rug for a nap. Purrada had seemed to forgive the interruption, and the dog and was purring. Katherine grabbed a marker and added Ida's name to the whiteboard. Her involvement in Amber's mystery had triggered suspicions, and so had Michael's USB information that she'd obtained and reviewed on her computer this afternoon.

Ida had her precious, family history to protect—she'd built her whole life around hiding a big secret. There was the pile of newspapers in Michael's room that he said he knew nothing about. Ida lived there too, so planting evidence to frame Michael and protect herself would have been easy. She remembered how Ida had told her at the Biographies Breakfast about fearing Michael and his suspicious actions. Katherine checked Rob's email again on her phone, opening the attachment about the puzzle winners for the paper. Yes, there was Ida's name, number eight in the top ten. But she wasn't at the shed. She was in the gift shop and then in the runway show. And why murder Brenda?

Katherine rubbed her hands together and whispered, "Yes." Hobbs had rolled onto one side and fallen asleep. Katherine paused in thought about how cute the dog was and how amazing it was that the animal could switch off his ferocious side in a way that seemed so easy and natural.

Her mind wandered to Jason and how he had an on/off switch too. She sighed as she thought about times when he'd let his gentle side show—his care with the library kids, his connection with Hobbs, his arms around her for that dance. She thought how he'd softened since she'd known him, and maybe she'd softened too? But sometimes his switch got stuck on rough.

Purrada posed in front of the laptop screen. That motion brought Katherine out of her daydream. "No, no paws on the keys." She grabbed the cat and put her down on the floor. She sat down and concentrated on the screen in front of her and the picture she'd texted herself of Amber's mystery purse. She had been through that donation box, and she would of course have noticed this gem. She thought back. The box had been in her office the night of the gala. She hadn't given it to Amber until Saturday morning. Michael had interrupted Brenda in the office and told her Ida was looking for her. When she walked out Friday night, had Brenda hidden this purse in the donation box, knowing it had the letter in it? Was she trying to keep that evidence safe from Ida? Did Ida know Brenda was investigating her family? Did she confront her? When?

She tapped her foot and swiveled her chair between dog and cat. "This is aggravating." Hobbs panted in his sleep, and his paws twitched in fast swipes as he chased something, or someone, in his dreams. Purrada gave a mew and stared at the dog.

Katherine got up and started pacing, waking Hobbs. She paused a few times in front of her whiteboard, but she just couldn't put it all together. She paced out to the kitchen for a glass of water. On the counter by the sink was an irresistible box of leftover cookies. She popped one in her mouth and grabbed a couple more. On impulse, she opened the catch-all drawer and took out the mysterious stone from the watering can in the shed. She rubbed it between finger and thumb as she took her water toward her office to shut down her computer when a glance down the hallway showed lights on in the gift shop. Wrinkling her forehead in surprise, Katherine went to turn those off.

The silence of the museum seemed almost unnatural. Katherine had become used to a high level of commotion with guests and workers. She hesitated as she approached the entry. She moved forward with caution into the shop.

Amber had left everything neat and in order. Katherine was proud of getting this museum going and staffed so well. It would continue to run well with her back in L.A., soon. She was delighted with the displays. Amber had a knack for using an eclectic inventory, creating inviting displays with curb appeal.

Putting her glass on the counter so she could munch on her cookies, Katherine savored the vanilla creme filling. What a tiring day it had been, filled with new revelations. She shuddered, looking out the window as she reminded herself that the killer was not only on the loose, but may be after her. A noise in the alcove startled her. She turned in a sudden panic, thankful when Hobbs ambled into the room.

"For Heaven's sake, get a grip," Katherine said to herself. She popped the remainder of the cookie into her mouth and went to the French doors to check they were locked. Hobbs sat down beside her, and she patted his head, then scratched behind his ear as she stared across her side yard.

She admired the rare, clear October sky and the half-moon shining brightly. Her new outdoor lights had the yard very visible. She was happy with the landscaping. The old, majestic fruit trees were undisturbed by the short rhododendron hedgerow now planted behind them. It separated the meadow portion of the property. She was pleased she'd been able to keep the pretty gazebo in place in the center of the yard. It highlighted the roses. Then it all became clear. The gazebo had been between the gift shop and the shed. Even with the yard floodlit, you wouldn't have been able to see the shed through the gazebo. No one could have seen the shed from the gift shop that night. Ida's words at brunch popped into her head. "I saw the light on in the shed when I was looking for Michael. It was right before the fashion show."

Ida had lied to her about seeing the shed light that night. Why would she lie about a thing like that? Was it because she needed a place to pretend she'd been, because the place she really was at that time was in the shed? Ida had possible motive, means, and now opportunity. Katherine examined the stone in her hand. It shone a deep blue in the light, possibly like a sapphire, torn from an antique, bridal mesh purse held by a 1920's style runway model.

Her gran's comment from earlier popped in her head, and she said it out loud, "I was so concerned about the cats in the neighborhood, when I should have been watching out for predatory birds. You're looking one way, and the killer swoops in from the other direction."

Katherine put her hands on her hips and explained to Hobbs, "Now I have to prove it. The Historical Society building may have the evidence. I won't know until I go there and find it. And Ida's not going to help me. I wonder if I could get in long enough to look around. I'm not going to disturb anything but, if it's really her, I could stop a murderer with the right evidence. I don't have enough now that the police would search her place. What do you think, Hobbs? How about a walk? Do you want to go for a walk? And maybe catch a killer?"

Hobbs stood up and gave his tail a wag. Energized, Katherine ran over to the lights and switched them off as she rounded the corner and headed back to her office to put on shoes and load up a purse with tools she might need on this night excursion. She burst into the office with Hobbs hot on her heels and grabbed a couple of items off the table as Hobbs barked and bounced behind her. She headed toward the closet for shoes and purse. As she did, she glanced at Purrada who yawned and stretched out a front claw lazily in her direction. Katherine paused with second thoughts. Then she looked out the French doors and remembered the night of the gala and the prowler in her yard, who was no doubt Brenda's killer. This time she might get that shadow in the night. It was worth the effort, for Brenda. And if she found nothing, well, then she and Hobbs would walk home. But she didn't think she was wrong.

Chapter Thirty-Seven

It was well past midnight by the time Katherine and Hobbs made their way out the back door. It always surprised Katherine how quiet Hobbs' paws padded as he walked off the porch and down the wooden stairs. On the other end of the leash, Katherine clomped alongside in her ankle boots. They crossed the yard and turned into the alleyway, toward the center of town. Katherine glanced over at her grandparent's cottage with the cheery light behind the curtains and the curl of smoke at the top of the chimney. She wished she was headed out to pay them a surprise visit and curl up for a midnight hot chocolate and chat. That was not in the cards tonight though. Resolute, she kept moving toward Bayside's shops and buildings and downhill toward the waterfront.

The ever-popular alleys of Bayside were dark and empty tonight. It was manageable, though, with the dim lights from the backs of the buildings. As they kept moving, Hobbs gave a quiet growl to one of the large, metal garbage bins. An ugly, startled possum stood on top. The animal froze in place except for his head turning with its natural, agonized look following them in watchful attention.

Katherine quickened her pace, nervous about creatures of the night, including certain human ones. She shivered and gathered her jacket closer, not from the weather, but from the thought that her analysis of the killer may have come too late.

As Katherine approached the iconic fountain roundabout, the sounds of the falling waters grew louder. At the point where her alley intersected with this road, Katherine turned the other way, toward the Founders History Museum. They walked along the road for a couple of blocks and then cut through City Park toward Ida's old, brick refuge where she protected Bayside history and the legacy of her founding family.

They entered the park and, in the darkness, Katherine's claustrophobia caught in her breath as they were swallowed by the trees. A tug on Hobbs' collar turned the dog back to sit with Katherine, who got on her knees to paw through her KW crossbody. It was reminiscent of a Louis Vuitton signature style vinyl. She searched for her flashlight. She put her cell on vibrate, since she was now in stealth mode. There was an abrupt rustle and snap of leaves on the ground as she turned the light on. She caught sight of a creepy ground movement, a rat scurrying through leaves. Hobbs barked, and Katherine moved away from there, pulling on his leash to follow. Did Hobbs sense this wasn't just a walk? Was he switching on his police skills?

They skirted the edge of a soccer field. Hobbs sniffed the air. Jason had told her Hobbs could smell and distinguish several scents at once. Maybe he detected a tantalizing ham and cheese sandwich abandoned by some ball player, the tree trunk another dog had recently visited, and a wandering cat, or maybe the scent of a killer.

Taking special care to be quiet now, she kept her light hidden close to the ground. They paused at the end of the tree rim. She stared at the back entrance to the old brick schoolhouse turned museum and the glass window in its back door. She turned off her light, stooped down, and whispered in Hobbs' ear one of the several German commands she'd learned from Jason. "Warten." Hobbs gave a whine but did as he was told, sat and waited. Katherine ran low to the ground into the depths of the alcove of the back doors. She hoped that no one intercepted her and that Hobbs remained vigilant from the trees.

She leaned against the building. A low growl sounded like Hobbs in the distance, then the sound of leaves rustling although there was no wind. There was no movement in the trees. Now she couldn't even see Hobbs, but she sensed him. She pushed on the basement door's metal bar. The bar was locked shut. She wasn't getting in that way.

Katherine stayed in the shadow of the building as she looked for entry. She went into the parking lot. She could still see the forest from the dark lot. The only vehicle parked there was the museum curator sedan that Ida used for giving speeches and carrying traveling exhibits that she loaned to libraries, schools, and other venues.

Katherine walked to the side door, and it was also locked. She ran back again to get another look at the glass doors and noticed the opening for a package drop. Trembling, she pulled on its large bar that served as a handle, but it didn't budge. Was there a lock on it too? No night drops allowed? She pulled on it hard, not thinking about the noise. It groaned open.

She couldn't see the bottom of the drop. It was a way she could get in, but she was terrified whether she'd be able to get out at the other end. What did it dump into?

She snapped on her light and flashed it in the drop again. It was a chute that went below this floor. Katherine choked back the knot of claustrophobia caught in her throat. She thought about all that had been stolen from Brenda, her family, and her friends. She brushed away the sudden flood of tears with her coat sleeve and stood looking at the darkness, sniffing. She took in a deep breath and let it out. Pulling the garbage bin closer to the chute, she climbed on top of it. She hesitated and scooted around to go in feet first. Another bark in the forest and, in that instant, she lost her balance and slid.

Chapter Thirty-Eight

She wasn't expecting dark when she landed. There were no night lights in the building. The slide down the chute backwards had been long and tight. She landed hard on a wood floor. Feeling around, she determined she was in a bin. She ignored her dull headache and leaned forward to straighten up. A couple of packages shifted underneath her. She started to stand and hit her head hard on a ceiling. She groaned as her dull headache roared. That's when panic surfaced. She reached up with both arms and felt solid wood. She slid her fingers along the surface in many directions. No opening. She crawled back to the chute opening and slid her hands along its edges, but there was no break in the lid. If she couldn't find a way to open this top, would she be able to somehow climb her way back up this steep, slippery slide? If she couldn't open the lid and step out, and if she couldn't climb up and get out, when was anyone ever going to check on this bin, and who would check on it? Would it be the killer? She was trapped, as if inside a tight, latched box clutch. One of those with the allure of sparkles on the outside, but the designer's tragic mistake of black lining inside so nothing could be seen within. Katherine screamed. Then she screamed again.

She thrashed all around her to find the flashlight that she'd dropped in her fall. She fumbled around and finally wrapped her fingers around the smooth, round shape. It flooded the space with light, and she squinted from the abrupt change, then she shrank back as her eyes adjusted and showed what she'd feared. The chute emptied into a bin that had a top secured all across it. She pushed it again and could see it was somehow locked down. Her claustrophobia closed in on her. She leaned back in the pile, raised both feet flat against the top, and started kicking hard. Her solid thuds went on for what seemed like an hour.

Weakness was an unfamiliar feeling for Katherine, and she wore it like a DIY purse kit sold in dollar stores - something long on amateur and short on style, with a garish design that should be hidden from the public. A few last, weakened kicks against the lid, and her legs fell down, leaving Katherine stretched out, lying across the bottom. It seemed to her that she'd always been strong and independent. She blazed trails and, when she ran into trouble, she worked harder and found a way to make success. She never needed anyone. She was the one who took care of people. Yet, here she was, alone, trying for a solution to her own troubles, and she couldn't think of any way out. What wasn't she thinking of? She fought back tears as she tried to remain calm despite feeling her skin crawl and hearing her labored breathing. How much oxygen was available to her locked in this bin?

She thought of her sons and worried she might never see them again. Wait, she had her cell phone. She'd call someone for help. She could call the police. No, then she might be rescued and arrested for trespassing or something. Detective Grace had warned her off sleuthing. She'd be excited to have an excuse to stop Katherine. And she still didn't trust Rob. If she called him, he might decide to turn it into some big news story, and she didn't need that kind of front-page coverage. If she called Jason, would he consider this a conflict of interest with his job and turn her in? Besides that, would he be upset that she'd left Hobbs cooling his paws on the grass outside? A call to Jason just now did not sound appealing.

Maybe Amber? Katherine didn't want her to end up in trouble. She wondered if Michael would be able to pick locks to get in and no doubt find a creative solution to free her, but he was in jail. Then she thought of the one person available that she could call. "Oh no. Really?" Katherine blurted out to no one as she tried to think of any other person. She was desperate. She pulled her cell out of the pocket of her Louis Vuitton and it lit up as she put her finger against it to unlock it with her print. She clicked on the contact before she could change her mind. As the call rang, the clip art of the coffee mug silhouetted by the moon glowed.

It sounded like the cell picked up on the other end and that familiar, slow, drawn out, alto voice came over the line. "Hello, it's Moonjava…"

"Help. It's Katherine. I need…" Katherine stopped talking as she heard the music. *All we are is dust in the wind.* Katherine rolled her eyes. "What? Oh, please pick up."

Life's too short brothers and sisters. Dust in the wind. And then the music stopped, and MJ's voice came back. "That is my message to you, friend. Now please leave me a message and experience the beauty of reaching out to another."

Beep.

"MJ, call me back right away. I need you. It's an emergency. Please help me. You can't find me. You have to call me to find me. Please." Katherine clicked to end the call. With MJ's usual lack of any sense of urgency or of time, Katherine's hope for a rescue was disappearing like dust in the wind, and she was out of answers. That time she always feared was here, that time when she didn't have the right answer or the perfect solution. Today she could not design a perfect ending.

She sat cross-legged and hunched over. Shivers enveloped her body as she hugged her knees and rocked. She closed her eyes. She was surprised when she thought of her great gran's bombing of London story. How she wished she could hear it one more time right now.

Her great gran had survived a London bombing in the basement of a store in the rubble of a building and was able to crawl out between destroyed buildings on either side despite her fears. A shiver curved all the way around Katherine's bent spine. Self-confidence was what got her through hard times. She could find the right answer to every situation through persistence, hard work, creativity and luck. Why was she giving up? She'd had the wrong answer when she ignored that first death threat note. She'd made fatal mistakes. Was she punishing herself? She straightened up her posture, until the back of her head hit the lid again. She put her cell back in her purse, lay down on her back, and raised her feet up. It took some kicking, but finally she thought she felt some give in what locked down the wooden lid. Was she raising it?

She reached over and turned the flashlight back on.

Focusing it on the edge of the lid, she kicked. It bounced up and down a little. She sat up and pushed it with her left hand and could see the locked latch on the outside. Looking closer, she had an idea what could help.

She reached down to the charm attached to her purse. She unclipped the purse chain that had a gold brass padlock and key. Pointing the flashlight on the bin latch, she saw that padlock was about the same size. The key on her purse charm might unlock this bin. She tilted her head to hold the flashlight against her shoulder and tipped up the wooden top with her head. It took some fidgeting to get the bin lock tilted toward her, but she could see that her kicking on the lid had also stretched the lock so that its hard grip had loosened. The key on the charm fit inside the lock's hole. In fact, it slid around inside with all the extra space because the key was a small misfit. Tightening her resolve, craning her neck, and twitching her arms and hands around in different directions to get the right grip, Katherine cursed when the flashlight fell from between her shoulder and cheek. She continued to play with the key in the lock, twisting it different ways and pushing it up farther. No luck. The padlock remained closed.

As she groaned and pulled the key out, Katherine was breathing heavily and sweating. Her fingertips were cold on the metal, and that's when she thought of using the chain on her convertible crossbody. She unhooked the clip on the chained shoulder strap and with some effort slipped one end through the loop of the padlock. If she could just pull hard enough and at the right angle, the padlock might break open. She braced her feet against the side of the bin when her cell vibrated. She vowed that no matter who was calling her, she was going to ask them for help. The screen lit up with a full moon over a coffee mug.

"MJ, help me. I'm locked in the basement of Ida's museum. I can't get out, and I'm afraid to call the police for help. Please, come and help me.

"Katherine, take a deep breath. Inhale."

"No, not your yoga now. I'm stuck in a bin. I don't know how much oxygen is in here so I'm not going to breathe deep. I need you here to help me please."

"Stuck in a bin? What's going on? Never mind. I'll get over there. Ida's museum? Okay. I'll call you back when I get there." MJ hung up.

She double checked that the cell was on vibrate. In case someone sinister surprised her and got here first, Katherine didn't want to be discovered because of a call back. Once the phone was back in the purse, she braced her feet against the side of the bin again and pulled hard, using the chain. The padlock started to bend. Katherine raised her hips up and pushed up with her head on the lid and at the same time pulled harder, and the padlock snapped. It was open. She raised the lid in triumph and stood up.

Thank goodness for bargain priced old locks. She reattached the chain and pushed her purse behind her hip so it could rest on her back. Katherine had never been so grateful for freedom. She breathed deep, happy. That's when the lights went on in the room. Katherine froze. What she focused on first was the gun.

Chapter Thirty-Nine

It wasn't a large handgun, although it was held in two fists clenched together around the handle. The double barrel, one on top of the other, loomed large in Katherine's vision, because it was pointed at her face. She also noticed that one finger was on the trigger. She moved her eyes along the barrel and up to the face of her captor. The look that met hers was cold and maniacal. The eyes were in constant movement up and down Katherine. The gun never moved though. Katherine thought of her gran's comment on one of MJ's meditations - it's the people you think you know who hide secrets from you best. She was now meeting the real Ida and her secrets for the first time.

Katherine hoped Ida had no idea she'd figured out that Ida had killed Brenda and framed poor Michael. A heat wave broke out on Katherine's face and traveled through her body. Sweat beaded on her forehead and under her arms. Traces of sweat traveled down her back. Her purse started vibrating. There was no recognition in Ida's expression since the purse was soundless behind her back. Katherine started to raise her hands. With her right hand she poked in the front purse pocket as if scratching her back. Had she pushed on the right part of the cell screen to answer the call? Could MJ hear them?

"What are you doing?" Ida shouted.

Katherine raised her voice. "You're scaring me with that gun, Ida Hansen. It's okay. I know I'm in your museum basement. I'm raising my hands up in the air so you can see I'm not doing anything. See, I'm moving my arms up slow." They were at shoulder height. She stuttered, "Ida. I'm sorry. I got stuck down here in your museum basement at closing. You don't need a gun. It's just me. I was stuck, but now I can go home."

"You always think I'm so stupid, Katherine. But you know what? You're the one who's stupid, and now you're going to die. You've been a lot of trouble."

At those words, there was a tremendous pounding in Katherine's chest and a pain as if her heart was wrenched apart and then twisted. "I know who you really are, Ida Hansen. You're a murderer. You killed Brenda. You disgust me. How could you?" Katherine gasped.

"Someone had to shut her up. You were the one who deserved to die. Your silly purses. Your shallow fashion decorations. You make a mockery of the glory and importance of history. History is to be preserved, admired. History should be studied and explained to people, presented in a proper way for people to memorize and appreciate. I can explain what people need to know about history. Teach them what I know. You throw sequins and lace onto displays and it's like a joke. You're a joke, Katherine—a dangerous joke."

Katherine withstood this crazy tirade in shocked silence. Then she spoke. "You're so threatened on your throne of Bayside local history that you have to kill? We could have shared history. We could have collaborated and taught each other. But instead you're a miserable, common thug. You've let down your

Bayside founding family that you evangelize."

"Shut up! I am the representative of the founding family. I personify Bayside."

"No, you disgrace Bayside."

Ida gasped and then struggled to catch her breath. She frantically scratched the top of her head with one hand. She stepped toward Katherine, waving the gun. Her hand tensed around the handle, white knuckles and a trigger finger. Caught, trapped and no way out, Katherine's back was against the wall.

Ida screamed, "You're wrong!" Her gun sagged as she added in a bitter tone, "You take back what you said, right now!"

Katherine kept her eye on the gun. "Bayside is a good town, full of people who are friends and family and spend their lives helping each other, creating and finding beauty in life and trying to do the right thing. These people deserve better than you. I know that you killed Brenda. You stole her life and stole her away from all who loved her, away from all her good works. You took her from her kids, from Russ. You've gone out of your way to frame a truly innocent young man for it and ruin his life. Why would you do this to Brenda? To Michael? Bayside deserves better than you."

"Listen to you, of all people, you defending Bayside. That's rich. You never even lived here full time. You didn't grow up here, you visited summers and holidays. You're a visitor. Even now you keep telling us how you're just here for a while. You're going back to your beloved Rodeo Drive. Well, you should have gone back to your artificial home and celebrity life. You never belonged here."

"I belong here far more than you, Ida. It's not a pedigree that makes a place home. It's love that shows you belong. It's certainly not hate, which is what fills you. You were determined to lure Brenda away from everyone at the gala. She had found out about your relative who got away with murder. You couldn't let that skeleton in your closet be known, could you? You thought you could get away with murder too. You got Brenda out to the shed and killed her with the purse I gave her. Were you trying to implicate me?"

Ida's face darkened and caved in on itself. She groaned and shook the gun at Katherine as she shouted, "How did you know about that? Theodore Hansen was no murderer. It's a lie. I have the right history records. You're talking about a lie." Ida slowed down now as color came back to her face, and she cast a forced smile. "That purse hanging at your place was a last-minute inspiration. The two of you had made such a big deal about your friendship and how Brenda treasured the purses you gave her, such a material friendship. A fitting ending for her."

Katherine's stomach turned, she was so sickened.

Ida laughed. "You don't like to hear that do you? Yes, you caused the opportunity for Brenda's murder. And now you're going to cause your own because of all your snooping. You should have let dead dogs lie."

"I won't let your family get away with murder again. History will not repeat. You won't frame Michael. You had the access to frame Michael. And it always sort of bothered me that you were late to the runway show—"

"Oh, your precious show," Ida spat out.

"It wasn't about the show, it was about how there

316

was no reason for being late. You were excited to be in it, so why would you risk missing it by being late, unless you were in a grave fight and couldn't get back."

Ida shrugged. "Ridiculous. There's no evidence there. No one else will think twice about it with Michael in jail. I've planted plenty of evidence that will convict him. Your accusations will die with you. Your efforts will kill you."

"You can't see the shed from the gift shop porch door, Ida. You told me you were looking for Amber and you were upset because there was a light on in the shed. But you can't see the light on in the shed from that windowed door. Even if you crane your neck and step as far over to the side as possible, it's not there. You weren't in the shop looking for Michael. You were in the shed."

Ida's complexion blanched, and she shrank back. Her left hand dropped down and stroked her chin a couple of times. Her right forefinger never left the trigger, although the barrel sagged.

Katherine paused and studied Ida's expression. A strategy formed in her mind. "I know you put that little story in your statement to the police, didn't you? That's why I let the police know to check on the view from that shop door."

Ida gripped the gun with both hands again. "I can fix it. I will fix it. You can rest in peace that I'll fix that when you're dead. You've been very helpful for once, at the end of your life."

"You can't fix the sapphire stone that came out of your purse that night as you struggled with Brenda, as you forced that handkerchief over her mouth. That was found in the shed. That's evidence, and the stone will fit exactly in the space it left in your purse. You can't kill me."

"I can't kill you? Oh, Katherine, wrong as usual. I've killed before to save my town's place in history and my history. You're so easy to kill. Here you are. You broke into my basement. You surprised me and scared me. It was self-defense. I could shoot you right now and no problem. I have other plans, though. I don't want anything connecting me to you, because you're not worth the hassle. So, get moving this way, but slow. Don't make sudden moves or I will kill you here."

"Ida—"

"Shut up and do what I tell you or I'll pull this trigger right now, I swear I will." Ida took a couple of steps forward, holding the gun in front of her.

Ida's loud and desperate tone echoed her previous hysteria. Katherine hoped MJ could hear them on her phone. Not just the gun, it was Ida's red face and intense frown that scared Katherine. "Okay. I'm moving."

Ida stepped over to the side and waved the gun in the direction of the hall to the stairs. "Go. I'll be right behind you and if you don't do as you're told, you're dead. We're going for a drive."

Katherine moved forward, thinking she'd be able to grab that gun and knock Ida over, or kick her, or push her. There was no opportunity as Ida stepped back. She followed Katherine's every move with both barrels.

Katherine thought this door led to the parking lot on the side of the building. If Hobbs was still there, she'd be able to signal him once they got outside. Or maybe MJ would be here and help. Ida marched her straight out through the back room and into the old basement loading entryway. On the way through, Katherine noticed the chemistry table that Amber had mentioned when she told them about her love letter mystery investigation.

Katherine thought she could maybe slam the door in Ida's face and run for help. She slowed down to get ready and got a shove in the back. She stumbled and fell on her hands and knees. She glared back at Ida who pushed a button on the wall that opened the loading dock door to the outside. Ida threatened her, "My gun is on you. Move it."

Katherine got up, ready to run. There was a double beep, and the trunk popped open on Ida's Jetta sedan. Looking for MJ, or for Hobbs, Katherine wanted to run, but Ida tapped the gun right in the middle of her backbone. A motion detector light shot on as she made it out to the loading area. Ida shoved her against the back of the car and tried to hold a wet handkerchief against her face. Katherine fought back as she was shoved inside the trunk, and the lid slammed down.

Chapter Forty

Her eyes were open, yet she couldn't see anything in the dark. Katherine screamed and pounded and kicked inside the trunk. Panic seized her with a cold sweat and a large lump in her throat. She was trapped in the trunk of a killer's car.

She fought the tears that threatened. Frantic, she felt all around and above her. An odd, glimmer of light drew her attention. It was a small glow, in the middle of the trunk lid. There was a bump there. It was shaped like a small light switch. She pushed it a couple of times, and the trunk popped open. Without hesitation, Katherine was up and out of the trunk. She saw Ida against the building closing the door. She pointed the gun at her again as Katherine pulled the pepper spray out of her purse pocket and aimed her fingers at Ida, screaming as loud as she could, "Hobbs Fuss! Attack! Hobbs!"

Ida looked around but held the gun on Katherine in an eerie silence. She laughed. "No one is coming to rescue you, and you don't bring spray to a gun fight. You're about to die, and Michael is going to prison. I win."

Katherine despaired that Hobbs wouldn't come. Did she get the command wrong? Then a thunderous growl preceded a wild leap by Hobbs onto Ida, knocking her backward, hard into the building wall.

The gun flew high into the air. Ida fought the animal. Regaining her senses, Katherine grabbed the gun where it fell and pointed it at Ida. She commanded Hobbs, "Pass auf, Hobbs! Guard!" The dog stopped his attack but stood by, growling and vigilant.

Katherine pointed the gun at Ida and shouted, "Don't move, Ida. You lose." Ida cowered, seemingly more afraid of Hobbs than of the gun. With her free hand, Katherine reached for her cell phone. She was surprised to see who was on the call she'd started when she was on the other end of the gun. Headlights lit up the parking lot as a police car turned in. Jason got out with his cell phone in his hand.

He signaled to Hobbs, then pocketed his phone and walked forward with handcuffs. He flashed Ida a smile and said, "Hello, Ida, you're being taken into custody for the attempted kidnapping of Katherine Watson and for questioning in the murder of Brenda Dirling." He cuffed her and recited the Miranda rights. "Do you understand your rights?"

Ida protested, "You've got the wrong person. I'll sue you."

Hobbs gave a growl as another car pulled in behind the patrol car. Rob got out and started taking pictures as he ran up.

"Do you understand your rights?" Jason repeated.

Ida sneered at the dog next to her and said, "Yes." Just then Katherine's Mustang glided onto the scene. MJ stepped out amid faint strains of Bob Dylan's *Blowin' in the Wind.*

Chapter Forty-One

Chills traveled Katherine's spine as she absorbed the looks of love from those in her office that Saturday morning. She was perched on the edge of her desk next to the picture of her sons, excited from their email they'd be home soon. Outside the window, she saw Reggie finishing the landscaping before the Sunday memorial. Her reverie was interrupted by the loud tapping of her gran's cane on the floor. "But, Katherine, whatever made you decide last night that it was Ida who did it?"

The room quieted down and gave Katherine their attention. She noticed with amusement that the Ladies of the Round Table were sitting in their usual order around her conference table. They'd each received an excited call from Pam. Her grandfather sat on the easy chair with Purrada nestled in his lap, enjoying his pets. Amber stood in the back of the room by the door to the kitchen. MJ leaned by the whiteboard, and Katherine gestured toward it.

"The board tells the process of elimination. Rob had lost the building heights battle against Brenda for his mother's business, but he was exerting revenge through his articles and editorials, not contemplating murder. His photographer corroborated they weren't separated the whole evening."

Peggy raised her hand. "Yes, we know about that.

It's surprising that you suspected dear Anthony Marconi."

Katherine nodded to her and then gave into wistfulness. "I've learned a lot about Anthony. At one point, he appeared to be a scorned lover, driven to prevent anyone else from being with his love. Although he is certainly a romantic, he's no murderer and is useless with chemistry for the knockout handkerchiefs."

Katherine leaned forward and pointed at the board as she explained, "I discovered that Tom Corey, with the 'T' embroidered handkerchiefs, was scheming with Judith in her capacity on the city council. They were both driven by greed, wanting to raise the building heights for development and investment prospects. Brenda was their primary obstacle. They were on video at the gala at about the time of the murder arguing, no doubt, about how best to carry out the paperwork shuffle to get around Brenda and city code. They are dangerous, but for different reasons."

Katherine took a deep breath and added, "Leslie is passionate and thinks she was wronged by Brenda. She could have researched the paralyzing chemicals, but she had nothing to do with the notes. And why would Brenda meet Leslie at the shed during the Gala? That only left two people who could have it all—motive, means, and opportunity. And then in the end there was just one."

Their review was interrupted as the French doors to the porch opened, and Jason and Michael walked in with Hobbs behind them. Purrada pawed the air toward the dog and then settled back into purring for petting. Michael had his saunter back, and he gave Katherine an extra broad smile. He scanned the room, and his gaze rested on Amber. Katherine's heart grew heavy as Amber crossed her arms and turned away from him and back to Katherine. Everyone else cheered for Michael. Amber's expression softened, and she wiped a tear from her cheek.

Katherine gave Jason a conspiratorial look. "I could see how Michael could be framed by Ida. The newspapers with the jumble letters cut out left in his closet, and she knew he was in some trouble for the City Hall hacking, which put him at odds with Brenda. It was Ida who used the chemicals in her basement. She was a jumbles player, even a prizewinner with the paper. The family history she'd built her life around was at risk from Brenda's research into the 1920's murder trial. Ida was even using her old relative Theodore's handkerchiefs to silence people. Once Amber told me about the letter she and Michael found and what it had revealed, all I had left was her opportunity to get to the shed, until I realized she also lied about being in the gift shop."

Her gran started clapping. "Bravo!" And everyone else joined in.

When the clapping stopped, Jason added, "Detective Adams has opened an investigation into the council members' potential conflict of interest. That will be read into the council meeting minutes on Tuesday night. The current building height restrictions will remain in place until the investigation presents conclusions."

Another cheer, and then Amber announced, "How about snacks and coffee for everyone in the café? Follow me."

As the room emptied, Pam said, "Thank goodness

you're safe, and the killer is in jail. I knew Michael was innocent. I had suspicions about Anthony Marconi, and others at the Round Table suspected others, but Ida of all people! We have a special surprise for you, Kat, in the new exhibit room." She took her husband's arm. "Shall we show her now?" Her husband nodded, and they started walking with Katherine and MJ following. Her grandfather stopped at the 1940's doorway and winked at her as her gran nodded. "Go on in, dear."

A full, new display case was lit up with a spotlight against the one wall that no longer had sketches or notes taped to it. Katherine walked away from the group toward the exhibit to get a good look. Her eyes fell upon a beautiful picture of a young woman with hope shining in her dark brown eyes with the long lashes. She wore no makeup, yet her high cheek bones and smiling lips were glamorous against the gray background. She wore a plain, button down and long-sleeved shirt, fitted so that her lithe figure showed. The shirt was tucked into the band on her plaid skirt. Katherine recognized her great gran's initials embroidered in the well-worn bag next to the large binoculars. She pointed to it. "Could that be Great Gran's real bag?"

She wiped away tears when she turned to look at her family, as Purrada strolled into the room, and Amber leaned in the doorway. Together they gave her an animated countdown, "One, two, three, surprise!"

Her gran breathed an audible sigh. "I was able to get the remnants of her old bag restored thanks to MJ and your staff in Los Angeles."

Katherine clasped her hands together in total enjoyment. There was the radio set placed next to the historic bag, a notepad and pen, along with original photos of the English countryside showing planes flying overhead.

Other purses and bags were placed next to pictures of other women of the WWII era. She skimmed the stories. She relived the warmth of each story's strong familiarity and recognized women's names as friends in her family's stories.

Katherine was shaking all over. Despite the lump in her throat, she managed to squeak out, "Thank you."

Her gran's eyes sparkled. "Oh, I'm so glad you're pleased."

Katherine paused, tingling all over. Her hands clasped over her heart, and her eyes dampened. She delighted in this motley group of family she loved. "It's all so thoughtful." Katherine cleared her throat. "I have a confession. In my life, I've been carrying a tote bag heavy with pride and hurt and anger. It's stuffed full of every life event I felt was unjust. I'm weighed down with it, because I carry it everywhere I go. I look in my tote, and I can't find what's meaningful because of all the old junk that's in the way. I'm dumping all that out now and making room for joy and gratitude and the space to help others. The designer designs, but it's the woman and what she does with it that makes the bag special." She stopped herself, gave a laugh, and added, "MJ, I've got a meditation for you today!"

"Lay it on us, girl."

Katherine's voice broke. "It was embroidered by Great-Gran. She put it in my beloved, much mocked croc purse - You are fulfilled when you do the impossible for someone else." There were nods, and her voice grew stronger and steadier. "Selflessness reverberates within the heart, the soul, and the imagination. It's love. That's where home is, and belonging feels good."

Chapter Forty-Two

Katherine was comfortable in her favorite jeans and a fitted, pale blue turtleneck as she meandered through her museum's rooms Sunday morning, padding on the wooden floors in her comfortable loafers. She approached the eclectic display that was Brenda's collection of purses, donated by Russ. There was energy from the blend of the antiques, to the working crossbody, to the waterproof scuba wallet, and the old multi-tasking mommy bag, and the evening clutch. It was an energy that represented all that Brenda's life had been and her many interests and valued contributions to others. Katherine angled the coveted, antique leather Bosca a little lower and widened its opening so the exquisite dove gray, silk lining would catch the light better.

Of course, Brenda would have laughed at the time Katherine had spent Saturday trying to get this purse exhibit just right for her friend. Katherine said out loud, "See my dear, accomplished Brenda, behind every successful woman is a fabulous handbag." As she leaned forward with the tissue from her jeans pocket to dust off one of the pictures of Brenda, Katherine imagined Brenda's retort giggling in her head, as she read the inscription on the photo frame - *in front of every bag is a fabulous friend.*

Katherine reached into the paper bag she'd left on

the small round table beside the exhibit and took out the old picture of two little girls dressed up in their mothers' heels and discarded dresses, with feathery boas hanging from their shoulders and lip stick smeared across their lips. They were holding hands and modeled long curls and beamed of big dreams. They held up shiny plastic purses, as they posed for the camera and laughed at each other, best friends. Next to this picture, framed in a shadow box, was that first purse that Katherine had sewn for her second grade and forever best friend. It was the one that Brenda had cherished all these years. It was the one that helped bring justice to a killer who'd robbed them of years to come. She put the picture in the center of the exhibit, next to the photo collage of Brenda and her family

She walked onto the front porch. This odd October weather brought sunshine streaming through the tree branches and flooded the yard with vitality. Would she be too warm in her turtleneck on this unseasonable day? MJ steered people over to the side yard for the dedication. Katherine thought, *a week ago these people were my guests, but now like magic my guests have become friends and family.*

Michael skulked the yard, with furtive looks from the sidewalk. His devastated posture sank his shoulders, and he leaned on the short fence as if he'd once held the missing key to a treasured code for an enchanted life ahead but had tripped dropping the key into an endless, dark pit.

Katherine's heart sank as she realized he must be looking for a glimpse of Amber, wishing to reconcile. Amber had been heartbroken by Michael's good intentions to send her away, and their love story seemed destined for the history shelves. Katherine walked over to him.

At first, she just stood next to him, with the short picket fence between them, looking across the yard with him. He spoke first. "Thank you. I didn't think I'd ever be proven innocent, but you did it. I didn't think anyone would ever believe me." He put his hands in his pockets and shifted on his feet. "Except Amber, she always believed me." He lowered his voice into a whisper. "Is she here?"

"Yes. She's probably already over at the memorial. Come with me."

"She doesn't want to see me. She says she doesn't understand why I said what I did. She's hurt. When I tried to talk with her, she was crying and just took off."

MJ walked back toward them now. "Welcome, Michael. Katherine, shall we dedicate this beautiful new space in Brenda's memory? The future awaits and from here it's looking sunny, especially for October in Bayside."

Kat nodded and gave Michael's arm a tug. "Come on, Michael, whatever the future brings, we'll face it together."

MJ picked up on the sentiment. "At the right time, we can all use a little help from our friends."

Michael stepped over the picket fence. Katherine greeted friends as the three of them walked over to the side yard where a small crowd had gathered. Her gran spoke and laughed with Anthony. Katherine was overjoyed to see Russ, Christine, and Danny standing by the ribbon with the big bow that was waiting to be unraveled. It extended across the gateway of the new Brenda Dirling meditation garden and nature reserve.

Katherine ran over to them. "Russ. Thank you for coming. I wanted to see you today. I want you, Christine, and Danny to want to be a part of this living memorial to Brenda and all she stood for. Having you all here makes it the best day it can be."

Russ nodded. "Thanks. You know how hard it's been, but today, and here, I can feel Brenda."

"Are you going to cut the ribbon?" Christine asked.

Katherine hugged her and held out her arm to Danny who joined in. "Let's untie the bow, and then we can all walk into the garden. Come and help me, all of you." Katherine gave each of them an end to the intricate bow, and then she grabbed the remaining loose end.

Now Katherine turned around to face the small crowd that had gathered. She waved her hand. "Hello. Hello, and welcome everyone." Among them were her grandparents who held each other in their arms as always. They were surrounded by a full attendance of the Ladies of the Round Table. Moving closer to the ribbon was Rob, grinning at her as he was pointing to direct his photographer for specific shots. His exclusive, syndicated front page article on Ida's arrest had been in the Saturday paper, and the Sunday edition included his full featured article on the investigation.

A rumble came from the street, building in volume until the motorcycle with the sidecar pulled up to the curb. Jason got off the bike and grabbed a small, potted plant out of the storage. He signaled to Hobbs who jumped to his side. Jason gave Hobbs something as they walked forward, but Katherine was too captivated watching the man to notice what it was. He walked with his dog up to the edge of the gathering and stood by

MJ. Michael had moved next to Amber, and Katherine saw him pull something out of his pocket and show her in the palm of his hand. It looked like wilted flower petals, and that almost made Katherine laugh until she saw Amber take them in her hands, smile at Michael and stand by him. His mouth dropped open.

Katherine took a deep breath. "Welcome to Brenda's garden, where everyone is always welcome, and everyone is a friend. That's how Brenda lived."

Katherine nodded, and they all tugged on their ends of the bow and opened a delightful retreat. The people started to walk in, commenting on the variety of new plants, the water features, the bird feeders, and the hopes that this spot of beauty would flourish.

As Jason walked toward Katherine, she moved forward to him. There were those sparkling, deep blue eyes again. "I'm so glad to see you."

"I brought a new plant for your garden."

"Daisies! I know enough about gardens to recognize daisies." Katherine was pleased with herself. With the development of Brenda's garden, she was starting to learn about plants.

Jason laughed. "You're right. They symbolize a new beginning with purity, innocence and loyal love. And, since these are yellow, they have the added essence of good luck."

"That's just right." Katherine's hands shook as he put the pot down on the ground beside the entranceway. "And I have something for you too." Katherine took some folded papers out of her pocket and handed them to him.

"What's this?"

"That's a current picture of Robby from an email

that includes where he is, at Lackland Air Force Base, near San Antonio. There's also adoption paperwork if you're interested, and, well I hope that you don't mind that I meddled."

Jason swept her into his arms, and she caught her breath, thinking they might be headed for a kiss. As her eyes closed, Hobbs interrupted in a begging position. He pawed at Kat's jeans leg with a whimper.

Katherine stepped back, but Jason didn't let her go. She asked Hobbs, "What is it, pup?"

Jason shook his head, laughing. "Hobbs, your timing needs work. He wants to give you the rosebud."

"That's sweet of you, Hobbs." Katherine smiled at Jason as she reached down and petted the dog. He dropped the flower on the ground, and she picked it up and looked at Jason. "Thank you." She scratched behind the dog's ear as he sat down on the lawn. "What a pretty color. I didn't know roses could be a lavender color. It's seems so delicate."

"Purple roses are for enchantment. They're for magical times and unexplainable things. They're for extraordinary people."

Katherine blushed as she inhaled the flower's fragrance. "It's a time of extraordinary old friends, and new ones."

Katherine let it all sink in through her full being, including the murmur of caring and joyful voices in Brenda's new garden. Her museum in the beautiful sunshine and the purses that showed in the shop windows glowed in the background. In the distance the deep, long bellow of the ferry horn, and just then the scent of the rose tickled her nose.

Jason gave her a disarming smile. "You are

extraordinary." Then he kissed her.

As they parted, they held hands, and Katherine said, "Shall we walk through the garden?"

Jason nodded. "The forecast said this summer weather is about to break. Tomorrow we'll be under water in a normal, wet, Seattle fall. Let's enjoy this heyday while the sun shines."

Hobbs barked. Purrada strolled up almost nose to nose with Hobbs who was staring back at her. "Wow, do you think even they could become friends?"

"It's the first miracle of Brenda's garden, maybe." Jason grinned.

Behind the animals on the driveway, a familiar car pulled up, and two scruffy young men got out. Katherine immediately recognized the weary faces, along with the Kenneth Cole bags she'd given each of them. "Oh, Jason, my sons are home. I'll be right back."

MJ walked up then and pointed to the men greeting their mom. "Well, look who's here! Tighten the strap on your messenger bag if you've got one, Jason. Now things could really get exciting. Right on! I might even stick around."

A word about the author...

Wendy Kendall has a passion for purses and stories of the women through history who carried them. Her cozy mystery *Kat Out of the Bag* is the first book of the In Purse-Suit Mystery Series.

Wendy is a blogger, editor, speaker, project manager, and syndicated columnist. Catch exciting author interviews on her two YouTube Podcasts—A Novel Talk, and also Kendall & Cooper Talk Mysteries.

She loves her two sons, Alex and Brad.

Visit her at:

wendywrites.org
https://sites.google.com/site/wendywriteshere/